The Hunter's Moon

The Hunter's Moon

M.R. Street

turtle cove press

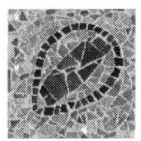

Published by Turtle Cove Press
www.turtlecovepress.com

Turtle Cove Press and the sea turtle mosaic design are trademarks of Turtle Cove Press.

Text Copyright © 2014 by M.R. Street
Cover design by M.R. Street
Cover image of howling wolf by Baccharus (Own work) [CC-BY-3.0 (http://creativecommons.org/licenses/by/3.0)], via Wikimedia Commons; background masked. Cover image of lunar eclipse by Juan lacruz (Own work) [CC-BY-SA-3.0 (http://creativecommons.org/licenses/by-sa/3.0)], via Wikimedia Commons; background masked.

All rights reserved worldwide. No part of this publication may be reproduced, stored in a retrieval system, or transmitted in any form or by any means -- electronic, mechanical, photocopy, recording, or any other -- except for brief quotations in printed reviews, without the prior permission of the publisher. Address inquiries to turtlecovepress@gmail.com

This is a work of fiction. Names, characters, places, and incidents either are the product of the author's imagination or are used fictitiously.

Library of Congress Control Number: In progress

ISBN: 0985943831
ISBN-13: 978-0-9859438-3-7

ADVANCE READER COPY

Dedicated to the Pack of Cousins
Kendra, Cody, Hannah, Allison, Derek,
Peyton, Cason, and Siyanna

In Memory of Cody James Essig
10.05.1994 – 01.04.2014

To look into the eyes of a wolf is to see your own soul.
                                                      --Aldo Leopold

PART I: THE RED MOON - AUGUST

CHAPTER 1

Jace pulls up on his Harley and buckles his helmet around the handlebars. He shakes his shaggy brown hair and leaps out of the saddle, a bouquet of wildflowers in his hand and a wide, lopsided grin on his face.

His smile vanishes as soon as he sees my mother and me on the front porch. Mama and I, like a pair of auburn-haired deer caught in the headlamps, hit by the news my friend Lisa just called me with.

We thought it was all over. We had beaten the curse. But Lisa's call made it clear -- the curse that turned my mother into a werewolf, and could have claimed me as well, isn't over.

Jace drops the flowers. I'm sure they're a birthday present for me. This is supposed to be my big night. August 10, my Sweet Sixteen birthday, dinner with Jace at a little outdoor bistro under the beautiful, honey-colored full moon, then a romantic walk along Mill Creek, just up the road from my new home in Lafayette, Georgia.

"What is it?" he asks. "Lani, what's wrong?"

"It's Stan."

"Lisa's dad?" He stands close enough that I can smell the scent of him, like dragon blood incense. "The guy Ben attacked?"

"I think he's turning into a werewolf." I punch Lisa's number into my cell and hold it to my ear.

Her voice chirps at me, "'Sup, Dude?"

"Lisa, I –." I start to tell her again to get away from there. Get away from the gallery and the thing that her father has become. But the voice on the phone is a recording.

"Leave your data and I'll call ya lata."

I click my teeth together, waiting for the beep. "Lisa, it's me, Lani. I'm coming to get you. To help. I'll be there as soon as I can. But you *have* to go somewhere safe. Drive south. Drive towards –"

"Atlanta," Jace says. "Tell her to take the exit for Jasper, about fifty miles north of Atlanta. Go to the Blueberry Hill B&B."

I leave the message and tell Lisa to call me.

"You mean, right now?" Jace asks. "He's turning into a werewolf *right now?*"

I look from Mama to Jace. "He could hurt Lisa. He could kill her. It's all my fault."

Jace touches the side of my face, then pulls me to him. "There is no way any of this is your fault. Do you have your keys? I better drive."

"You're coming too?"

"Of course I'm coming too."

I look in his ocean-blue eyes, amazed that he doesn't turn tail and get as far away from me as possible. "I -- I --."

"Would do the same thing for me."

As Jace takes his bike to the carport out back, Mama grabs my arm. "You can't go up there. He'll kill you both."

"I can't let Lisa handle this herself."

"Then I'm coming with you," Mama says.

I try to protest, but she shooshes me with a finger at my lips. A simple action, yet it sets a slew of emotions swirling. At first I feel like a little girl, which I mildly resent. But suddenly I realize this is one of the things I missed, growing up without a mother. The flash of resentment is gone like an afternoon rain shower.

"I've had the most experience with werewolves," Mama says. "I may be able to help. I'll be right back."

I nod.

"I'll get our things." Mama darts inside for her purse and my backpack.

As soon as we're all in the SUV, Jace peels out, leaving a double track of tread on the road. The sun is gone and the sky is streaked peach and purple outside the driver's side windows as we race north. The moon is low and huge in the Eastern sky. Will I ever again look at a full moon and just see its beauty? Or will it always carry an ominous aspect?

I touch Jace's thigh and he curls his fingers around mine. "This town, Jasper. How far is it from Lafayette? Is it far enough from Rock Bluff that Lisa will be safe? Will she be able to find it?"

"One question at a time," he says, squeezing my hand. "Rock Bluff's just south of the Tennessee border, right? Jasper's probably right at halfway between here and Rock Bluff. My grandparents have friends in Jasper. I mean, my grandfather does."

I feel a splinter stab my heart. His grandmother had been

killed two weeks ago, attacked by a werewolf. That werewolf had been Mrs. Stoat. Her son Ben was my best friend growing up in Cloud Pass, Tennessee. The same Ben who attacked Lisa's dad. All this death. All my fault. I know Jace doesn't blame me for his grandmother's death; nor does his grandfather.

Nobody blames me, except me.

Jace has gone on with his explanation, and I try to pay attention.

"Some of their old friends have a bed and breakfast. We can stay there while we're figuring out what to do."

"What *are* we going to do?" As everyone has told me, there is only one cure for a werewolf. It involves a silver bullet.

"I don't know, Lani." He brings my fingers to his lips and kisses them gently. Will our lives ever be normal enough that I won't be filled with guilt at his touch? The excitement that bubbles through me? I should be concentrating on helping Lisa and Stan. No-one's ever found a way to cure a werewolf."

"We have to, though. We have to find a way to help Stan."

"All I can promise is, we'll keep Lisa safe."

"That's not enough. We have to find a way to save Stan from the werewolf's curse."

I twist around to look at Mama. She's sitting as close to the door as she can get, her body tensed against the shoulder belt, as if without it she would bolt straight through the window. "Mama?"

She jerks out of her thoughts. "Yes, Sweetheart."

"You have to tell me about your family. About Romelia's

family, I mean."

"What do you want to know?"

"Your step-mother, Aurelia. How did your father meet her?"

Mama curls her legs up under her. "I was about six. My mother had just passed away. Papa was ... inconsolable. Somebody, I think it was his doctor, told him he needed a hobby to help him through his depression. He decided to do something positive in Mama's memory. She was always very artsy, loved going to galleries and taking crafts workshops, so he took up painting."

A knot forms in my chest and I feel a new connection to my grandfather, even though I don't remember him. I feel the same overwhelming sense of loss as when my dad died. It still sneaks up on me, out of the blue. This crushing realization that he's not here any more.

After he died, I moved in with Mama in Lafayette, in southwest Georgia. Making the mosaic around our front door helped ease my depression over losing my father. When I set in the moonstones that used to be the eyes of Boulder Man, the giant stone statue Dad made for me in our backyard in Cloud Pass, I felt Dad's presence behind me. Maybe I need to take up a hobby in Dad's memory.

I tune back in to my mother's story. "Mama always loved the colorful costumes and music at the Greek Food Festival, so Papa went there to paint. That first year, the festival manager saw his plein air painting and hired him on the spot to work at the weekly farmer's market. Papa set up a booth, painting quick studies of people strolling by. The musicians, the peddlers selling fresh fruits and vegetables. Lots of children and dogs. The market was on Saturdays, so I would go with him. Sometimes Papa painted pictures of me, too."

Mama looks out the window as if more than the landscape is passing through her mind. "One day a group of strangers came to the market. I could tell they were strangers, not just because I'd never seen them before, but because of the way the vendors watched them."

"Let me guess," Jace says, looking at Mama in the rearview mirror. "As if they were going to steal something."

Mama nods. "There were maybe a dozen men and women, and one child. A little girl not much older than me. The men were dressed plainly. Slacks, long-sleeved shirts, and vests. Most wore hats, regular men's hats. A few wore scarves wrapped around their heads. That was exotic and fascinating, but the women!"

Mama whistles, a long, drawn-out note. "I couldn't take my eyes off them. They were so beautiful. So exotic. One of the women walked by so close to Papa and me that I could smell her perfume and the breeze blew her scarf across my face.

"Papa reached out and touched her arm. She whirled and snatched her arm away from his grasp. She started to curse at him, tell him she hadn't stolen anything. Papa apologized and explained he only wanted to paint her portrait. She said she had no money, and Papa said that was okay. He would pay *her* to sit for him, *and* give her the portrait. She agreed, but only if the little girl, her daughter – could be in the painting, too."

"The woman was Aurelia, and her daughter was Aunt Romelia, right?"

"That's right, Sweetheart. I asked Papa if I could be in the painting, too. Papa said no." Mama sighs deeply. "Before that, Papa had let me have anything I asked for. That was the first time he ever told me no."

"That must have hurt you a lot," Jace says. "Especially having just lost your mother."

"When you're a child, and you feel like you're being replaced in the heart of the only person you have left, that is what wounds the deepest."

We fall silent and I drift in and out of wakefulness, lulled into fitful dreams by the rhythm of the tires on the road. I visualize the scene that must have occurred after my cell disconnected. Lisa's father, Stan, usually a big teddy bear of a man, now transformed into a different creature, a raging, bloodthirsty wolf. In his frenzy, he wouldn't have recognized his own daughter. How could she possibly have escaped?

It isn't the east when they mean do you mean Western?

CHAPTER 2

I don't know how long I've napped, but when I wake up, the sky is perforated with stars and the moon is full and yellow on the (eastern) horizon. Mama is asleep in the back seat. Jace stifles a yawn.

"Do you want me to drive?"

"I'm okay. We're almost there."

"Where exactly is 'there'?"

"My grandparents are part of this B&B network. They're friends with the owners of Blueberry Hill in Jasper."

He's still talking about his grandparents as if they're both alive, like I talked about Dad after he died. Like I still do, sometimes. I don't correct Jace. What good would it do to remind him that his grandmother is dead? He might decide he doesn't want to help me save Stan. He might decide to get rid of the werewolf and truly end my family's curse, once and for all. *How can I think this way? He's not like that. He's on my side.*

"How do you know they'll have any vacant rooms?" Now it's my turn to yawn. I turn my moonstone ring with my thumb, rotating it around and around my finger.

"I called ahead while you were asleep." Jace glances at me and strokes my hair before focusing his eyes back on the road. "We'll stay there, at least for a couple days. Until the moon is well past full."

"He could still be lycanthroping," Mama says.

"We didn't mean to wake you up," Jace says, looking at Mama in the rearview mirror.

She waves off his apology. "You need to be prepared. If you intend to confront him, you could be in mortal danger."

"Mama, I know that werewolves can be active at any time, no matter the phase of the moon, or even whether it's day or night. Romelia told me. And I've seen it myself." I strafe my fingers through my tangled, rust-red hair. "But this is different. I think Stan will recognize Lisa, like you recognized me."

"When I was a werewolf, my mind was untamed. Instinctive. Some part of me was still human enough to grasp right from wrong. Do all werewolves think that way? I don't even know. But I do know that you can't trust your life to how you *think* he will act."

"Your mom's right, Lani," Jace says. "We'll think this through before we head to Rock Bluff."

Of course he's right. They both are. I need to stop thinking with my heart and start thinking with my head, or I might end up ripped limb from limb by a werewolf.

If Stan changes again, and isn't confined, Lisa will be powerless to defend herself. He'll attack her the way Ben had attacked Stan, ripping off Stan's arm in his powerful jaws.

But Stan won't stop with an arm.

Lisa is so small, so confident of her ability to fight back, and worse, so trusting of her father, that she'll be totally helpless. He'll rip her to pieces. And then go for the rest of us.

We pull into a gravel parking area lit by solar lanterns hung from old-fashioned lampposts. The only other vehicle is a tan-and-wood-tone Volvo station wagon. It looks like it just rolled out of the showroom. I don't know what Lisa drives, but I don't think a Volvo is her style. Of course, I would never have seen myself driving a Mercedes SUV. But then my long-lost Aunt Romelia sacrificed herself for Mama and me, and left me her Mercedes.

As we climb the back steps to the bed and breakfast, a light goes on. A second later, the door opens and a petite, pale blonde teen stands at the top of the stairs. Her hair glows white in the moonlight. "Jace Lovari," she squeals. She sprints down the stairs and pounces into his arms.

"Hi, Alex. Long time, no see." He peels himself away from her.

"I can't wait to tell you about my summer! Intense," she gushes. She seems to notice Mama and me for the first time. "So, you're dating sisters now, Jace?"

He laughs and wraps his arm around my shoulders, pulling me to his side. "No, just Lani."

"I'm Lani's mother, Melani," Mama says.

"You're kidding. You're not sisters? What's your secret to staying so young-looking?"

Mama doesn't explain that during the ten years she was a werewolf, the diet of human flesh kept her young. Now that she's not a werewolf, I don't know if she'll age like a normal human or if she'll start aging in dog-years, like my dad did when he refused to yield to the werewolf compulsion for human flesh.

"Thanks for the compliment," Mama says. "And thanks

for putting us up for the night."

"No problem. I'm Alex Book. My parents run this place. The house is empty tonight, so you can take your pick of rooms. If you need to stay more than one night, though, you're going to have to bunk up. A big crowd arrives tomorrow. Re-enactment folks."

"Thanks, Alex." Jace holds the door open and we go inside through a small bar area with four barstools. A mural of a pasture dotted with grazing horses, a mansion on a hill in the background, graces the wall behind the bar.

"This is the best room for wifi," Alex says. And there'll be coffee and newspapers in the morning. 'Course, there'll be a full, made-to-order breakfast in the dining room, too. We start serving at 6AM."

We walk down the hall to the front lobby. Alex ducks behind the registration desk and retrieves a handful of keys. "Let's go upstairs and you can pick your rooms. We're empty tonight, but almost full the rest of the week. There are three rooms on the second floor, and three more on the top floor. The carriage house out back has two more rooms, with a connecting door. But both those rooms are kind of small. Nice for a romantic evening away from all the bustle of the main house." She cuts her eyes at Jace, but he's not paying attention. Or is he pretending not to notice her remark?

"All four of us couldn't fit in one of them if we need to stay more than one night," Jace says.

"Four?"

"We're expecting Lani's friend any time now."

"Yeah, then, the carriage house is definitely out."

Mama and I pick the largest room on the second floor. It has a queen-size bed and a bathroom en suite, as do the other rooms, but this one also has a camelback sofa by the window. It will be crowded if all four of us have to room together, but I plan to go on to Rock Bluff first thing in the morning, anyway. I think the others will agree.

Jace takes the room across the hall, and we reserve the last room on the floor for Lisa. We go downstairs to the bar to wait. Jace finds a pitcher of sweet tea in the bar fridge and pours us all glasses. I draw tic-tac-toe patterns in the condensation on my glass. I notice Mama is doing the same with hers.

A car rumbles into the parking lot, and Lisa whirls inside as if she is racing a storm. Her Goth mascara is streaked across her cheeks; her purple-black hair is tangled.

"I'm a hot mess," she says as she drops a small canvas duffel bag to the floor. "And not just 'cause it's August." She embraces me with skinny arms.

"Did he hurt you?" I ask.

Lisa shakes her head against my shoulder. "He didn't touch me. He hurt his arm, though. The one he still has. Broke his bedroom window. Then he went to the gallery office and made me deadbolt the door."

I push Lisa to arm's length so I can look at her face. "Can he get out?"

"No, but I don't know how long he can stay in there, with no food, no water. No nothin'."

Lisa wipes her face, only succeeding in further smearing

her mascara.

"I'm so sorry about … all this."

"You have to be Mrs. Morgan. You look just like Lani. It's not your fault."

Her words are like a punch in the chest. I know whose fault this is. Mine.

"So, how are we going to solve this?" Jace asks. He pours a glass of tea for Lisa.

She takes it in trembling hands and sits down on one of the barstools. "I don't know. I don't know."

I sit next to her and rub her back. "Not with a silver bullet, that's for sure. I don't want anyone else to die." *Not because of me.*

"Frank, Lani's father, overcame his lycanthropy," Mama says. "Is Stan strong enough to do the same?"

"Dad *mostly* overcame it, except for the one time when he attacked Ben's father," I remind her. "There can't be any exceptions with Stan."

"Then we have to think of something else." Jace puts the pitcher of tea back in the little fridge and rests his forearms on the bar in front of me.

"What else is there?" Lisa asks.

"Something that's never been tried before," I answer. "Mama, you were telling us about Aurelia and her family. Where did they come from?"

"Before they came to Lafayette? They traveled around the country for a long time. I think Romelia was born in upstate New York."

"Where was Aurelia born?"

"Romania."

"Same as my grandparents," Jace says.

My eyebrows shoot up. "Did your families know each other in Romania?"

"Well, yeah. My grandparents were the ones who invited Aurelia and her family to come to Georgia, when they were tired of the winters in New York."

"But when Romelia met your grandmother at the B&B, she didn't seem like she knew her. In fact, she was pretty ticked off that the old owners weren't there any more."

"Romelia didn't like any Roma,' Mama says. "I think she was ashamed of being Roma, and blamed her problems on her heritage."

"She brought her problems on herself. I'm glad she had a change of heart, and I don't mean to speak ill of the dead, but she just about destroyed our whole family."

"I know, sweetheart. I wish with my whole heart things could have been different."

"Wait, your families are all from Romania?" Lisa looks around at us. "That's where my brother Carson is. He's doing his college internship for a chemical engineering company."

Mama raises one thin, arched eyebrow. "That might be useful."

I can't imagine how a chemical engineering intern, half the world away, can help us cure Lisa's dad. Then it hits me. "You think there might be a chemical antidote for lycanthropy? Something botanical?"

Jace slaps his palms on the bar. His eyes are wide with excitement. "It could work! Mixing western science with Old World herbs and spells."

"We just have to find the right combination," Mama says.

"Leez, do you think your brother could do some research? Find out if there are any local remedies that mention werewolves?"

She lowers her head.

"You haven't told him?"

"I told him that Poppy had come down with a bug."

"How can you keep something like that from him? He needs to know about your dad losing an arm, even if you don't tell him it was a werewolf."

"Poppy didn't want to tell him about his arm. He said Carson will notice something's missing when he comes home." She looks up at me. "And Carson wouldn't believe me if I'd told him Poppy was a -- a werewolf. I hardly believe it myself."

"What if we go to Romania?" I ask. "We could do the research."

"School starts next week," Mama says. "I'm not sure going half-way around the world is the best plan."

"Then what is the best plan?" Jace asks. "I don't mean to be disrespectful, Mrs. Morgan, but I don't think there's any other way."

"I've got a passport," Lisa says. "And I know a bit of Romanian."

"I know the language," Jace says. "And I have a

passport, too."

My hopes fall like a bird shot out of the sky. "I think I used to have a passport, but I don't know where Dad kept it, or even if it's still valid."

Mama opens her purse and hands me a blue-covered booklet. "I have it with me."

I open the passport to the page with my photo. It's several years out of date, but the passport doesn't expire for another two years. "Why would I need a passport, anyway? Dad and I hardly ever left the state of Tennessee, much less the country."

"He wanted you to have one, in case –." Her voice trails off.

"In case we had to leave the country to escape you," I finish for her. "How did you get it, if it was supposed to be a way to keep you away from me?"

"Romelia gave it to me after your father died. Along with a few other personal items of your father's."

"I'm good to go, then. What about you guys? Do you have yours?"

"Mine's in my car," Lisa says. "I take it everywhere. You never know when you're going to get invited to a big art show in Italy or when your brother's going to need to get bailed out of jail in Romania. Seriously, SP – you know, Stan – thought he and I should both have passports in case something happened to Carson while he was overseas."

"Do you have yours with you?" I ask Jace.

He shakes his head. "But Nicu can bring it to me. That's

my grandfather," he tells Lisa. "I'll give him a call. Can he bring you all any clothes or anything?"

"Good thinking," Mama says. "Tell him Aurelia has the key. She can throw together a few things for Lani."

I look up at Mama and it's like looking in a mirror. We have the same auburn hair and green eyes. "What about you? You should go, too."

Mama bites her upper lip. "Believe me, I'd be much more comfortable about my sixteen-year-old daughter going to Europe if I were going, too. But I don't have a passport. Besides, someone needs to stay here to help Stan."

Lisa stands up, scraping the bar stool legs against the hardwood floor. "No, Mrs. Morgan. You have to stay away from him. I'll stay. He's my father. I can handle him. But he could … he could kill you."

"You say he's locked up where he can't get out?"

"The gallery office has a deadbolt that locks with a key on both sides. Poppy doesn't have a key in there with him."

"He's going to need daily help to survive." Mama takes Lisa's hand in hers. "Not just during the times when the werewolf urge is strong, but for his amputation care, meals. This is a way I can help. Let me do this."

I place my arm across my friend's rail-thin shoulders. "I think it's a good idea, Leez. But he's your dad, so it's up to you."

Lisa looks from me to Mama to Jace and back to me. Tears stream from her eyes as she nods silent agreement.

"Did you bring clothes or anything with you?" I ask.

"Just for the night."

"Alex is about your size," Jace says. "I bet she'd let you borrow some clothes."

"Alex?" Lisa asks.

"Her parents own this place."

"I don't even know her."

"No, it's okay," Jace insists. "She's really sweet."

A prickle of jealousy crawls up my spine and entrenches itself like a tick at the back of my neck. I roll my head around on my neck to dislodge the feeling. I've never had a boyfriend, and I don't know how guys talk about their ex-girlfriends. But I don't want to become a suspicious drama queen.

"Thanks," Lisa says, sniffling back the tears.

Jace wraps an arm around my waist, then extends his other hand to Lisa. "By the way, we haven't officially met. I'm Jace. Jace Lovari."

"Lisa. Lisa Puckett. I remember you from the gallery. Oh, and Lani, happy birthday. I'm sorry I ruined it for you."

"You don't have to apologize. This isn't your fault."

"Aaaggghhh!" Jace grabs his chest and slumps against me.

Panic sweeps through me. "Jace! What's wrong? Are you okay?"

"I forgot your birthday! Well, I remembered it. I got you flowers. I don't know what happened to them."

"I'll settle for a birthday kiss."

"In front of your mom?"

"Yep!" I know I'm grinning like a possum but I can't help it.

He slides his hands up the sides of my face, brushing my tangled hair off my cheeks. He leans close, and I wait until just before his lips brush mine before I close my eyes and forget that there's anybody here except for Jace and me.

Mama clears her throat and taps her cell phone. "I'll go online and buy airline tickets for the first available flight."

"I have money," Lisa says.

"So do I," Mama insists, "and I'm going to use it."

"Sorry to interrupt."

We look up and see Alex with a tray of sandwiches.

"Thought y'all might be hungry."

"Thanks, Alex." Jace takes the tray and sets it on the bar. "Do you think you could drive us to the airport in the morning?"

"No prob." Alex removes the plates of sandwiches and condiment caddy and flips the empty tray vertically under her arm. "Where you going?"

"Just a quick trip to get some folk medicine for my father," Lisa says. "He's sick and, um, not responding to standard treatment."

"Yeah, I know. Jace said he had a nervous breakdown," Alex says.

"He kind of turned into a lunatic overnight," Lisa says, and it's not a lie.

"I'm sorry to hear that. I'm happy to help however I can."

"Can she borrow some clothes?" Jace asks. "She won't have time to go home to get anything before we leave."

"Sure 'nuff." She squeezes Lisa's shoulder. "Just come to my room when you're through with your sandwich, and you can choose whatever you like." As she turns to leave, Alex asks, "What time does your flight leave?"

Mama taps a few strokes on her phone. "Three-fifty-five tomorrow afternoon."

"Okay. Let me know when you want to head out. I'll be ready when you are."

I take a few bites of my sandwich, but I'm not real hungry. I hold my elbow to my face to hide a yawn.

"Why don't you kids turn in," Mama says. "Tomorrow's going to be a long day."

"What about you, Mama?" I stand behind her and hug her, resting my chin on her shoulder.

"I'll be upstairs as soon as I buy the airline tickets and make some other arrangements."

"Arrangements?"

"I need to be prepared to handle Stan's ... situation."

"Mama! Not a silver bullet!"

Lisa's face blanches.

"No. No." Mama looks at Lisa, then pulls us both into a tight hug. "Please don't ask any questions. But I promise you, no silver bullets."

CHAPTER 3

The next morning, I walk downstairs, thinking I must be the first one up. But as I walk into the dining room, I hear soft voices and laughter coming from the kitchen. I knock on the swinging door and it opens a few inches. I push it the rest of the way open. "Hello?"

Alex and Jace are standing in front of the stove, so close together that they could have tied one apron around the both of them.

"Oh, hi, Lani." Alex slides away from Jace.

"Good morning, Beautiful," Jace says. He taps a spatula against a cast iron skillet and moves the pan off the gas burner before he comes over to me and kisses me on the cheek.

Why didn't he kiss me on the mouth? It was good enough for in front of my mother, but not in front of Alex?

"Do I have morning breath or something?" I ask.

"No, but I've got onion breath," he says. "You don't want me kissing you with this mouth."

"How did you sleep?" Alex asks. She's standing at the sink now, washing a huge red beefsteak tomato.

"Great. The bed in that room is so soft, I couldn't stay awake if I wanted to."

"Funny, that's not what Jace said last time he was here." She flicks water off her fingers at Jace.

"Knock it off, Alex!"

I'm not sure if he's talking about her bedroom talk or the water game, but either way, I'm with him. I know he's been with other girls. I just don't want them rubbing my nose in it.

"He said it was the softest bed in the house."

"Alex…"

She moves close to him, wiggling her hips and her ponytail with each step. "But he wasn't in the mood for sleeping."

"You know, I appreciate you letting us stay here and all." I step between Alex and Jace, my back to him.

He wraps his arm around me and kisses the top of my head. "It's okay, Lani," he whispers into my hair. "She's just messing with you."

"I know when I'm being messed with," I say, gritting my teeth. I wrap my arms on top of Jace's. "And I know I don't like it."

Alex is about three inches in front of me. Her teasing grin suddenly fades. "I didn't mean anything by it. Honest. Friends?"

It's hard to stay upset with her while Jace is embracing me. Not only is he showing *me* I'm his choice; he's showing *her*.

"Yeah. Friends."

As quick as a cat, Alex pounces on us, hugging us both. We tumble to the floor in a heap. Alex rolls off me and I'm left kind of sitting in Jace's lap.

"Ow, my butt," Jace says. "This is exactly why I only have one girlfriend at a time."

Alex giggles, then breaks into full-blown belly laughs.

It's infectious. Soon Jace and I are laughing too.

Lisa and Mama appear at the door. "Gonna let us in on what's so funny?" Lisa asks.

We pause long enough to catch our breath, but one look at Alex and I break up again. Alex and Jace join in and we laugh like a trio of hyenas.

***

Alex makes us Southwestern omelets. She asks if Jace has ever made me one, and lets me know she's the one who taught him.

But Alex's teasing comments don't bother me any more. "Yours are almost as good as his," I tell her.

"Delish," Lisa says.

I'm on my second cup of hot Earl Grey when Jace's grandfather and my step-grandmother Aurelia arrive.

"Nicu," Jace says, using his Romanian nickname for his grandfather, "This is Lisa. Her father's the one who's hurt."

"Nice to meet you. Can I help you with those groceries?"

"And I'll get the cooler," I say.

"*Nu!*"

I pull my hand back as if bitten. I've never heard Jace's grandfather raise his voice.

Nicu hands the cooler to Mama. "I've got this," she says. "Why don't you help Aurelia with her bags?"

Aurelia pulls first one lumpy suitcase from Nicu's truck and then another. Jace takes one and I take the other.

"You're walking funny," I tell him.

"I'm fine. Just a little sore from where you threw me to

the floor."

"Yeah, right."

"Mr. Lovari," Alex says, embracing Nicu. "So nice to see you again. I'm so sorry about Mrs. Lovari."

Nicu's face turns grey with his heartbreak. The loss is still so fresh, only six weeks ago. "Thank you, Alex."

"Is there anything I can do?"

"*Nu*, just your prayers."

"Can I help bring in your stuff?"

"Do you have a walk-in fridge where I can put this cooler?" Mama asks.

"Yes, ma'am." Alex reaches for the cooler. "I'll take it for you."

Mama twists to the side. "That's okay. I can carry it if you just lead the way."

From the protective way Mama guards the cooler, I'm pretty sure I know what's inside. A special treat for Stan.

"Do you have my passport?" Jace asks his grandfather.

"Right here." He pats his shirt pocket then withdraws the slender blue folio.

Jace takes the passport and sits on the couch. "Aaghh!" He winces and shifts his position, grasping the couch's arm and lifting his butt off the cushion. "I think I hurt my tail bone when we fell in the kitchen."

"That's not going to feel good on a trans-Atlantic flight," I tease.

"Broken tail bone is nothing to laugh about," Ivan says. "You should go to the doctor, Jace."

"Really, I'm fine. And besides, Melani already bought our tickets. The flight leaves Atlanta this afternoon."

"You will not be on it, I'm afraid," Aurelia says. "Listen to your grandfather. He is a doctor."

"He's not a doctor. He works in the hospital morgue," Jace says. He grins at his grandfather. "But your patients don't complain, do they, Nicu?"

"Again, Grandson, you should not joke about an injury to your tail bone. It could be very serious. You might even need surgery."

Jace exhales in defeat.

Mama and Alex return.

"The boy cannot go," Aurelia says. "He has serious injury to tail bone."

"I fell on it a little while ago. I guess I'll have to go to the doctor before I can go to Romania."

"Romania?" Alex asks. "You didn't tell me you were going to Romania!"

"Since my brother's working in Romania, we thought he might be able to help us find a remedy."

"So you're into alternative medicine? Cool. Has he tried Charlotte's Web?"

"Um, no," Lisa says. "But we'll be sure to give that a try, too."

I sit beside Jace. "I don't want to go without you."

"What's more important? My butt or Lisa's dad's, um,

problem?" He puts his arm around me. The movement must have caused him to put his weight on his tailbone again. He groans and readjusts to a more comfortable position, then pulls me close to his side.

"I wish I could be here to help take care of you. But Lisa's right. This trip can't wait."

"I'll miss you. Promise to be careful, Beautiful."

I smile at his new nickname for me. I like it a lot better than what he used to call me – Wolf Girl. That was before he knew the family history.

CHAPTER 4

I get out my Kindle for the flight from Atlanta to Paris, where we'll have a two-hour layover until the flight to Bucharest. I scroll through the index of books I've downloaded, but don't see anything that overrides the thought that keeps spinning through my mind: *What if it doesn't work.*

I look over at Lisa. She flips the pages of the in-flight magazine and exhales loudly as she reaches the end.

"Anything interesting in that mag?"

"Oh, yeah, lots. Anything good on that Kindle?"

I shake my head. "I can't concentrate."

"Me neither. Why don't you tell me a little history."

"History?"

"Your history. You know, what brought us together on this journey."

I lean close so none of our fellow passengers can hear. I tell her how my mother's step-sister, Romelia, had been in love with my father when my parents were dating. Romelia thought that putting a curse on Mama, turning her into the worst monster imaginable, would make Dad leave Mama and fall in love with her. Instead, Dad's love and empathy for Mama only grew to the point where Dad took on the curse himself.

"When Romelia realized that the Romanian curse she used would be carried through Mama's bloodlines to me, and that it would claim me when I turned sixteen, she got all remorseful."

"Why sixteen? Is that, like the magic year for werewolves?"

"It's the Romanian age of majority. When you are eligible to vote, to marry, to inherit property. Or in my case, to inherit the curse."

"So what did she do?"

"She decided to end the curse. But the only way to do that was for me to kill my mother. It had to be me, because I was Mama's only living blood relative. Part of the curse."

"That's a lot to lay on an almost-sixteen-year-old."

"Tell me about it."

"Here, let's think about something else for a while." Lisa gives me one of her ear buds so we can both listen to her iPod. Her eyes are closed as she sings along to the song.

I nudge her arm. "Seriously? *Two Tickets to Paradise?* We're going to Romania, not the Bahamas."

"How do you know it's not paradise? Carson seems happy there."

I roll my eyes at her.

"Okay, how about this one?" She rotates the dial on her iPod to an even older, cornier song.

"Geez, Leez! What decade are you from?"

"Stan brought me up on the moldie oldies. You know, LPs and SPs?"

"Lisa Puckett and Stan Puckett?"

"Long-playing records and short-playing records."

"Don't you have *any* music from our generation?"

She slides the dial through her playlist. She gives me one of her ear buds so we can both listen. The tune is by The Neighborhood.

"This I can take."

As the plane banks, the mirrored towers of Atlanta's skyline glisten in the afternoon light.

I close my eyes and think about the coming autumn, when Jace and I can put our hands in each other's sweater pockets, like in the song lyrics. I daydream that I weave my arms inside his sweater, next to his warm chest. He pulls his sweater over his head and flips it inside out over my head. I'm caught with my arms pinned at my sides inside the inside-out sweater. He kisses me gently on the lips and says, "It's an inside-out, upside-down world, isn't it, Wolf Girl?"

"Don't call me that." The sound of my voice snaps me from my reverie.

"Call you what?" Lisa munches a Biscoff cookie. The in-flight magazine and a plastic cup of cola are on her tray.

I shake my head and the ear bud pops out of my ear and dangles at the end of its wire. "Nothing. I must have dozed off. Can I have one of your cookies?"

Lisa pulls the other ear bud out of her ear and places it on the tray. She moves the magazine, revealing an unopened pack of cookies.

"Thanks." I bite open the plastic wrapper and devour both cookies. "Have you ever been to Paris?"

Lisa sips her drink and hands it to me to take a sip.

"Poppy and I come every year or two. We like to keep

up with the international art scene."

"That sounds cool. Maybe I could come with the two of you next time."

Lisa breathes a deep sigh. "I don't know if Poppy will ever travel again, other than to the morgue and the graveyard."

My chest squeezes up with the memory of my own father's last breath.

"Lisa, I don't know how we're going to do it, but I promise you. The three of us will come to Paris on the best fine-art-and-live-bait road trip you ever dreamed of."

"Thanks, Lani. When you say it, I can almost believe it."

"You better believe it, girl. We're not going halfway across the world to come home empty-handed. Now, tell me what you told Carson about us coming to visit."

"I told him Poppy isn't getting better and that someone suggested herbal remedies." Lisa pokes my nose with her straw, which is still in its wrapper. "Don't give me that look. As I recall, your father didn't tell you that your mother was a you-know-what until he absolutely had to."

I roll my eyes at her again. "Leez, I was a child. This is different. Carson is an adult."

"If I had told him about the attack, he would have felt like he needed to come home. This job means so much to him. If he left, he would lose it, along with his scholarship."

"Then why does he think we're coming to Romania?"

"I told him Poppy had come down with a bug and traditional medicine wasn't working. Carson said it was quite a coincidence. For the last month or so, he's been collecting information on local remedies. He actually asked if I wanted to come to Romania to help him."

"That's awesome! Maybe he's discovered some secret cure already. He just hasn't told you because he doesn't know your dad needs it."

"I'll tell you what secret he's discovered. A girlfriend."

I gasp exaggeratedly and raise my eyebrows. "He has a girlfriend that he hasn't told you about?"

"Not a word until I told him we were coming. He hasn't told me much about her, just that she's local, but speaks perfect English. She's a scientist herself, but he didn't meet her at work. In fact, he didn't say where she works, just not at his company."

"Local, huh? Maybe she'll be able to help us."

"Lani, I'm not sure I want to tell Carson the truth about Poppy's, um, situation. Much less, spill to a complete stranger."

"We'll scope her out, see what she knows. I'll leave it to you to decide whether her knowledge and local experience are critical, and if she can be trusted enough that you feel comfortable sharing the details with her. But you've got to tell your brother. Otherwise, how's he going to help us? Besides, he deserves to know. Stan is his father, too."

***

We have a two-hour layover in Paris, with our bags checked through to Bucharest. "Let's go to the Platinum Lounge for some munchies," Lisa suggests. She serpentines through the crowds at Charles DeGaulle as I do my best to keep up.

"I'm not a Platinum member."

"I am. I can bring a guest. As much as Poppy and I travel

--."

Lisa stops suddenly. She pulls me to her side and leans her head against my shoulder. "I just hope we find what we need."

"We will," I say, hoping it's true. I try not to think about what could happen to Lisa's dad if we *don't* find a cure for lycanthropy.

"This place is the bomb," I tell her as I look around at the Futurama-style club for the rich and swanky. The space is huge but packed with people, mostly businessmen in slim, dark suits with slicked-back, David Beckham hairstyles and women with Coach and Versace carry-ons. "I'd never be allowed in a place like this by myself."

"Sure you would. You fit right in."

"Just 'cause I'm with you. You increase my cool factor by an order of magnitude."

"Please, girl. All they care about in here is if you got the little blue card."

Despite Lisa's assertion, heads turn as we walk in, as if the regulars know I'm an intruder. Maybe because I'm wearing skinny jeans, a T-shirt that commands, "Do not read the next sentence. You little rebel -- I like you," and my crappy-looking but ultra-comfy ankle boots. Lisa is wearing a ruffly pink camisole that Alex lent her, and the same black jeans from yesterday. Our outfits scream, *Imposters! Vagabonds! Attention, cool, rich people! Keep an eye on your wallets and diamond-studded handbags!*

We sit in cushy chairs beneath impressionist art

THE HUNTER'S MOON 33

mounted in humongous gilded frames. "I can't believe I'm in Paris! These paintings are gorgeous."

"Lani. This is just the airport. Some day we'll come back to Paris, and I'll take you to the Musee D'Orsay, the Louvre, the Rodin. We'll go to some of the galleries along the Tuileries and at Montmartre."

I grin at her like a possum.

"What?" she asks.

"You said that like we'll definitely be back."

"Yeah, I guess I'm starting to think positive."

A server brings us a bowl of trail mix. "Can I offer you ladies something to drink?" she asks in a silky accent. Not French, but definitely what Lisa would call *continental*.

"Two LaCroix Limes," Lisa answers for both of us. "In the can, with straws, *pozhaluysta*."

I blink at Lisa as the server moves to the next group of travelers. "How many languages do you speak?"

"I know a little bit of lots of languages."

"Because you travel a lot?"

"Not really. When we're looking for art, Poppy and I mostly go to Paris and Venice. Once to Japan. I just like languages. Knowing different languages, even the little pieces I'm able to pick up, makes me feel less stuck in a little town."

"So how fluent are you in, say, Romanian?"

"Just enough to get me in trouble."

"Tell me something that would get me in trouble in Romania."

"Hmm." She taps her index finger on her chin. "I don't

want to get you thrown in jail."

"One notch back from that."

"How about, *Vă doresc cu pasiune?*"

"Va doo-rescue passee oo-nay? I like the sound of that. What's it mean?"

"I desire you passionately."

"I know you do, but what does it mean?"

"I desire you passionately."

"I know. I was kidding."

"Me too. But you might need that when you get back home to Jace."

I sigh. "Ah, yes. But what about something for the guys who are going to be knocking themselves out to date us in Romania?"

"Hmm, we *are* two gorgeous American women." She pops her gum as she thinks. "How about, *Las-o baltă, tu pămpălău.*"

"Which means?"

"Forget about it, you wimp."

"Laz-oh-balta, too pampa-low. Perfect!"

In a few minutes, the server returns with two green Coke cans and two straws. Lisa pops her top and swigs straight from the can.

"Why'd you ask for straws if you're going to drink it that way?"

Lisa removes the wrapper from her straw and flattens it. She folds one end over like a ribbon and slides the other end through it. Twisting the wrapper back and forth, she soon has a pentagon shape, which she pinches to make five points.

I look at her miniature star. "That is so cool."

"I leave these wherever I go. I think of them as a kind of a good luck charm for whoever finds them."

"Luck? I don't think I believe in luck." *Now I'm the one thinking dark thoughts.*

"Lani Morgan, you are one of the luckiest people I know."

"Seriously?" I slump into the cushy velour-covered chair and sip my cola through the straw. "How do you figure?"

"You survived a werewolf attack. You freaking escaped a curse on your family that would have turned *you* into a werewolf."

"But I'm bad luck to you and Stan."

"That is pure, 100% bull crap. You did not attack Poppy. Quit beating yourself up over what happened."

She aims a sesame stick at my mouth.

I open wide and she pops it in. "Besides, you are flying halfway around the world with me to try to save him. That is a true friend, not bad luck."

"I know, but –."

"Need more reasons? You found your mother, who is alive, thanks to you. And you have a gorgeous boyfriend who is crazy about you."

"He is pretty gorgeous. But crazy about me? I don't know. He seems pretty tight with Alex."

Lisa sips her LaCroix. "I just met both of them, but I'm a pretty quick study of people. They might have been a couple once. But that was before you came on the scene. What did you expect, he'd save his virginity for someone he'd never met?"

I know I'm blushing, and Lisa sees it. "For realz? You're saving yourself for someone you never met?" She arches an eyebrow. "Or maybe someone that you've met now? That is so Jane Austen."

My phone buzzes. "It's Jace."

"See? It's like you're connected telepathically. You were thinking about him, you were thinking about saving yourself for him, and voila! He texts you. What's he say?"

"He asked how we are. He says Mama's with Stan, and they're both okay."

"Thank God."

My phone chimes again. "He's going to the mall with Alex. They're going to get gelato and see a movie. He's bringing a pillow for his butt."

"So tell him to have fun. He is *not* going to do anything to break your trust. Seriously."

I text him back.

> At airport in Paris. Have fun. Miss you.

He immediately texts back.

> Miss you too. Next time you're in Paris, I promise I will be there with you, mon amour.

I grin my possum grin, all teeth. I know I look goofy, but I can't help it.

Lisa pulls the phone from my hand and reads the text. "See, he's crazy for you. Text him, I desire you passionately."

Before I lose my nerve, I do.

He texts back,

> Now I need a cold shower.

Lisa tilts her head back and gulps the last of her water. "So are you going to hook up with him?"

"Leez, I just turned sixteen."

"Lots of girls have done it by sixteen."

"I know. And where I come from, lots of kids get married in their teens. My friend Billie Mae Wrenfield got engaged last month. She's getting married in November, when she turns seventeen. But that's not me. I don't want to marry someone just to get married."

I think of Ben, my former best friend in the world. He wanted to marry me to save me from becoming a werewolf, a fate he himself was unable to avoid.

Poor Ben. He couldn't help what he became. Maybe if I'd married him, it would have saved us both.

Another life ruined because of me. Literally. I shot him with the silver bullet that ended his life. I only hope I ended his misery as well.

"Where'd you go, girlfriend?" Lisa pulls me out of my brown study.

"I was just thinking about Ben."

"Your so-called friend from the mountains?" Her jaw sets.

I nod slowly. "I wish you could have known him before he died. The real him. The only time you met him...."

"I know." She crunches her LaCroix can in her fist and puts it back on the table. "I didn't meet your friend. I only met the werewolf."

Lisa balls her hands into fists and squeezes them between her thighs. "I gotta tell you, Lani. I really hate him."

"Don't think I'm trying to stand up for him, but he couldn't help it. It's no excuse for what he did to Stan."

Lisa's bangs hang across her forehead like curtains, but behind them I see fierceness in her eyes. "You know what I hate worst of all?"

I shake my head.

"I hate having hate in me. It leaves a bad taste in my mouth. It makes my lungs tighten up."

"What can I do to help?"

"You're doing it. You're being my friend." She smiles and looks at her watch. "We better get to the gate."

As we leave the club, I look back over my shoulder. The server is clearing our table. She puts the empty coke cans and the bills we left as a tip on a round tray, then reaches back down and picks up the paper stars Lisa made. She holds them in her palm and smiles, then slips them in her apron pocket.

I tuck my arm through Lisa's. "So what do you think your brother's girlfriend is like? Something out of a vampire movie? Or a regular home girl like us?"

"Knowing Carson, she's probably some mousy little lab rat with huge spectacles and clothes from Goodwill."

"Hey, I love clothes from Goodwill!"

"Me too, Sistah!"

"What about Carson? Does he like thrift-store shopping?"

"You saying you want to invite him to go shopping with us?"

"No way, Leez! It'll be just us girls."

"What if he begs, pleads, gets down on his knees?" Lisa's voice quivers with faux woe.

"I'll tell him, *Las-o baltă, tu pămpălău.*"

We both break out laughing and can't stop, all the way to our gate.

***

The tiny plane we board for the four-hour flight to Bucharest feels like a coffin. It's cramped and airless. The windows are glazed with age. I feel my chest tense up. I crack my knuckles – a nervous habit from childhood that I thought I had outgrown.

Lisa, on the other hand, settles in to her window seat and pulls a Romanian-language brochure out of the seat pocket in front of her. In a few minutes, her head nods forward and she is asleep.

I check out the other passengers. Our side has two seats in each row, and across the aisle is a single row of seats. Directly across from me is a young woman in her early 20s who looks like she needs another sixteen inches of leg space. She's wearing a hot pink, halter-top dress and black spider web leggings. Her only jewelry is a silver necklace made of some sort of coins strung together. It's clunky and exotic and I wonder how much it cost.

Her complexion is milky, her blonde hair is almost white, and when she looks at me, her blue eyes are almost colorless, as clear as the water in the Garnet River back home in Cloud Pass. I look away quickly so she doesn't think I'm staring at her.

The other passengers are nowhere near as striking. The men wear navy or tan jackets over rounded stomachs, dress slacks, and lace-up shoes. The women wear faded print dresses and most of them hold lumpy cloth bags on their laps.

Are they as normal as they look? Or do some of them have deep, dark secrets like Lisa's and mine? Maybe one of these people is a vampire, coming home to Dracula's Transylvanian castle. The pale girl hasn't seen the sun in months, by the looks of her.

Vampires! Who needs them when you can open a can of werewolf any time you need a dose of monster to liven up your day?

Despite my flippant thought, the one thing I can't get out of my mind is how urgent our situation is. We *have* to find a solution to the werewolf curse. Something that doesn't involve a silver bullet. I never want to shoot any living thing again. Even if it's a werewolf.

As the plane bumps through turbulence and the engines drone, I try to doze, but my mind won't turn off.

After about ten minutes, I whisper, "Lisa? You awake?"

"Am now."

"I'm sorry."

"It's okay. She yawns and stretches her arms as much as possible in the cramped space. "What's up?"

"I can't sleep. All I can think of is werewolves."

Lisa slips the brochure into her bag. "Then why don't you tell me what you know about them?"

"Mostly what Romelia told me. My step-aunt? You met her at the gallery?"

Lisa nods. "I remember her. I thought she was some sort of heiress."

"Except there was no family fortune, just a family curse. And she wasn't the heiress, just the babysitter for the heiress to the curse."

"Vous."

"Moi. So, that's the first thing. You don't have to be

bitten by a werewolf to become one. Romelia put a Roma curse on my mother that turned her into a werewolf."

"A curse, huh? I thought that curses were just in fairy tales."

"You probably thought werewolves were just in horror movies, too."

"Good point. I wouldn't have believed it if I hadn't seen it with my own eyes."

"Cursed by her own sister. Well, step-sister, but still."

"There's a reason step-sisters have a bad reputation. Ever hear of Cinderella?"

"Well, Romelia made up for putting the curse on Mama. I don't know if she knew taking the silver bullet would release Mama and me from the curse, or if she just felt she should be the one to die."

"How did you have the courage to shoot at your own mother?"

"I knew I couldn't shoot her in cold blood, even when she was in werewolf form. Mama saw my hesitation, and knew I wouldn't shoot her just to save myself. She turned to attack Aurelia, my step-grandmother. Mama knew I couldn't let her hurt someone else."

"What'd she do?"

"She lunged for Aurelia. I fired the gun. But Romelia jumped in between me and my mother. It was the most selfless act I've ever seen. When the bullet hit Romelia, she and Mama kind of changed places. Romelia turned into a werewolf, and Mama changed back to her human form for good. Romelia died, but she freed Mama from the curse, and me as well."

"Did you have to use a silver bullet?"

"Yes, that time and for Ben."

"So, curse or be bitten by a werewolf to become one. Silver bullet to kill one. What else?"

"True love."

"You can cure a werewolf with true love?"

"I don't think so. But my dad *became* a werewolf out of love for my mother."

"For realz? That is empathy exponential."

"I guess you could say he died for her. He became a werewolf, but he wouldn't -- um, this is kind of gross."

"Lani. I've seen my father's arm get ripped off by a werewolf. I think I can handle anything after that."

"Okay. So, he wouldn't eat people. If a werewolf doesn't eat human flesh, he ages like a dog. Seven years to one human year. That's what happened to my dad. He refused to give in to the urge to attack and feed on people." I take a deep breath. "Well, he attacked one person who was going to kill my mother."

"What happens if the werewolf *does* eat people?" Lisa grimaces. "I guess this is where it gets gross."

"You've seen my mom. She's barely aged at all since I was five."

Lisa's eyes grow wide. "She killed people?"

"No, but what she did is just as awful. While she was locked up at Hunt House, Jace's grandfather brought her dead body parts to eat."

Lisa sits up and her face turns pale. "He killed people for her?"

"Shhh!" I look around, but none of the other passengers seems to have heard. Or if they did, they don't speak English. The pale girl across the aisle is engrossed in a fashion magazine. "No! He works at the morgue. Sometimes bodies come in all mangled from a car crash. Sometimes, arms or legs are, you know, severed. So she never had to kill anybody. She never even bit or scratched anybody. I'm thankful for that."

Lisa is silent, chewing on her right pinky fingernail.

Maybe I've told her too much. She's revolted by what my mother did.

I open my mouth to defend Mama against the indefensible, when Lisa cuts me off with the look in her eye. It's somehow fierce and fragile at the same time. Like Lisa herself.

"Do you think Jace's grandfather can help my dad," she asks. "Like he helped your mom?"

I exhale with relief. She understands. "What do you think was in the cooler he brought to the B&B?"

The aroma of steamed vegetables and prime rib *au jus* wafts through the air.

"Mmm, lunch," I say. "Perfect timing."

Lisa giggles and I think, *Finally*. I know how hard it is to be happy about anything when your father's deathly sick. Even a little laughter is a good sign.

"*Bon appétit*," she says.

CHAPTER 5

We debark the plane directly onto the tarmac and crowd with the other passengers through a single-wide glass door into the Customs area. Then we're bustled into the airport arrivals area, where mobs of family and friends greet our fellow travelers.

"There he is. Hey, Carson!" Lisa waves and starts pushing through the greeters and travelers toward a tall, square-jawed guy with shoulder-length brown hair. He could be a younger, beardless version of Stan.

"*Stea*," the pale girl from our flight shouts, inches from my ear. "I missed you so badly!"

She charges between Lisa and me with her arms extended, ready for a long-awaited embrace ... with Carson?

She throws her arms around his neck and kisses him all over his face.

"You're early," Carson tells her. "I didn't think you'd be home until tomorrow."

"Change of plans," the girlfriend says.

Lisa is as stunned as I am. "This is the girlfriend?" she whispers to me.

"She's no lab rat," I observe.

"And her clothes definitely aren't from Goodwill."

Finally, Carson notices Lisa and me. "Sissy, you made it!" He scoops Lisa in his bear-like arms and swings her around, oblivious to the people he's knocking her into.

"Put me down," Lisa says with a laugh. "This is my friend, Lani Morgan."

I extend my hand and Carson shakes it vigorously. "Pleased to meet you. Carson Puckett, at your service."

The pale girl clears her throat.

Carson pulls her to his side. "And this is Tatiana Petrescu."

"It's an honor to meet Carson's sister." She has a slight, exotic inflection that reminds me of my step-grandmother's accent. "*And* her friend."

"You speak English?" I ask. "We could have talked on the plane."

"I beg your pardon?"

"You were sitting right across the aisle from me on the plane from Paris."

"Pity. I love nice, long chats on trans-oceanic flights." I'm surprised by the icy tone in her voice.

"I'm sorry," Lisa says, "could you pronounce your name again? Ta-she-anna?"

"*Da*, Tatiana. You have very good pronunciation. But you can call me Tasha."

Carson reaches for Tasha's bag. "Do y'all have any checked bags, or just your carry-ons?"

"Just this," I say.

"Same." Lisa slings her bag over her shoulder.

"I won't be that lucky with you, will I?"

Tasha pinches his cheek. "You know me better than that,

Stea."

Carson laughs. "Don't I! Let's get to baggage claim, then."

As we walk, Carson asks Lisa, "So how's Poppy?"

Lisa glances sideways at me, silently asking me to let her break it to Carson in her own way. "About the same," she says. "He's not responding to the drugs they've got him on. I even went up to his ginseng patch and brewed him some tea, but I think he needs something stronger."

"And you think the locals here might have something that will help him?" Carson is obviously skeptical. "Why didn't you check with the locals in Rock Bluff?"

"You think I didn't try that already? You don't realize how sick he is, Carz. You're the chemist in the family. I thought you'd be happy to help."

"Easy, Sissa-Leezy. Of course I'll help. I'm sorry I'm not home to help out more. Maybe we should all fly back tomorrow."

"No, we can't!" My interruption takes us all by surprise. They look at me expectantly. Lisa's eyes are wide, and I know she's afraid I'm going to tell the whole story, right here in baggage claim. "Lisa told me that if you leave, you'll lose your job."

"They'd probably let me take some time off for a family emergency. But even if they couldn't hold the position for me, it's just an internship. It's not more important than my father's health."

"Then you should stay here and help us find a cure." I

remember Jace's words. "Carson, you and Tasha have the perfect combination of knowledge, modern chemistry, and ancient remedies."

"Ancient is correct," Tasha says. "Humans have been here for tens of thousands of years. Romanians have acquired much medicinal knowledge in that time."

"Do you know any of the local healing lore?" I ask her.

"Of course. I've been sharing some of my family's remedies with Carson."

"She's a treasure trove. I'm sure we can find something to help Poppy."

"There's one." Tasha points at a shiny white suitcase with black polka dots approaching us on the baggage carousel.

Carson lunges for it and pulls it to the floor in front of us. "Damn, this is heavy!"

"Three more, just like that. Plus my quiver case. Ah, there it is."

"You traveled light this time."

Tasha picks an invisible piece of lint off Carson's jacket. "We should stop at the mall and let the girls shop. When in Romania, you want to look Romanian, no?"

I'm about to answer that I don't see anyone else dressed like Tasha. But Lisa doesn't look offended. In fact, she has a big smile on her face.

"I doubt your Versace dress came from a mall in Bucharest," Lisa says. "It's Donna, not Gianni, right?"

Tasha's white-blonde eyebrows raise and she flashes a brilliant smile. "I like her style a lot better than his, don't you?

May he rest in peace."

"It's gorgeous. So is your necklace. Is that designer as well?"

"You could say that. I designed it myself. These coins are called *lew*. The old currency of Romania."

"They still are the Romanian currency," Carson says.

"These are from earlier, *Stea*, when they were pure silver. I love designs that express our history. Here." Tasha unclasps the necklace and hands it to Lisa.

"Beautiful work." The coins are soldered to tiny metal circles through which the chain is threaded. "Where do you get something like this done?"

"I have a silversmith in Bucharest. He is my favorite. He can make anything I ask him for. I just draw a sketch of what I want, and he produces it, exactly to my specifications."

I think about my step-grandmother, Aurelia, going to a silversmith for a special purchase. I shiver at the memory of what she commissioned: a silver bullet. Actually, silver bullets, plural.

"I'd like to meet him. Poppy and I might be able to commission him for some pieces for the gallery. Does he do large work?"

"Any size. Any item. Like I said, anything you could possibly ask for."

"Turn around," Lisa says. "I'll put this back on for you."

Tasha hooks elbows with Lisa on one side and me on the other. "We will find exactly what you both need to wear to fit in while you're in Romania. And after that, we will stop for dinner on the way home."

"Do we really have time to go to the mall? Don't we need to get started researching?"

"I need to decompress after my travels," Tasha says. "It was a stressful trip."

"Where did you go?" I ask.

"A little town outside Paris."

"What were doing that was so stressful?"

"Family business."

From her tone, I know that the conversation is over.

Carson pays for a cart to haul our luggage to the car. Tasha carefully positions a canvas sack on the top of the stack. "Did you say that's a quiver case?"

"That's right."

"What's it for?"

She arches a pencil-thin eyebrow. "What would you think it's for?"

"To carry a quiver?"

"That's right," she says again, this time with a note of sarcasm.

"Do you have arrows in it?"

"Why would I need a quiver if I had no arrows?"

"It just seems like something the airlines would have a problem with."

Tasha flips a pink suitcase lock that's attached to the zipper of the canvas bag. "TSA certified," she says. "Anything with a lock on it like this, they don't blink an eye at. They know they can open it and examine the contents any time they want to."

"Is that everything?" Lisa asks.

"I hope so," Carson says with a grunt as he pushes the cart toward the exit. "Nothing else will fit."

***

The mall reminds me of the run-down K-Mart in Knoxville. The aisles are wide with dingy terrazzo floors. The lighting is dim, and the racks of clothes are sparse, like a picked over buffet that probably was less than bountiful to begin with.

Tasha darts ahead from rack to rack, occasionally pausing to run a sleeve or pants leg through her fingers. She pulls out a frilly white skirt and holds the hanger at my waist. "This would look darling on you."

"Me likey," Lisa says. "You have great fashion sense, Tasha. How did you wind up in chemistry?"

"I would have to move to pursue a fashion career. My family needs me here right now." Tasha walks slowly around the rack. "Here, Lisa. This is cashmere. You would look smashing in it."

She hands Lisa a neon-purple shell with a low-slung cowl neck.

Lisa holds it to her chest. "Let's go try these on, Lani."

Our purchases safely tucked into cloth bags – which we had to buy as well – we head on to the next destination.

"Museum of Trash?" I read the English translation on a sign beneath the Romanian words.

"Y'all wouldn't believe how much this country recycles," Carson says. "They're way ahead of the U.S."

Carson points at a sandwich sign that stands on the pavement beside the door. The hours are chalked in. "Bummer. They close at Noon on Thursdays."

"We will have to take you to see some other sites," Tasha says.

"Remember, we're not here as tourists."

"Of course not. But when will you be able to return to Romania? You need to experience our culture while you are here."

"Don't tell me we're going to Dracula's castle." I roll my eyes. "Birthplace of the vampire legend?"

"It's a very historic cultural site, but I'm afraid you will not find vampires at the castle, Lani."

"Damn my luck."

"Maybe before we go home," Lisa suggests. "If our flight schedule allows some time for exploring, I'd like to go to a museum or something with ancient Romanian history."

"How ancient do you want?" Tasha's eyes glitter with excitement.

"How ancient do you got?" Lisa responds.

"Thousands of years. In fact, tens of thousands of years. Did I not tell you this?"

Now Lisa's eyes twinkle. "Seriously?"

Tasha nods. "Have you heard of *Peştera cu Oase?*"

I repeat the term slowly, trying to get the pronunciation right. "Pesh-terra coo Wassa. What's that?"

"The Cave with Bones. Are you familiar with it?"

Lisa shakes her head vigorously. "Human bones? No,

thanks. I thought you meant ancient art work. I'm not into bones and skeletons and all that spooky stuff."

"No?" Tasha cocks her head at me as we walk toward Carson's car, an antique Volvo that looks like its main components are rust, dust, and duct tape. "Maybe you are not interested in bones and skeletons and all that spooky stuff. But perhaps your friend is."

"What makes you say that?" I ask.

"You sounded disappointed about there being no vampires at Bram Castle. I assumed you are into vampires, ghosts, that type of thing."

"I was being sarcastic. I don't believe in vampires, and I have no interest in them."

"What about *pricolici?*"

"Pree coh-leech?" Lisa asks.

She is unfamiliar with the word, but I'm not.

I come to a stop and my bag slips from my shoulder. "It means werewolf."

Before I can reposition my bag, a tiny hand snatches it out of my grasp.

"My bag!"

I watch as a barefoot little boy races the opposite direction down the sidewalk, clutching his prize close to his side like a running back with a football. He is joined by two other barefoot boys, all of them dressed in grubby hand-me-downs. They all disappear into the crowd.

"Well, that's the last time you'll see that skirt," Carson says. "Damn Gypsy kids. If you don't keep your eyes open and hold your bags close, they'll rip you off in a heartbeat."

I almost forget what made me drop my bag in the first place. "Why do you automatically assume they're Roma?"

"Ah! Thank you, Lani," Tasha says. "I have tried many times to teach Carson to call us Roma. You might not know by looking at me, but I am Roma. And so were those boys, unfortunately."

"Why unfortunately?" Lisa asks.

"Because every time the Roma steal your bag or pickpocket your valuables," Tasha explains, "it emphasizes the stereotype."

"I should have warned you earlier," Carson says. "They'll steal you blind. Or at least, steal your heart." He squeezes Tasha and smiles at her with total adoration.

"A Roma stole Lani's heart, too," Lisa says. "Didn't he?"

I smile my possum grin again. I can't hide that I'm as head-over-heels with my Roma boy as Carson obviously is with his Roma girl.

Tasha adjusts her necklace so the heavy silver coins are more evenly aligned around her throat and chest. "You know Roma in Tennessee?"

"Georgia, actually."

"And these Roma, are they of Romanian descent?"

"Yeah, the ones I know are. Why?"

Tasha shrugs. "Small world, that is all. Is the name Cojocaru familiar?"

"No. Jace's last name is Lovari."

"A good Roma name."

"My step-grandmother is Roma, but I don't know what her last name was before she married my grandfather."

Back in the Volvo, Tasha looks at me in the rear-view mirror as Carson winds his way onto a four-lane road. "I'm sorry about your skirt. We'll have to find something else for you tomorrow."

"Damn Gypsies," Carson mutters again.

Tasha glares at him, but in a gentle way that shows she's more exasperated than upset with him.

"I mean, damn kids. Is that better?"

She pinches his arm.

Carson squirms away. "No harassing the driver!"

Tasha turns to look at Lisa and me. "We Roma are hard workers, proud of our heritage, and eager to move into the future."

"I know," I say, stealing a glance at Lisa. "We're counting on it."

Carson turns off the highway and winds through tree-lined streets with three-story-tall apartments on either side. The buildings are weathered and grey, the architecture unadorned except for brick-red arches. The ground floors of the buildings are occupied with shops.

I don't know anything about building design, but my father was a builder. He had a simple yet elegant style, displayed in both our home in Cloud Pass and the chapel he built for the Methodist church. I think I inherited his taste in architecture, and I think he would have liked the uncomplicated pattern on these apartments as much as I do.

"Is this it?" Carson asks. "I haven't been here in a while."

"Just there." Tasha points and Carson turns at the next intersection.

"Where are we going?" I ask.

"Dinner," Tasha says. "A little spot the locals like."

"Off the beaten path of the tourons," Carson adds.

"Does Romania get enough tourists to beat a path?" I ask.

"If it's a goat path, it only takes two or three," Carson says. "Plus a goat."

After a couple more blocks, Carson banks the car on the sidewalk and parks at an angle. Just ahead of us, an opening between buildings leads to a shady courtyard.

As we walk toward the courtyard, a pack of dogs walks by in the opposite direction. All three dogs are lean to the point of starvation, brown, with curly tails. They trot by with barely a glance at us. I watch them go by, and notice that one of them, slightly taller than the other two, watches me as well.

He stops and turns to look at us.

"Hey, pup," I say.

"Don't call them," Carson says. "There are a lot of stray dogs in Bucharest. You never know; they could have rabies."

The big dog takes a step toward us.

Lisa flinches and ducks behind her brother.

Carson waves his arms in the air in a shooing motion. "Get!"

All three dogs tuck their tails and scamper away.

As we approach the courtyard, three men standing at the

entry stop talking. Their heads swivel as they eyeball Tasha. One of the men whistles a long note.

"I'm telling your wife," Tasha says.

The men laugh and swat each other with their hats. I don't know if they understand English or just the tone in her voice.

Inside the courtyard, kiosks line the walls, and tables and chairs are grouped in the middle. The air is thick with the savory scent of grilled meat.

"You girls find a table," Carson says. "Tasha and I will get us all some dinner."

We claim four vinyl-cushioned chairs and a laminated-wood table and wait for Carson and Tasha. "So, Leez, what do you think of your brother's girlfriend?"

"She's a knock-out. Not what I expected at all, but I can see why Carson likes her."

"C'mon, Leez. A woman is more than a sexy body in a painted-on dress."

"True. Not all women have sexy bodies and painted-on dresses. The others must have something else going for them. Maybe they're librarians."

"You chauvinist." I swat her arm. "Tell me what you think of her, as a person."

"She knows her way around a fashion mall. She's friendly. I guess she's smart, if she's in chemical engineering."

"Do you think we can trust her?"

"I don't know. She has the local remedies that we need. If we tell her what we're looking for, she could point us to the ones that might help. What do you think of her?"

"I think she's going to help us find a cure for your dad."

Lisa smiles so wide her dimples pop. "Then she's my new best friend."

I put on an exaggerated pout. "Hey, what about me?"

"I love you too, girl."

***

After a dinner of lamb kebabs and roasted veggies, Carson drives us to the center of Bucharest. "This is Lipscani, or Old Town."

He parks on the curb in front of a small grey house tucked between apartment buildings on Ion Ghica Street.

I step out of the car into the chilly night air. I hadn't noticed when we were eating dinner, but the temperature has dropped now that the sun has gone down.

Lisa rubs her arms and looks up at the two-story building. "You rent this house?"

"Just part of it. The owners have the upstairs."

Tasha unlocks the door. Carson hauls her luggage inside and dumps it in the corner next to an ornate grandfather clock. He and Tasha take off their shoes and deposit them in a wicker basket on the other side of the door; Lisa and I follow their lead.

While Carson takes Tasha's luggage to one bedroom, Tasha leads us to the second. She gestures at a vase of deep red crocuses on the dresser. "I told Carson to put fresh flowers in your room, to welcome you."

"Thank you, Tasha. How do you say 'thank you' in Romanian?"

"*Mulțumesc.*"

"Muhl tsoo mesk. *Mulțumesc,* Tasha. I love the color red."

The red flowers remind me of my father, who had a passion for gardening and from whom I inherited my love for the color red. Tears prick at the corners of my eyes.

"That was very thoughtful of you," Lisa says. "Especially since you were traveling yourself."

Lisa and I throw our bags on the bed, which is wider than my twin bed at Mama's and my house in Lafayette, but narrower than the double bed in my room at my home in Cloud Pass. The house where my dad raised me as a single parent. He was a carpenter and a stone mason. His father had built our house when Dad was a little boy.

When we moved back to Cloud Pass, Dad embedded moon stones in my bedroom's door frame and in swirling patterns around the room's walls. As a five-year-old, I didn't know then that the moonstones were to protect me from something awful: My own mother.

"You okay?" Lisa whispers.

"Yeah. Flashback moment. Thinking about my dad."

"I get those about my mom sometimes. For no reason, I'll just start thinking about her. After all these years, it still hurts. Like this crushing weight on my chest."

"When did your mom pass away?"

"When I was six and Carson was ten."

"Is it okay to ask what happened?"

"She had been sick with cancer, but she was getting

better. Then one day, she was ringing up a customer at the cash register. She had an aneurism. One minute, she was fine. The next minute, she was gone. I didn't get to say goodbye, or tell her I loved her one last time. The last thing she said to me was, 'Go comb your hair. It's a rat's nest.'"

She slides her hand across the side and back of her head and sighs. "That's why I keep it short. So it's easier to control."

Tasha knocks on the bedroom door. "Let me show you the rest of the apartment."

"I'll fix us all some drinks," Carson adds. He puts a kettle of water on the gas stove. "Hot Romanian tea good for everyone?"

"I love hot tea," I tell him.

"Sounds great," Lisa says. "I was getting a little chilly."

Tasha shows us around, starting with the tiny kitchen. The ceiling is draped with dried herbs that hang from crisscrossed strings. Carson rubs his chin as he studies the selection. He plucks a few stems, which he tosses in a tall silver teapot.

A table and two wooden chairs crowd one cramped corner of the kitchen. Books and papers are stacked in both chairs, on the table, and in tumble-down piles on the floor under the table. Carson squares a stack of papers. "Sorry for the mess. This is our research."

There's also a bathroom that consists of a pedestal sink and a tiny shower, and a separate water closet with the toilet and a sink. The master bedroom is the same size as our room but with a queen-size bed. It looks like a battleground between Tasha's and Carson's styles: Metallic surfaces bare of any clutter occupy one side of the room, while the unmade bed and a wooden dresser with drawers that are overstuffed with man-clothes indicate Carson's overgrown-college-boy taste in décor. Carson's side is winning the battle.

Last is the cozy living room, where I take a seat on an ultra-comfy couch draped with a quilt. I recognize the quilt's wedding-band pattern from one of the quilts my father had in our house. Feeling completely at home, I curl my legs up under me.

"I think I'll use the water closet," Lisa says.

Carson brings out a tray of china cups and the silver teapot and sets it on the little table in front of the couch. He pours me a cup of steaming hot tea and sits on the other end of the couch. Although there are two perfectly good rocking chairs, Tasha sits between us, a tight fit.

"So tell me," she says as she pours tea for herself and Carson. "What are Carson's father's symptoms?"

I blow on the tea and take a sip. "Um, he has a fever," I ad-lib.

"Go on. What else?"

"I'm not sure. You'll have to ask Lisa."

Fortunately, Lisa returns, saving me from digging a hole I couldn't climb out of. "Ask me what?" She washes her hands at the kitchen sink and pours herself a cup of tea.

"We need to know exactly the nature of your father's illness if we are to help find a cure." Tasha looks at Lisa. "*Exactly* the nature."

Lisa paces in the tiny area between the table and the two

chairs. She sets her tea on the table.

She looks at me for assurance.

I nod.

"Okay. Here it is. About six weeks ago, Poppy was attacked by a wolf."

Carson jumps to his feet. "Sissy! Why didn't you tell me?"

Tasha and I stand, too.

"It's like Lani said. I didn't want you to race home and lose your job. I thought I could handle it."

"How badly was he hurt?"

"The wolf, um, bit his arm off at the elbow."

Both Carson and Tasha gasp.

"Sissy, you really should have called me!"

Lisa is crying now and Carson goes to her and folds her in a bear-like hug. She is so tiny next to him, yet anyone could tell they are brother and sister.

"So do you think Poppy's infection was caused by the wolf, or something he picked up at the hospital? A MRSA infection?"

"It … It." Lisa is too choked up to get the words out.

I clear my throat. "It was definitely caused by the wolf."

"How do you know?" Carson asks. "Do you think it was rabid?"

Lisa takes several deep breaths. "They gave Poppy the rabies series at the hospital, just in case. But that isn't the problem."

Carson holds his sister's shoulders and looks down into

her eyes. "What is it, then?"

"The wolf that bit Poppy?" Lisa looks from Carson to Tasha.

"Tell us," Tasha says. Her pale blue eyes are wide, but her expression is less one of fear than of some sort of voyeuristic excitement.

Lisa takes another deep breath. "It was a werewolf."

Ha!

CHAPTER 6

Carson looks at his sister in disbelief. "The hell are you talking about?"

I can't blame him for being skeptical. If I hadn't seen werewolves with my own eyes, I would think Lisa was crazy, too.

It's hard to talk about, but I know I have to tell them my story if we want them to help us find a local remedy that will help Stan.

I recount the whole story, beginning with my Aunt Romelia's unrequited crush on my father.

"So you never knew your parents were werewolves?" Carson asks. "How could you not have known?"

"I thought my mother was dead. I thought she died when I was five, and Dad and I moved to Cloud Pass. And my dad? I don't know. I guess there were signs."

"Like what?" Carson spits the question as if he's a prosecutor and I'm on the witness stand.

"He got old before his time. I thought it was from the stress of being a single parent. He said he saw my mother. He said she was a werewolf. I thought he was hallucinating because of his fever. It's not like lycanthropy – being a werewolf – is a disease that you suspect when your father gets sick."

I tell them how my best friend, Ben Stoat, had become a werewolf. My father had attacked his father when Ben's father tried to kill Mama. Then Mr. Stoat became a werewolf and attacked his own family, killing Ben's sister and turning Ben and his mother into werewolves. As I recount the story, all the deaths press in on me like the lid of a coffin. By the end, I'm exhausted. I slump down on the couch and rub my face, pressing my palms into my eyes.

All is silent except a ringing in my ears, until Tasha says, "We can help you."

I raise my head and look at her. My eyes feel puffy and red, and a headache is beginning to pound behind my right ear.

"How?" Lisa asks.

An impish smile plays on Tasha's face and her icy blue eyes twinkle as she fingers the coins on her necklace. "I have my grandmother's remedies and notes, including some references to the *pricolici*."

"Werewolf remedies?" Carson asks. "You didn't tell me you had anything like that."

Tasha shrugs. "You're looking for cures for cancer, migraine remedies, ways to retain memory as people age. Your work is much more serious than silly folklore."

"Doesn't seem so silly, now." Carson is fuming. He paces in front of Lisa, knocking his leg into the table. Lisa's cup tumbles to the floor, shattering and sloshing tea across the rug.

Carson rubs his shin. "Why didn't you tell me Poppy had been attacked? It's not like he got a little scratch. His fricking arm was ripped off at the elbow, for Chrissakes."

Lisa, cowed by her brother's outburst, pulls her legs to her chest, making herself into a tiny ball in the chair.

"Carson, don't blame her," I tell him. "She called me as soon as she knew Stan needed help. She called you as soon as we made the connection that you might be able to help."

Carson stands in front of his sister, his arms board-stiff at his sides and his fists pumping. "But I'm his son! You should have called me as soon as he was injured. To hell with the job. He needs me."

Lisa raises her tear-streaked face to him. "Yes. Poppy needs you."

He exhales loudly through flared nostrils. His lips are set tightly together.

Tasha steps to his side and rests her hand against his shoulder. "*Stea,* calm down. She is doing what she can. She is asking for your help."

"At least you called, eventually." He holds his hands out to Lisa.

She stands and he embraces her in a fierce hug.

"Tonight, Carson and I will look through our research that we have here."

"I'll check some of the information from my company's intranet," Carson adds.

"What can we do?" I ask.

"Tomorrow, after breakfast, you girls can assist with the research," Tasha says. "Tonight you should sleep."

I think of the stacks of papers spread throughout the apartment. "Do you think you have any information about werewolves?"

"Hopefully not just information. Hopefully, somewhere

in all this mess, we'll find the cure."

That night I can't sleep. I check the time on my phone. Eight PM Eastern time. That means it's 3 AM local. I've never traveled overseas before, but I know if I don't go to sleep on Romanian time, I'll have jet lag in the morning.

I'm afraid my tossing and turning will wake Lisa, who is curled in a ball like a little kid, on the very edge of the bed.

I get up and tiptoe out to the kitchen for a glass of water. The house is completely dark except for a thin, grey light peeking through the kitchen window from a streetlamp. I peer into the cabinets until I find the glassware. I fill the glass with water from the sink and raise it to my lips.

The front door opens with a creak. Startled, I drop the glass on the floor, where it shatters.

"Two broken glasses in less than two days." Tasha props her canvas quiver case by the front door.

"I'm really sorry." I pluck pieces of glass off the floor as best I can in the dim light and set them on the counter.

"It can only mean good luck, I'm sure." Tasha turns on the light over the stove and joins me on the kitchen floor.

"How do you figure?"

"Haven't you ever thrown a glass in the fireplace?"

I shake my head. "I've seen it in old movies. What does it mean?"

"It could mean a joyful occasion. It could be done to dispel misfortune. It could break a string of deaths." Tasha holds a shard of glass to the meager light from the tiny appliance bulb in the stove hood. The light refracts through the glass and creates a rainbow on the floor.

"But one thing it definitely means…." She grins and raises her eyebrows. "I get to go shopping for new glassware."

We place the glass shards in a tiny tin bucket under the sink, and Tasha sweeps the floor.

"Do you normally stay out so late? I heard you come in late last night, too."

"Family business," she says. "Nothing to concern yourself with."

As she bends over to brush the glass particles into a dust pan, the light catches her necklace.

Something's odd about it. It takes me a moment to realize what it is. "Tasha! You lost one of your coins."

She puts her hand to her throat, touching the exact spot on the necklace where the coin is missing. "Oh, well."

"You don't sound terribly upset."

"Another trip to Dalca the silversmith. I guess there are worse things in life."

***

Breakfast is big. So big, we take it out back to the garden. A picnic table under a gazebo offers space for the bowls of fresh fruit – sliced apples, plums, wedges of watermelon – as well as a basket of fresh-baked bread and a platter of thinly sliced venison and cheese. The gazebo furnishes shade; the mid-August morning sun, and with it the temperature, is already starting to rise. Despite the heat, Carson has brewed a fresh pot of tea, this batch flavored with mint, and he pours for us all.

I build a venison sandwich, spreading a thin layer of

mustard on the meat. I add a few slices of apple to my plate. The venison is moist and any gaminess is tamed by the earthiness of the bread.

Carson and Lisa choose only fruit, cheese, and bread, but Tasha creates a huge sandwich with multiple layers of venison and cheese.

"You've got a real Dagwood sandwich," I say.

She looks at her sandwich. "No, it's *carne de vânat*. In English, venison. Are dogwood trees even edible?"

"Their bark is worse than their bite," Carson says.

I giggle at his quick pun. "Dagwood. He's a cartoon character who makes huge sandwiches."

"He could really wolf 'em down, too," Carson says.

Lisa drops her fork on her plate with just a tiny bit more clatter than necessary. "No dog jokes, okay? No wolf references."

"Sure, Sissy." Carson leans in to put an arm around Lisa's shoulders. "But you don't need to be so sensitive."

"Me, sensitive? You're the one who lost your temper last night."

"C'mere, Sissy." Carson touches his forehead against Lisa's. "I was upset last night. Confused. You dropped the bombshell on me that Poppy was attacked by a werewolf. I guess I was mad at myself for not being there to protect you and Poppy."

"There was nothing you could have done. You probably would have tried something heroically stupid, and been attacked, too."

"How long have you known about the *pricolici*, Lisa?" Tasha asks. "Werewolves, that is."

"We know what it means," Lisa says. "When the wolf attacked Poppy, I didn't know it was a werewolf. I thought it was a regular wolf or a wolf-hybrid. It knew commands, like it was housebroken, so I knew it wasn't wild."

Lisa had told me that the wolf obeyed her when she told him to sit. Then he left when she told him to get out. I remember remarking to Ben once how well his mama had trained him. He was very obedient, with perfect manners. Until he turned into a werewolf. That's when most of his housebreaking flew out the window. At least he listened to Lisa before he killed either her or Stan.

"What are you thinking?" Tasha's question makes me look up from my plate, where I have absent-mindedly picked apart the bread from my sandwich, forming a tiny mountain of crumbs.

Tasha, Lisa, and Carson are all staring at me. I wipe the corner of my mouth with my thumb, thinking maybe I have a glop of mustard.

"Oh, were you talking to me?"

"Yes, about werewolves," Carson says. "How long have you known they aren't just a legend?"

"Just a month, month and a half."

"How many werewolf attacks have you seen?" Tasha asks.

"I've seen a werewolf kill one person." Jace's grandmother, Natasha, was hiding right next to me when the werewolf grabbed her by the throat and broke her neck. The memory of Natasha's death stings, but I can't dwell on that right now. "I've been attacked by two werewolves. Three, if you count my mother, but that was different – she was trying to provoke me to kill her. And I've seen Mama in her werewolf form fight two other werewolves."

Tasha sits up straight. Her eyes are as wide as a kid watching the shark handler at the Atlanta Zoo at feeding time. "You've seen werewolves fight *each other?*"

I nod.

"Why were they fighting?" she asks.

"Two wanted to kill me. One wanted to save me."

Tasha pushes her chair back from the picnic table. "That's impossible. Werewolves do not have human emotions."

"Yeah. They do." I clamp my molars together to avoid saying something hurtful. After all, she *is* going to help us, even if she doesn't know as much about werewolves as she thinks.

"They have one emotion only. Their insatiable need to feed on human flesh. It is all they care about."

Blood pounds in my temples. "You're wrong. You don't know what you're talking about."

"Lani, chill," Lisa says.

"But I've seen it," I insist.

"I didn't say that you hadn't," Lisa says. "I'm just saying, we better hope Tasha knows *something* about werewolves. At this point, it's Poppy's only hope for a cure."

I take a deep breath. Then another. "You're right, Leez. You're absolutely right. Tasha, I'm sorry. I truly hope you can help us."

Tasha's face smoothes into a smile. I brush off the feeling that it's the same expression a teacher gives a preschooler who apologizes after being naughty.

"Carson and I have lots of notes from what we found out last night."

"Anything about werewolves?"

"Not directly, but some interesting leads," Carson says.

"We'll share those with you first, then go to the libraries," Tasha adds.

"How many libraries are in Bucharest?"

"There is the national library, the museum libraries, and there are several private homes with impressive libraries."

"But we don't have access to private homes," Lisa points out.

Tasha's eyes gleam. "You do if your last name is Petrescu."

"Are you famous?" I ask.

"My family goes back many centuries in Romania. You might call us famous, yes."

"What are you famous for?" Lisa asks.

Tasha shrugs. "Being Petrescus."

***

The notes Tasha and Carson have taken are piled in heaps on the table in the kitchen nook. More piles are stacked under the table. More papers and notebooks and journals are piled in the closet in the room Lisa and I share, and in the cabinets, and in Carson's dresser drawers, and on almost every other available surface in the tiny apartment. The only areas that are exempt are the room Lisa and I share (which I feel was also used, prior to our arrival in Romania, for storage of the volumes that are now on the closet floor), the living room (likewise), and Tasha's half of her and Carson's bedroom. That area, I am 100 percent certain, was never covered in disorganized clutter of any kind.

Lisa and I curl up on opposite ends of the couch. Carson sits cross-legged on the living room floor, and Tasha brings us each stacks of papers to look through. She doles them out like a teacher handing out assignments. "The words you are looking for are *pricolici*, which means werewolf or werewolves; *remediu*, which means remedy or cure; and *antidot*, which of course means antidote. You might also see *poțiune*, *vraja*, or *farmece*. Potion, spell, magic. *Magic* or *magie* also mean magic, very easy to recognize."

"What's the Romanian word for snake oil?" Lisa asks.

"I'm not familiar with snake oil."

"Then I've got some you can buy," Carson says. "Cures everything from dandruff to erectile dysfunction."

Lisa and I snicker behind cupped hands.

"I do not have either dandruff or erectile dysfunction," Tasha tells Carson. "But maybe you could use it yourself."

"Bwah!" Lisa erupts.

We both laugh so hard tears stream down our faces.

Carson turns red, then joins in our laughter. "Walked right into that one, didn't I?"

Tasha slaps the papers in her arms onto the table. "What

is it? What is so funny? I cannot help it if I do not understand all your American idioms."

"Don't worry," Lisa says. "We're not making fun of you. But I think, when we find the cure for lycanthropy, we should call it 'Stan's Snake Oil.'"

"Patented and trademarked by Puckett, Petrescu, and Morgan, Inc.," Carson says.

"Will the esteemed colleagues of Puckett, Petrescu, and Morgan please buckle down and search through these papers," I say. "Or we'll be patenting and trademarking a bunch of nothing."

"And that won't help Poppy," Lisa adds. "Tasha, can you write down the words we're looking for?"

Tasha pulls a long sheet of butcher paper from a roll in the kitchen and writes the words with a thick black marker. Even with the clunky marker, the script is swooping and graceful.

"Wow, your handwriting is beautiful," I tell her.

"Do you always write like that?" Lisa asks.

"It's how I learned," Tasha says modestly.

"It's very calligraphic. Even a list of words looks like poetry."

"Actually, she does write poetry," Carson says. "She's very good. Very romantic, but not sappy."

"I'd like to see it sometime," I say.

Lisa nods. "Me, too. Maybe after dinner, you can read some to us."

Tasha shakes her head. "I would be too embarrassed."

THE HUNTER'S MOON   75

"Three against one," Carson says. "But for now, it's to the Batcave!"

"Where are we going?" Tasha asks. "I thought we were staying here and doing research."

"We have *got* to introduce this girl to proper American culture," Lisa says. "Maybe we'll read some bat poetry after dinner."

She runs her finger down the first page in her stack. Suddenly she gasps. She looks at the sheet of butcher paper. "Is that word potion?"

Tasha looks at the word Lisa is pointing to. "*Nu*," Tasha says. "*Porțiune* is portion. But it is close. Keep looking."

For hours we comb through the documents. Some are photocopies, some are clippings taped to the page with passages highlighted and notes squiggled in the margins. Carson must have written these notes; they appear to be in English, but some are less decipherable than the Romanian texts.

When my stomach rumbles, I put my hand over my belly, but the noises are so loud that everyone looks at me.

"Must be lunchtime," Carson says. "Wanna give me a hand in the kitchen, Sissy?"

As Lisa and Carson rattle around in the kitchen, Tasha and I continue to scour the papers. I turn a page and read at the top, "…*leac pentru licantropia.*"

Lycanthropy!

I wave the paper in the air. "I think I found something."

Tasha takes the page from me and I point to the top line on the back. She flips the paper over and reads the entire sentence, *"Există doar un singur leac pentru licantropia."*

Lisa and Carson rush over and we all crowd around Tasha.

"What does it mean?" I ask. "That's the word for 'cure,' right? And *licantropia* -- That has to mean lycanthropy."

"*Da*, Lani. It means, 'There is only one cure for lycanthropy.'"

"Woohoo," Lisa cheers. She and Carson high-five.

I can't join their celebration. By Tasha's lack of excitement at my discovery, I know she is thinking the same thing as I am.

Lisa squeezes my shoulders. "What's wrong, Lani? It means there's a cure!"

"I've heard that phrase before – that there's only one cure for a werewolf."

"You know the cure?" Carson asks. He slaps a handful of papers against his thigh. "Then why in blue blazes did you girls come half-way around the dad-gum world looking for it?"

Lisa shushes him with a sweep of her hand. "It's not really a cure, is it?"

I shake my head. "Tasha, translate what it says next."

"The bullet must be pure silver, or no less than zero-point-nine-nine-five quality. For the best result, the *pricolici* should be shot in the heart. To ensure the beast does not revive, and to send the soul to heaven, the corpse must be burned."

Lisa slumps to her knees, clutching several pages in her hands. She wads them up and throws them toward the fireplace. "No. Oh, Poppy, no." She crumples to the floor and covers her face with her hands as she weeps.

I look around at Carson, Tasha, and Lisa. "We're not giving up. We'll find another way."

Carson kneels beside Lisa. "That's right, Sissy." He strokes her hair until she calms down. She holds her arms out to him and he pulls her to her feet.

"There has to be a cure, and we're going to find it."

I grab a handful of papers and wave them in the air. "We can't stop looking now."

"We've barely started," Carson agrees. "Look at all this paper! Somewhere in here is Poppy's cure."

"You gonna be okay?" I ask Lisa.

She nods her head. "Let's get back to work."

"Wait, what about lunch?" Carson asks.

"Okay, okay," Lisa says. "We'll eat lunch and then it's back to the Batcave."

"What is it with this cave of bats? Is it near the *Peştera cu Oase*?"

"Tasha, please make my brother rent some *Batman* DVDs and introduce you to an American icon." Tasha points at Carson. "And be sure you get the TV series so she sees the *real* version."

Lunch is soup and home-made bread. "The bread came from my grandmother," Tasha says. "I hope it is not stale."

"It's all delicious," I tell her.

"That reminds me," Lisa says. "I brought you a present."

She dashes into our bedroom and returns with a jar, which she flourishes in the air like a bouquet of flowers pulled from a magician's hat. "Voila!"

"Is that what I think it is?" Carson practically drools.

"Yep! Peanut butter."

"Your sister is a saint! A national hero," Tasha says, beaming.

Carson opens the jar and looks like he is about to dip his finger in the peanut butter.

"Use a spoon," Tasha says. "And don't be a glutton with it. You never know when we'll get more."

Later, with our stomachs full of too much soup, bread, and peanut butter, we return to the job of combing through the reams of notes, news clips, and ancient documents.

We work until the light from the sun grows dim, then turn on lamps and continue searching straight through dinner. Even Carson doesn't complain about the missed meal. Finally, though, Tasha says, "Time to stop for the night."

I straighten the pile of documents I've just finished pouring over. "We haven't found any more reference to werewolves or cures or any of the other buzzwords we've been looking for. Do you think it's time to look at some different sources? Like the libraries you were talking about?"

"*Da*. Tomorrow we will focus on the libraries of Bucharest."

CHAPTER 7

I was expecting a communist-era concrete building with all the charm of a prison. The National Library of Romania is nothing like that. Although it was built during Communist rule, it's been rehabbed into a thing of beauty. With its soaring walls of glass, it reminds me of the Tower Building in Knoxville, only blue instead of green.

Inside is just as impressive, airy and modern. A large area of the floor is made of frosted glass with images of letters that seem to float just below the surface.

Tasha presents her library card at the circulation desk to gain entry to the library.

When we try to follow her, the librarian-slash-security guard blocks us. *"Doar ei."*

Carson fishes some money out of his wallet. The librarian slips the bills in his pocket and lets the rest of us pass.

"You know what this is," I whisper to Lisa. "Library bribery."

"Say that three times fast."

I laugh. "With a spoonful of peanut butter in your mouth."

Lisa snaps her fingers. "Hey, I should have brought more peanut butter! No telling how many bribes we'll have to pay while we're here."

The library has an impressive collection of manuscripts,

old Romanian newspapers, and rare books in multiple languages. "Will they really let us touch these documents?" I ask Tasha.

"Most of them, yes. You'll know if you handle something that you shouldn't have."

"How will we know?"

"They'll cart you away in shackles," Tasha deadpans.

Lisa and I look at Carson. "She's kidding, right?" Lisa asks.

"Well, they haven't arrested Tasha or me."

"Yet," Lisa says.

Tasha sorts through the astounding quantity of materials, pulling out the most likely sources. Carson, Lisa, and I claim a table near a blue-hued window that is as tall as the stained-glass windows in the United Methodist Church of Cloud Pass.

Thinking about those windows at my church makes me think of my father. He installed the intricate glass windows when he built the church. It took him and a team of expert glass handlers a week to put the main window in place, a three-piece wonder of stained-glass craftsmanship that rose the full two-story height of the church.

Lisa elbows me in the ribs. "Quit daydreaming. We've got work to do."

"Sorry. I was just thinking about my dad."

"Flashback moment?"

"Yeah. It's these windows. They aren't even stained glass, but they remind me of watching my dad put in the windows at our church."

"Memories are like that," Lisa says. "Something you think is totally unrelated will remind you of your dad – or in my case, my mom – and suddenly, you can't think of anything else. Sometimes, it's a good thing. Like I guess the stained-glass memory is for you, judging by the smile that was on your face when you were sitting there just now, staring at the window."

"Before you so rudely interrupted my thoughts."

"Sorry about that."

"After your mother died, did you ever have memories that completely overwhelmed you? Like, not bad memories, but memories that make you so sad because of what you've lost, that you're almost crushed with grief?"

"I still do. It doesn't happen as often as right after she died. But somehow that makes it even more agonizing when it does."

We're quiet for a few moments, then simultaneously take in a breath and exhale with a sigh. I smile at Lisa. She nods and we hunker over our assigned stacks of papers.

As the day passes, reflections from the windows travel across the floor, the desk, and the piles of documents like a sundial's shadow. I blink and look up when a blue-hued sunbeam charts its path across my face. The wide swath of sky visible through the nearby window is melting from blue to purple.

"What time is it?" I ask Lisa.

She checks her watch. "It's one o'clock our time, so that's –" She ticks off the conversion from Eastern to Eastern European

Time on her fingers. "Eight PM here."

Carson walks by with a stack of books. "You mean we worked straight through lunch? No wonder my stomach is growling."

"Enough for today," Tasha says. "Let's get some dinner. We can return tomorrow."

"Do we just leave everything on the table?" I ask. "It'll be here when we come back?"

"*Nu*. The librarian will reshelve everything."

"How will we know what we've already looked through?" I ask.

"I'll write it all down," Carson says. He pulls a tiny notebook and pen from his shirt pocket. Tasha points at a document and whispers instructions to Carson. He scribbles the information and nods when he is ready for her to go on.

While they catalog our progress, Lisa and I look out the plate-glass window. On the brown grass lawn, which has a bluish tint, two little boys kick a soccer ball back and forth. They stop their game and run toward a woman who helps them put on coats. As they walk away, hand-in-hand, the smaller child breaks free. He runs back to retrieve the forgotten soccer ball, then rejoins his family.

"Ready to go?" Tasha asks.

We cross the street from the library to a sidewalk bordering a narrow, winding canal. Following the waterway, we occasionally have to step aside to avoid teenage boys on skateboards. Old women in babushka scarves and clunky shoes clutch their purses tightly under their ample bosoms as they pass.

I hear music up ahead, growing louder as the sun gets lower. Carson opens the door of a two-story building with a sign hanging from two chains: *Tavernă*. Instantly the music blares more loudly. The trio on stage is led by a barefoot woman with an electric ukulele. The music is sweet and sad and frenzied, all at once.

The tavern is packed; only two tables are empty. A waitress bounces over to us in time with the music and directs us to the table that is closest to the door, furthest away from the band.

Tasha speaks to the waitress, pointing to each of us in turn. The waitress licks the tip of her pencil, scribbles on her notepad, and twirls away.

"What are our plans tomorrow?" I yell to be heard over the music and other people's conversations.

"Back to the library, I guess," Carson says.

The waitress deposits bottles of water in the middle of our table.

"Actually, I think we should visit a private library," Tasha says. "The owner is a friend. He has an eclectic collection that might prove fruitful."

"How much do we tell him about what we're looking for?" I ask.

"Only as much as he needs to know."

As dinner arrives, the uke player strums the opening lines of Stairway to Heaven, but the song quickly morphs into something that sounds more traditionally Romanian, a festive tune that lifts my spirits, even though I'm tired as a rock. I dig into my dinner, willing myself to slow down so I can enjoy the textures and flavors. Mamaliga or cornbread wrapped around gooey cheese, cabbage rolls, and for desert, *crema de zahar ars*, a light, delicious flan with glazed caramel topping.

Later, we go back to the apartment, where Lisa and I crash on the living room sofa.

"Who wants plum wine?" Carson asks.

I shake my head. "I'm not twenty-one."

"In Romania, the age of adulthood is sixteen," Tasha says. "You may have some if you like."

I look at Lisa. "I will if you will."

We exchange a grin.

"Let's do it."

Carson retrieves four wine glasses from the cupboard. He cradles a dark purple wine bottle in the crook of one elbow and arranges the stems of the four glasses between his fingers.

"That's a real talent, Carz," Lisa says.

"I'd juggle, but we're running low on glassware."

"I'm really sorry about that," I say.

Tasha helps Carson with the glasses, arranging them on the little coffee table. "He's not really worried about breaking the glasses. He's worried about wasting the wine and staining the rug."

"Nah," Lisa says. "He's just worried about the *stain* on his clown college application."

I sip the wine tentatively. It's sweet and a little tangy. Despite it being legal to drink wine here in Romania, I still feel a tinge of guilt.

"Is something wrong with the wine?" Tasha asks. "You do not like the flavor?"

"No, it's good. I just never drank alcohol before."

"It takes a little getting used to," Lisa says.

"How would you know?" Carson asks.

"Don't get all big-brother on me. You're the one who bought me my first wine cooler."

Tasha stands and stretches, covering a yawn with her elbow. "It is time for bed. We have another big day ahead of us tomorrow."

Although I've only had a few sips of my wine, she takes my glass from my hand and pours the contents down the sink. She returns for Lisa's and Carson's glasses. Then she turns off all the lights except the little appliance light in the stove hood.

"Okay, night-night," Tasha says. She pulls Carson from his chair and drags him toward their bedroom.

"Geez," Lisa whispers as we go to our room. "You think she could show *some* subtlety. I'm his sister. That little scene was TMI."

"Or maybe she really is just tired."

"Right. Well, I'm going to take a shower before bed."

"I'll take one in the morning. I'm exhausted."

I shimmy out of my jeans and lie down in bed, but even with my fatigue, I can't get to sleep. I plump the pillow so I can read something on my Kindle.

Lisa comes back into the room, wrapped in a towel.

"Can I ask you something?"

"Sure. You can ask me anything." Lisa towels off and changes into flannel pajamas.

"Do you think it's easier when someone dies when you are expecting it?"

"No way. It's never easy when someone you love dies."

"My dad was sick, but I didn't think he was going to die."

"Same with my mom. She was sick with the cancer for a long time, but we thought she was getting better. I read a lot of books on cancer for kids. So I kind of knew what she was going through, and that it was normal to be afraid."

"Did that help prepare you?"

"When she died, she was gone." Lisa snuggles under the covers and curls into a curled-up cat position. "Nothing can prepare you for your mom being gone."

"Yeah, I guess you're right." I turn off the light on the nightstand between the two beds. "Does the light from my Kindle bother you?"

"No. Read as long as you like."

"Good night, Leez."

"Good night, Lan."

Eventually, I realize I'm reading the same paragraph over and over. I power off the Kindle and place it on the nightstand beside the lamp. As I reposition my pillow, I hear the front door open and close. Carson or Tasha must have left something in the car, I figure.

I don't know how long I've been asleep when the squeak of the front door wakes me up. I get out of bed and tiptoe to the bedroom door, opening it a sliver. In the darkness, I see the slender silhouette of Tasha, her hair glowing in the light from the kitchen. She takes her quiver case off her back and, holding it by the strap, creeps to her bedroom door. Quiet as a ghost, she slips inside and soundlessly shuts the door behind her.

I'm groggy and can't process this right now. In the morning, I'll ask Tasha what was going on.

CHAPTER 8

Another day, another walk into the heart of Bucharest. This time, Tasha leads us to a wrought-iron gate set in a tall concrete wall. Behind the gate is a small but lush garden in front of a narrow, three-story house. Rounded gables on the corners make the house look like a miniature castle.

Tasha pushes a buzzer on a keypad beside the gate. While she waits for an answer, she thrums a rolled-up scroll against her thigh -- the paper on which she wrote the list of important Romanian words.

A moment later, static barks from the keypad's speaker.

Tasha pushes another button and yells into the speaker.

The gate clicks and we walk through the garden. As we approach the house, the door opens and a skinny old man in a tuxedo opens his arms wide.

His smile is just as wide, showing yellowed teeth that are tiny like baby's teeth but perfectly straight. "Tatiana! Why do you stay away so long?"

"Oh, Decebal, you sound just like my grandmother." Tasha accepts his embrace with one arm, extending her other arm to the side so as not to crumple the scroll. "May I introduce you to my friends? This is Decebal Cojocaru."

He hugs us warmly as Tasha tells him our names. "Please to call me Decebal." I can smell his aftershave or cologne, heavy and floral, when he kisses my cheeks.

"So tell me," Decebal says as he leads us into his house. It is dark, with rich wood paneling and hardwood floors. "Tell me about this *pricolici*."

I grab Tasha's elbow. "How much did you tell him?"

"That we are looking for a cure for a werewolf. We are requesting access to his personal library. Do you want me to lie to him?"

"No, of course not." I look at Decebal. "I hope I haven't offended you, sir. I just … it's just …." My face and neck burn with embarrassment.

"You do not want me to think you are crazy for such superstitious beliefs, *nu*?"

"That's right."

"In Bucharest people know me as a bit of an eccentric. This is because of my broad acceptance of multiple beliefs, whether it be religion, folklore, or what they refer to as my obsessive-compulsive behaviors. Tatiana brought you to the right place."

He opens double doors made of shiny black wood, revealing a spacious room bright with sunshine from skylights and lined floor to ceiling with bookshelves. In the center is a long pub table with banker's lamps at either end and barstools all around.

"I would recommend starting …." Decebal taps his chin with one long, skinny finger as he moves about the room, considering the books filling every shelf on every wall. He stops pacing and spreads his arms wide in front of one section. "Here."

Decebal rings a small crystal bell, and a butler appears. Decebal tells the man something in Romanian and the butler bows and leaves.

"Coffee, tea, and pastries are on the way. In the meantime, please make yourselves at home. If you need me, just ring this bell." He leaves the bell on a pedestal table by the doors to the library, which he closes silently behind him.

Tasha unrolls the scroll with the key Romanian words and places the paper on the table. She secures the top with one of the banker's lamps. "Get me a book," she tells Carson.

"Which book?"

"Any book. A heavy one."

He picks one that must weigh ten pounds and brings it to Tasha. She spreads the scroll flat and places the book on the other end.

Soon the butler returns with a giant silver tray loaded with pastries, a coffee urn, a teakettle, china cups, a tiny pewter pitcher of cream, a bowl of sugar cubes, and a small jar made of beveled glass. Decebal follows behind the butler like a puppy sniffing the treats.

The butler unfolds a serving table and places the tray on it. Decebal motions for us to help ourselves, then takes a pastry himself. "Mmm, heavenly. Jakob makes the best pastries in the world -- except for your grandmother's, of course, Tatiana."

"*Mulțumesc*, Decebal. I will tell her you said so." Tasha bites into a pastry. "It is very good, Jakob."

"Now, tell me," Decebal says, dabbing the corners of his mouth with a napkin. "Who is this *pricolici*, and how do you intend to deal with him? Did the silver bullet not do the trick, as the Americans say?"

"We are *not* trying to kill him!" Lisa's voice shakes. "He's my father, and we are going to cure him!"

"Oh, my dear." Decebal scurries to her side. "I am so sorry for misunderstanding. When Tatiana said she needed a medicinal 'cure' for the *pricolici*, I assumed she meant a tranquilizer of sorts. A sedative to put the beast to sleep to make an easier target. I do apologize, my dear. Please forgive me."

Lisa nods, takes a few deep breaths. "Of course. I don't guess you have many visitors looking for a werewolf remedy."

"You are the very first. Please, may I refresh your tea?"

"Thank you," Lisa says, her voice still shaky. "That would be nice."

"Do you take sugar? Cream? Honey?"

"Honey, please."

Decebal removes the glass lid from the beveled jar on the serving tray. He dips a tiny glass wand into it and drizzles honey into Lisa's tea.

He insists on refreshing all of our drinks and encourages us to eat more pastries. "I'll let you get back to your work. Remember to ring the bell if you need any assistance."

We search through Decebal's extensive collection, using our established method of skimming the texts for words that might be connected to werewolves and remedies.

"Remind me not to choose research librarian as a career," I tell Lisa, rubbing the back of my neck.

"I think I'll become a dockworker," Lisa says. "Less

backbreaking."

When the light fades, we pack up our notes and ring the bell. Decebal and the butler both respond to the summons.

"We're done for the night," Tasha says. "May we leave the resources on the table?"

"Yes, of course," Decebal says. "They will be here when you return."

***

Days turn into weeks as we roam from library to library. The university, other private libraries, back to the National Library. After two weeks, we are no closer to a cure.

Exhausted and depressed from our lack of success, we return to Decebal's home.

"What about your grandmother?" he asks Tasha.

Carson shakes his head. "We already scoured all her recipes when we were looking for folk remedies."

Decebal's eyes glitter as he arches his eyebrows. "But you were not looking for *pricolici* remedies, were you?"

"Why didn't I think of that, Decebal? Now that you mention it, I am sure I saw references to *pricolici* in some of Dama's books."

"I wish you'd thought of that two weeks ago," Lisa says, a tiny edge of frustration in her voice that reflects my own feelings.

Tasha shrugs. "We were there for a totally different reason. It barely registered at the time." She reaches for my hand and caresses the moonstone ring on my index finger. "I think you will all like my grandmother very much."

CHAPTER 9

Tasha tells us her grandmother lives in Oltenita, a small town outside Bucharest on the banks of the Danube River.

"Seriously?" I ask. "*The* Danube River?"

Tasha laughs good-naturedly. "No, the *other* Danube River."

"I guess I always thought the Danube was in Austria, or maybe Germany," I admit. "I never expected to find it in Romania."

"Romania is full of surprises."

We bump along in the Volvo, a greenish-blue river snaking its way beside the highway on our right, summer-scorched farmlands on our left.

"Like what?" Lisa asks.

"Well, you already know about *Peştera cu Oase*, the Cave with Bones, so that's not a real surprise."

"What's so special about it? Is it like the Catacombs in Paris?"

Tasha rolls her eyes. "Pssh. Those bones are modern bones. A few hundred to a thousand years old. To see *really* old bones, I mean the bones of our ancestors' ancestors, you must go to the Cave with Bones."

"How old are the bones in the cave?"

"Older than dirt," Carson says. "Thirty-five *thousand*-year-old bones were found there."

"That's amazing," I say.

"Tell them about something else, Tash. One of Romania's quirky national treasures."

"We have a merry cemetery. It has colorful wooden crosses for the grave markers."

"Merry is good," I say. "But can you stay away from topics related to bones and death?"

"Sure, sure. Let me think." In the rearview mirror I see Tasha scrunch her mouth from side to side in thought. "Ah! Did you know we have bears? And wolves? The most of any country in Europe."

A shiver jerks Lisa's body like a taste of bad medicine. "Are … are they werewolves?"

"They are just common wolves," Carson says with a soothing voice. "And they're up in the mountains. You won't run into them here."

We all grow quiet. The only noise is the car's purring little engine and an occasional groan from the shock absorbers when we hit a pothole.

I stare out the window. Beyond the stores and houses, a blocky cement water tower looms like a movie prop leftover from *War of the Worlds.*

Carson turns the car onto a narrow road lined with faded gingerbread bungalows. All the houses but one appear weatherworn, with faded, peeling paint and scraggly yards of sand and weeds. We stop at the only house that appears to have been well cared for.

Tasha's grandmother's house is painted a fresh

sunflower-yellow. Window boxes and hanging baskets overflow with a rainbow of flowers and ferny plants. A sign on the door says *Cazare*.

"Here we are," Tasha says. "Home of the best spiced-apple baker in all of Romania, my Dama."

The bounce in her voice feels forced, and it makes me like her a little more. She's trying to cheer up Lisa, wipe away the memory of the earlier conversations about wolves and bones and cemeteries.

Tasha reaches over and toots the horn before getting out of the car.

The front door swings open and a very large woman, tall and doughy, steps onto the porch. *"Nepoată,"* the woman says, opening her arms wide and shuffling down the porch steps. She embraces Tasha and they kiss each other's cheeks.

As tall as Tasha is, and she's wearing heels that add to her height, her grandmother is taller.

"Lisa, Lani," Tasha says. "May I present my grandmother. Dama, this is Carson's sister, Lisa, and her friend Lani."

"Bună ziua," the woman says to us. "Welcome, everyone!"

"Dama does not speak very good English. I may have to interpret for her.

"She speaks better English than I speak Romanian," I say.

Dama asks Tasha something in Romanian.

"Do you feel like having some tea and sweets?" Tasha

translates.

"You bet!" Carson says.

"Ha!" Lisa laughs. "When do you *not* feel like having some sweets?"

Carson leers at her and opens his mouth to reply.

Tasha holds up her hand like a traffic cop. "Don't answer that in front of my grandmother!"

We take off our shoes and leave them on the front step before going inside. The bungalow is tiny but neat as a pin. It's one large room, bright with sunshine streaming through windows on all four walls. Paintings of flowers and mountainscapes hang on the walls. The air is imbued with a warm, inviting aroma.

The furniture consists of a day bed, which I have the feeling Dama uses at night as well, and a half-dozen rocking chairs arranged in a crescent. The hardwood floor is covered with an oval rug of fabric scraps, very much like the one in our house in Cloud Pass.

Tasha and Dama enter a closet-like room that turns out to be the kitchen. They come back carrying a teapot, china cups, and a tray of pastries.

"Spiced-apple scones for everyone?" Dama asks.

"Yes, please," Carson, Lisa, and I answer in unison.

As I reach for a scone, the front door bursts open.

A tall, slender man stands in the doorway, hands on his hips, silhouetted by the morning sun. A faint scent of patchouli wafts in.

Dama addresses him in Romanian, *"Scoate-ti"*

something.

The man bends down and unties his shoes. His build and his movements remind me of a gangly foal. He tosses his shoes on the front step and shuts the door. "Eh, Tasha. Look what the cat drug in." His words are tinged at the edges with an exotic accent.

"I could say same thing about you," Tasha replies.

Dama smiles warmly at the man and gestures him forward with her arms outstretched. "What kips you away so long, *Copil meu*?"

Without the sun casting his features in shadow, I see he's not much older than me. His high cheekbones and dark eyebrows accentuate his eyes, which are the color of rich chocolate. I find myself comparing his features to Jace's, and feel my cheeks and ears burn.

He sniffs the air and exhales with a sigh. "If you would bake apple scones for me, I would visit more often."

"This is my cousin, Mihail," Tasha says.

"Please, call me Mike." He grabs Carson's hands in both of his. "You must be Tasha's new man. Quite an improvement from the last one. That guy was American, too. What was his name? Billy-Bob-Jim-Jack Jones?"

Tasha's eyes narrow to slits. "Enough, Mihail."

Carson puts on a hillbilly accent. "Mah full name's Carson-Cal-Goober-Sonic-Mountain-Man. But you kin jest call me Carson." He laughs and slaps Mike on the back. "Pleased to meet you, Mike. This is my sister, Lisa."

Mike covers the floor between Carson and Lisa in two

loping steps. He touches Lisa's hand to his lips. "Of all the flowers in my grandmother's house, I have never seen such an orchid as you are. But I have a feeling you are not as delicate as you appear, eh? Do you have a boyfriend?"

Lisa sputters, obviously flustered by the attention. "Uh, not exactly." She slips her hand from his and pulls me to her side. "This is my friend, Lani."

"If Lisa is an orchid, you are a wildflower."

Mike reaches for my hand, but before he can put it to his lips, I give him a firm handshake and then pull my hand away. "Pleased to meet you. I *do* have a boyfriend."

"I'm not at all surprised."

Although Mike's banter is flirty, his attitude is more home-grown charm than pick-up artist. He gives me the impression that he must have learned to talk this way from watching American movies. He speaks the words as if he's reading lines.

"I was expecting to see you in Bucharest," Tasha says. "I could have used your help the other night."

"Doing what?" I ask.

Tasha levels a half-lidded gaze at me. "Family business."

"I had to be somewhere else." Mike wraps Dama in a hug around her waist and picks her up. "But I'm here now!"

Dama laughs and slaps Mike playfully on the shoulder. "Put me down, *copil*."

Mike sets his grandmother down and pecks her on the cheek. "You know you love it, Dama!"

"Humph," Tasha says. She brings another cup from the

kitchen. "Can I pour everyone some tea?"

I bite into a scone and close my eyes in pleasure. The flaky crust gives way to cinnamony, stewed apple slices. "This is the best apple scone I've ever tasted."

"*Mulțumesc,*" Dama says. "Please have more."

While we eat, Tasha and Mike chat with Dama in Romanian.

At one point, Mike's eyebrows raise and he pauses over his teacup in mid-sip. He looks from me to Lisa. *"Într-adevăr? Pricolici?"*

"Yes, werewolf." I look around at the faces of strangers who may or may not be our allies. "So, now that the whole family knows why we're here, will you help us?"

Tasha and Dama confer in Romanian some more, with Mike tossing in a question here and there.

Dama grins at Lisa and me. *"Da.* We can help you."

My heart jumps into my throat, knowing what this means for Lisa. We both leap to our feet and squeeze our hands in celebration.

Dama says something else in Romanian.

"What did she say?" I ask.

"She said we should go to the museum," Tasha says. "To the library."

"Not another library," Carson whines.

Lisa jabs him in the ribs. "You call yourself a researcher?"

"Well, which is it?" Carson asks. "A museum or a library?"

"There's a big library *in* the museum."

"Kill two birds with one stone, then." Carson kisses the back of Tasha's hand. "Not that you'd ever kill a bird, or anything else."

"Where is this museum-slash-library?" I ask.

Mike's face brightens with a wide grin, exposing teeth that could have used braces when he was younger, but now add charm to his otherwise pristine face. He rubs his hands together. "Walking distance. Let's go!"

CHAPTER 10

Tasha decides to stay with Dama and help her around the house.

"Do you need my help?" Carson strokes Tasha's shoulders.

"Yes," Tasha answers.

Carson's eyes light up. "Awesome. What can I do? I'm good with leaky faucets, mowing, watering plants."

As he lists his manly abilities, Tasha turns him toward the door and gives his back a gentle shove. "You can get out of the house and let my grandmother and me work in peace. Now, go."

"Oh, is that how it is?"

"Yes, that is exactly how it is. Wait!" She turns him back toward her and embraces his face between her palms. After kissing him hard on the mouth, she tells him, "Now you can go."

"I'll be your tour guide," Mike says as we sit on the front steps to put on our shoes. His accent is like something out of a Russian spy movie. Fascinating and dangerous, more like a movie soundtrack than any one particular character. As he laces up his shoes, he half-hums, half-sings a line from the old Survivor song, *Eye of the Tiger.*

"I haven't heard that song in forever," I say with a laugh. "Where did you learn it?"

He stares at me in disbelief. "You must not listen to much music. It's a top American tune."

I give Lisa a quizzical glance, careful that Mike can't see.

"She just doesn't listen to the hip stations," Lisa tells Mike, straight-faced.

"Maybe I can teach you the lyrics to some popular American tunes."

His earnestness and the way he says *tunes,* like it has a "y" in it – *tyunes* – strike me as adorable.

He pats his shoes and leaps off the step. Spreading his arms wide, he announces, "Welcome to Oltenita. A city many hundreds of years old, named after my grandmother, Nita, whom we call Dama because she is the oldest woman in town and is older than almost all the buildings."

As he says this, Dama and Tasha appear at the doorway. "Mihail. You must stop spreading this, this *prostii*."

"She says it's nonsense," Tasha explains.

Mike stands with his hands clasped. "I beg your forgiveness, Dama. I was only joking."

"I am three months younger than the Widow Patrescu," Dama says. "And I'm younger than at least half the buildings."

Behind her, Carson lets loose his moose-call guffaw, and Lisa and I erupt in laughter, too.

Dama points her finger in the air. "Mind you, the Widow Patrescu was not born here. She is latecomer. Has only lived in Oltenita for seventy-five years."

Dama grins and shoos us with her apron. "Off with you."

As we stroll down the street, Mike continues his tour-guide banter. "This is a city of juxtapositions. The right word, yes? An ancient city becoming more important as a modern business and tourist destination. In fact, she is the heart of my budding entrepreneurship. Come, I will show you her virtues."

"What about her vices?" Lisa asks.

"Far too many to explore in one brief afternoon." Mike nudges me. "But come with me tonight, and I will introduce you improperly."

We walk as two pairs, Mike and me in front, Carson and Lisa behind us.

"What kind of business are you thinking about?" Carson asks.

"A tour boat!" Mike pulls Carson up to the front, relegating me to walk beside Lisa.

Mike's stride lengthens, accented by a little hop when he comes to an occasional rock or broken piece of brick in the road. "It will be special, romantic, like the Bateau Mouche in Paris. But my boat tours will cater to different lovers."

"You mean, same-sex couples?" Lisa asks.

He dismisses the idea with a flip of his hand. "No, how idiotic. I mean lovers of wildlife. The delta attracts hundreds of species of birds."

"Do you have a business plan?" Carson asks. "How much will it cost?"

I notice Lisa has been quiet, staring at her shadow on the road. But her brother's comment brings her back from wherever her thoughts have taken her. "Carson! Isn't that personal?"

"I don't mind a bittle bit," Mike says. "I am happy to report my finances are one hundred percent sound. I have many investors already."

Carson and Mike chatter about investments and business partners and return on investment, while Lisa and I enjoy the Oltenita countryside.

The road is bordered on one side by a high stone wall and on the other by a carpet of wildflowers. Beyond the wildflowers are yards with giant trees that look like hemlocks. The air is filled with the aroma of the trees and flowers, filling me with a profound homesickness for the mountains where I grew up.

Lisa points at a pair of huge, snowy-white birds with black wingtips that cruise overhead, disappearing beyond the treetops. "Pelicans! I haven't seen pelicans since Poppy took us to Myrtle Beach. Do you remember, Carson?"

But Carson is engrossed in his conversation with Mike about musical bands and river pilot's licenses and accommodating gourmet chefs on board a river cruise.

"My boyfriend is a chef," I mention, loud enough for the guys to hear.

Mike pauses to look over his shoulder at me. Without responding, he turns back to Carson and continues yakking.

"Guess I have to talk to you, Leez."

She tucks my arm in hers. "I don't mind *a bittle bit*."

Gradually, the aroma of flowers and trees exhaling fresh oxygen has been replaced by an oily smell, like diesel fuel at a gas station.

"And here we are," Mike says, pulling our party to a halt. In front of us, a broad river rushes past a busy waterfront. A half-dozen men direct a military-looking truck onto a barge. One man, wearing a turtleneck sweater and a wool cap, pulls on a thick rope and yells directions. Even though he is speaking Romanian, I can tell he is not happy with the progress.

"Hey, Vladimir," Mike yells. He waves at the man in the turtleneck.

"Eh, Misha!" The man throws the rope to one of the other workers and jogs over to us. He and Mike embrace, slapping each other's backs.

"This is my business partner, Vladimir Damiano."

Vladimir shakes hands with each of us, a hearty, two-fisted shake that just about knocks Lisa off her feet.

Lisa looks around at the waterfront. "Are we close to the museum?"

"Oh, I know, sorry, I know," Mike apologizes. "I wanted to show you the Danube before we went to the museum. It's just a little out of the way."

I look at the sludgy brown water. Smears of oil flash colors across the surface, reminding me of the prism from the glass I broke. "This is the Danube? But it's brown."

"I thought it was blue," Lisa says, echoing my own thoughts.

"This is a working port," Mike says with a shrug. "The river is cleaner upstream."

Vladimir asks Mike something. Mike looks at us and translates. "He wants to know if you'd like a boat ride."

"That boat looks kinda full," Lisa says.

Mike laughs. "Not *that* boat." He points at a disreputable-looking wooden houseboat. The name *Cozla* is peeling off the bow. "*This* one is my boat. Mine and Vladimir's."

Next to the barge, the houseboat looks tiny, insignificant. The barge could plow right through her without suffering a scratch. Meanwhile the houseboat would be so many matchsticks strewn in the barge's wake.

I point over my shoulder with my thumb, indicating the direction we came from. "We really need to go to the –"

"Sure, we'll go then!" Mike pulls Vladimir to his side and slaps the dockworker's chest. They nod and smile and talk excitedly.

"We really need to get to the museum," Carson says.

"Sure, sure," Mike says. "Right after the boat ride."

"I wish Tasha had come with us," Carson says as we climb aboard. "She could tell you the names of all the birds we'll see."

"Or she could have taken us to the museum," Lisa mutters.

"I don't want to offend Tasha's family," Carson whispers.

"Looks like it's an offer we can't refuse," I whisper to Lisa. "We can't find the museum without Mike."

"Just keep telling yourself, we're in Romania," she whispers back. "Not in a movie about the Russian mafia."

Vladimir backs the boat out of its slip, then hands the helm to Mike. The engine coughs and sputters, and engulfs us in a diesel-laden fog. As Mike steers the boat forward, we leave the noxious cloud behind.

With Mike at the helm talking with Carson, Vladimir joins Lisa and me at the front of the boat.

"The boat, she nice, *da*?"

"All she needs is a fresh coat of paint," I say with a smile. I don't know how much English Vladimir understands, but I try to convey my agreement with my tone and by nodding my head.

"So how do you know Misha?" Vladimir asks me.

"He's my friend's brother's girlfriend's cousin," I answer.

Vladimir smiles and nods.

Mike speaks in Romanian, pointing first at Carson, then at Lisa, then at me.

"Oh, okay. That is good," Vladimir says. "You have brought investors for our tour boat business."

"We don't know anything about boats," I say.

"Or investing in boats," Lisa adds.

"Is no problem! You can invest in the tour boat! Misha is working out details with Carson now. You can invest as family."

"*Nu!* No investments." Lisa's answer is final. No more offers she can't refuse.

Vladimir holds his hands up, palms out. "Okay, Okay. Am înțeles. I understand.

He looks so hurt, I want to offer consolation. "Next time we visit, we'll buy tickets for the tour."

Vladimir's face brightens. "Okay, okay. *Da.* Is good."

I turn back to the river, hoping to enjoy the scenery in peace and quiet, but Vladimir peppers us with questions. "Where are you from?" "What have you seen in Romania?" "What is the weather like in Georgia and Tennessee?"

One time back home, my friend Billie Mae hosted a foreign exchange student from Finland for three weeks. On the exchange student's first day at school in Cloud Pass, Billie Mae and the principal brought her around to introduce her to all the classes. We all bombarded her with questions until the principal decided the girl had suffered enough.

Lisa has clammed up, staring at the river. I have to carry the conversation as best I can, me not speaking Romanian and Vladimir speaking limited English.

"Where you go next, after river?" Vladimir asks.

"We're going to the museum."

"Why you need museum?"

Lisa whips her head around to glare at me, a warning.

"We want to learn about Oltenita while we're here."

"Hey, Vladimir," Mike hollers from the boat's cabin. "I need you here."

"Scuzati-ma." Vladimir bows to both of us and joins Mike in the cabin.

"If he's going to be a tour guide, he needs to learn when to guide and when to back off," Lisa grumbles.

"I'd like to hurry up and get to the library, too." I nudge her shoulder with mine. "But he's just trying to be friendly. How many American girls do you think he meets on the docks?"

"We should have told him, *Las-o baltă, tu pămpălău*."

Upstream from the marina and other buildings near the port, the riverbanks are wild with brush and reeds and an occasional stand of trees.

"I have to admit," Lisa says, "the river is beautiful. The water is dark but undeniably blue, now that we're away from the docks and all the pollution from the boats."

Lisa points to a tree up ahead. The tree is bare of leaves, but appears to be swathed in white flags. As we get closer, the flags become ibises. Dozens are perched on the tree, covering every limb.

"It looks both dead and alive at the same time," Lisa says. Her eyes are glassy.

"Like the river. So brown back at the dock, but blue and alive here."

Lisa swipes at the tears that have pooled at the rims of her eyes.

Smudges of mascara appear over her cheekbones. I rub at them with my thumb. "Bump-bump-bump-bump-bump." I hum the famous notes of *The Blue Danube.*

The corners of Lisa's mouth twitch into a grin. "Bump-bump, bump-bump," she replies.

And just like that, the magic of this historic river infuses me with hope. I can tell Lisa feels the same way. Maybe it can fill us with enough of its magic to help us find a cure for Stan.

***

Like everything in Oltenita except the flowers on Dama's front porch, the museum is faded. The once-grand façade is like a former beauty queen, still proud but more gloomy than glamorous.

When we walk inside, it's like cracking open an ordinary rock to discover it's a geode with a sparkling treasure inside. The floors are polished hardwood, the walls climb to dizzying heights before encountering the frescoed ceiling. Glass display cases line the walls, guarded by suits of armor holding spears, axes, and maces.

A tall but hunched-over man with slick black hair walks over to us. He wears a black suit that's two sizes too large for his skinny frame. He reminds me of the staff from the mortuary at my father's funeral.

Mike speaks to him in Romanian.

Carson whispers to Lisa and me, "He's asking about local lore. Where they keep their old reference books."

The man guides us to a pair of massive mahogany doors. Figures of angels and hunters, wolves and bears are carved in them. Opening the doors, he leads us into the library. The sunlit air is dusty and heavily scented with the smell of old books and old wood.

Old wooden bookshelves, crammed with books whose spines look as ancient and uncared-for as the building's exterior, line the walls from floor to ceiling except for where tall windows let in the sunlight.

A plump woman sits at a heavy oak table. She uses a magnifying glass to peer at the text in front of her, a scroll of paper that she handles gently with gloved hands. Her aroma is a mixture of eucalyptus ointment and a generous dousing of rose perfume.

The woman glances up at us, grunts a greeting, then returns her attention to the scroll.

The mortuary man gives Mike some instructions and leaves us where we stand.

"What do we do now?" I ask.

Carson scratches his chin. "I think we should split into teams. All these documents are in Romanian. Lisa and I both know a little, so she and I will work together. We'll start over here." He motions to the books lining the inside wall. "You and Mike start over there." He means the opposite wall, where the windows are.

"But what are we looking for?" Mike asks.

"Anything about werewolves or curses," Carson says. "Local potions, remedies, that sort of thing."

Carson and Lisa start at the closest bank of shelves.

I follow Mike to the stacks by the windows. He tilts his head sideways to look at the titles on the book spines. He pulls out several books and hands them to me. "Take these to a table and start looking through them. I'll keep looking for more."

I find a table at the opposite end of the room from the old woman and splay the books across it. I open one and am overcome with a sense of uselessness. The text is written in an archaic font. It's hard to tell what the letters are, much less to find the word *pricolici* hidden in the pages. I strafe my hands through my hair.

Lisa sits next to me and dumps an armload of books on the table.

"What's wrong?" she whispers.

"I feel like I'm the weakest link," I admit. "I wish I'd paid more attention in Spanish class. Not that it would help. Spanish isn't Romanian. Why did I even come? I'm useless."

"Be right back," Lisa says. She leaves me sitting alone at the table in the library. I look around. Carson and Mike are pulling books from the stacks left and right. The old woman turns her head away from the scroll and coughs into a handkerchief.

Lisa returns with an encyclopedia. "You know the words by now, right?"

"Yeah, I think so."

She opens the volume to a page that includes several alphabets. "This is Old Romanian. This is the Cyrillic alphabet that was used up until about 1900. And this is the modern alphabet. You can compare any letters you're not sure of."

"Thanks. What would I do without you?"

Lisa winks and makes a "chk" sound out of the corner of her mouth. "I think you would miss me a bittle bit."

I smile. "I'd miss you more than a bittle bit. I'd miss you a bittle bunch."

I get the sensation that someone is watching me. Probably the old woman with the scroll, wondering what we're doing. But no, she is concentrating on her work, peering through the magnifying glass and taking notes in a small journal.

I look the other way, behind me. "Whoa!"

Mortician Man is standing right behind me. I didn't hear

him approach. He holds several notepads in one hand and a bunch of ballpoint pens in the other.

"*Am adus asta pentru tine.*"

"Nandru says he brought these for us," Mike translates. "*Mulțumesc, Nandru.*"

"Oh." I feel my cheeks burn. "Thanks. *Mulțumesc.*"

Mortician Man -- aka Nandru -- puts the pads and pens on the table and walks away. I watch him as he silently glides across the room. The only sound he makes is the click of the twin mahogany doors closing behind him.

"Attention, Bran Castle," Lisa whispers in my ear. "Your missing Dracula has been located. Please come fetch him immediately."

"I don't think he escaped from Dracula's castle. A nearby funeral home, maybe."

"Be honest. If it wasn't all sunny in here, would you be so sure?"

We spend the next several hours pouring through book after book. I find lots of references to *medicină* and *poțiuni*, which after I get used to the calligraphy are easy to recognize: medicine and potions. In one book, I come across the words *remediu* and *pricolici* in the same sentence.

"Look at this!"

Mike crowds in behind me to look over my shoulder.

I point to the passage. "It means remedy, right? Remedy for werewolves?"

"Remedy, yes," Mike says. "But even better. It also means cure or recipe."

"And here." Lisa indicates a long list right below the reference I found. "These are the ingredients, the amounts, and the cooking instructions."

Carson pumps his fist. "Yes! Then we're on the right track in thinking we can devise a formula to cure Poppy."

"Woohoo!" Chill bumps of excitement prickle my arms, and I don't care what the other library patrons think of my outburst.

Lisa and I high-five. "I'll write this down," she says.

Mike looks at the page with the recipe, then the next page, and the next. "It doesn't say if they actually tried it, or if it worked."

"Why would they write it down if it didn't work?" Carson asks. He slaps Mike on the back. "I bet your grandmother will be able to whip this up for us."

Mike grins. "Maybe I can convince her to make some more spiced apple scones while she's in the kitchen."

***

Dama opens a door off the living room and pulls a string that dangles from the ceiling just inside. A light comes on, revealing a huge kitchen, complete with a six-eye gas stove and an oven set against a brick wall, a deep double sink, and the largest refrigerator I have ever seen, not just in Romania, but anywhere. A long table is dusted with whiffs of flour that escaped Dama's cleaning towel. Behind the table, against one wall, is a bookshelf crammed with ancient-looking books, like from the sixties.

"Can I look at these?" I ask.

Dama nods. "*Da*. Look at whatever you like."

I take a book from the shelf and open it to a random page. It's a cookbook. I can practically taste the sumptuous looking chicken in the photo. "Jace would love this."

"Your boyfriend?" Mike asks. He is standing so close to me that I feel like I'm getting sun burnt from his heat.

"Uh-huh. He's an amazing chef."

Unbidden, an image of Jace and Alex laughing in the kitchen of the B&B in Jasper pops into my mind. I mentally Photoshop Alex out of the picture.

Dama pulls a large metal pot from a cabinet and places it in the sink. "Misha, fill this with water and put it on the stove."

While Misha fills the pot with water, Dama looks at the recipe we brought from the library. "Mm-hmm. Mm-hmm. Hmm."

Next, she studies a row of books between a pair of gargoyle bookends on the bookshelf. She selects a dictionary-sized volume, its spine at least three inches thick, and blows dust off it. She splays the book open on the table and flips to the index.

"What is that book?" I ask.

"My favorite cookbook," Dama replies. "Full of old family recipes."

"I thought we had already borrowed all your family cookbooks," Carson says.

"This is different type of recipes."

Running her fingertip up and down the yellowed page of faded Romanian calligraphy, Dama finds the recipe she is looking for. She thumbs through the pages of the cookbook until she gets to the right page. "Here we are."

"What is it, Dama?" Tasha asks.

"Between my family recipe and recipe Lani found, is possible will work."

I hug Lisa. "It's going to work! I feel it!"

"I thought you said you were the weakest link. Then all you do is find the recipe at the library. Way to go, Sistah!"

Dama wastes no time preparing the concoction. "Mihail, one tablespoon dried wolfsbane! Tasha, two teaspoons sage!"

Her grandchildren jump to her bidding. As in Carson and Tasha's kitchen, Dama's basement ceiling is strung with twine from which all sorts of herbs and other plants are hung to dry. Dama calls out the names of herbs and plants (and, for all I know, noxious and hallucinogenic weeds), and Mike pulls the desired plants from the ceiling's upside-down garden. Again and again, Dama calls out the names of the ingredients and Mike retrieves them.

Tasha runs the stems between her fingers to dislodge the leaves into bowls that line the counter by the sink. She pinches the required quantity of each herb out of the bowls and rubs it between her palms over the pot of water, which is steaming at a near-boil.

All I can do is stand back and watch. Carson and Lisa are similarly mesmerized by the beehive of activity.

"It's like the elves in the shoemaker's shop," Carson murmurs. "Putting magic together at midnight."

"I didn't know we could just whip up a recipe, simmer

for a few hours, and make werewolf-cure chili," Lisa says.

"This must just be part of it." I think back to how diligently my step-grandmother Aurelia and Jace's grandmother Natasha had tried to find a remedy for lycanthropy. They had ancient Romanian volumes of their own, books that had been passed down from generation to generation in their families. The Roma didn't write down all of their lore, but if they couldn't find a cure in all their accumulated knowledge, I doubt Dama will be able to simply pull a cookbook off her shelf and produce a cure. I expected a fusion of modern medicine and ancient lore.

As if she hears my thoughts, Dama slams the book shut. "Turn down the stove," she orders Tasha. "We are done here."

"The cure? It's ready?" Lisa's eyes are wide with hope. She clutches her trembling hands at her chest.

"Nu," Dama says. "No cure."

Lisa's shoulders droop. She casts her eyes to the floor and holds her cheeks in her hands. "Oh."

Dama lifts Lisa's chin with a gentle finger. *"Nu există nici un leac ... încă."*

Tasha takes Lisa's hand in both of hers. "She says, there is no cure ... *yet.*"

Tasha, Mike, and Dama talk excitedly in Romanian. They speak so quickly, I doubt even Lisa or Carson is able to follow their conversation.

Finally, they all stop and look at us – the Romanians in a line facing the Americans.

"Dama says," Tasha pauses as if making sure her translation is accurate. "She says we need *praful de strămoșii*. The dust of the ancestors."

"That phrase came up several times in the books at the library," Carson says.

"What does that mean?" I ask. "Where do we find the dust of the ancestors?"

"The Cave with Bones," Lisa answers, her voice barely above a whisper.

Dama nods. *"Da. Peştera cu Oase."*

CHAPTER 11

Dama shoves cloth bags full of fresh breads and pastries at us as we prepare to leave Oltenita. *"La revedere, copiii mei.* Be careful."

Mike peeks through the car's open window, investigating the bag in my lap. "You didn't give them all of the apple scones, did you, Dama?"

She swats him away from the car and our pastry-laden bags. "More for you inside."

"Such an appetite," Tasha says, shaking her head. "He can't resist Dama's baking."

As we drive away, I breathe in the aroma of fresh-baked breads that fills the car. "Who can blame him?" I say.

Carson and Tasha chat about couples' things. Whose turn it is to do the laundry. What dish they should bring to the retirement party for one of Carson's co-workers next week. I wonder if this is Carson's way of dealing with his concern about his dad -- concentrating on routine things so he doesn't have to think about Stan's very un-routine problem.

When their conversation turns to their plans for matching tattoos, Lisa elbows me and offers me one of her iPod ear buds. We put our heads together so we can both listen, a habit that feels as natural as if we'd known each other for years.

After a few songs, Lisa sighs and pulls the ear bud from her ear. She hands it to me and slumps against the car door, her forehead against the window.

"You okay?"

"Just tired," she answers.

I think it's something more, but decide not to press her. If something's bothering her, I know she'll talk to me when she's ready. I figure she's thinking about Stan, or maybe she's made the connection about wild animals being in the mountains, where we'll be headed tomorrow.

After a few minutes of silence, she pulls out her cell phone. Lisa's head is bent, her fingers moving over her phone pad. "Poppy hasn't answered any of my texts. I hope he's okay."

"It's only about 5 PM at home. I'll see if I can reach Mama." I type a quick message.

> U OK?

A few seconds later, my phone chimes to indicate I have a text. A reply from Mama pops up on my screen.

> Nothing serious so far. Stan is getting antsy as the moon phases toward full.

> He won't answer Lisa's texts.

> Can't. He ate his phone.

Lisa is watching the text conversation. "Poppy ate his phone! What else has he eaten? I hope he hasn't hurt anyone."

"No, Mama said 'nothing serious.' I'm sure she would consider it serious if SP were eating people." I tap in

> What else?

> Don't worry. He hasn't eaten anything alive.

I show Lisa. "See?"

"Tell your mom that Poppy's on a strict diet of dry dog food."

"Not even canned?"

"He's been a bad boy. He doesn't deserve canned."

After I text this message, I text Mama a question that has been worrying me.

> I'm missing so much school. Will I get thrown out?

Mama texts back,

> I contacted your new school, and Stan called Lisa's school. You both have excused absences and a LOT of make-up work.

> I should get Xtra credit in Chemistry or Bio.

> I'll ask your teachers.

> Thanks, Mama. LHLH.

"What's that mean?" Lisa asks, looking at my screen.

"Love and hugs, and more love and hugs."

Lisa gives me a tight squeeze. "LHLH to you, too."

"Back at ya. And Mama sends love and hugs for all of us."

At Carson and Tasha's apartment, we pack the car for a morning departure.

"Are those tents?" I ask Carson as he shoves two large

canvas rolls into the car's miniscule trunk.

"You don't mind camping, do you?" Tasha asks. "The Cave with Bones is very remote."

"No, that's fine," I answer. "I like the outdoors."

"Poppy took us camping lots when we were little, right Sissy?"

"I think those are the same tents we used back then," Lisa says. "Are you sure they don't leak?"

"One of them leaks. You and Lani can have that one."

Lisa hands her brother a bedroll. "What about animals?"

"Sure, it's in a forest, so there are animals. But they won't bother us."

Lisa doesn't look reassured.

"Same as anywhere you go camping," I tell her. "You never let them bother you when you were little, right?"

"That was before a wolf attacked Poppy."

"It wasn't a regular wolf, Leez. Regular wolves don't attack people."

I remember Tasha's assurances when we first arrived: Bears and wolves are only up in the mountains.

The Cave with Bones is in the mountains.

"Besides," Carson says, "I'll be there to chase away any animals that get too curious."

When the packing is done, Carson and Tasha prepare dinner. While two of the loaves Dama sent home warm in the oven, Carson rinses tomatoes and cucumbers. He slices them with a small knife.

Tasha slides a long, vicious-looking knife from a wooden

block on the kitchen counter. It makes Carson's knife look like a plastic toy. She slices cheese from two half-wheels, one yellow, one white, and piles the vegetables and cheeses on a large tray, which she places on the living room table.

Carson brings the two warm loaves of bread, wrapped in cloths, to the table.

"What are the plans for tomorrow?" I ask as Carson pours the wine.

"We'll drive up to Anina. It's a full day's drive, near Anina in the southwest part of the country. We'll need to gather overnight supplies before we head out."

"Is it in the mountains?" Lisa asks.

"Yes, very picturesque," Carson answers. "Once we get there, we'll get some dinner and hire some locals to take us to the cave."

"Don't you have GPS?" Lisa asks.

"You have to have coordinates, and the exact location of the cave is tightly guarded information." Carson refills Tasha's glass and his own. I cover my glass with my hand and shake my head when he offers me more wine, but Lisa accepts a second glass.

"Why the secrecy?" I ask.

"The cave is a site of tremendous archaeological significance."

"In the mountains," Lisa adds.

"Right. The government wants to dissuade tourists and fortune seekers from damaging or stealing the artifacts."

Lisa gulps her wine like it was fruit juice. "By which you

mean the bones."

"Exactly."

"And what does that make us?" She takes her glass to the kitchen and sets it in the sink. Without turning around, she tilts her head back and exhales. "Grave robbers."

"This is different." I join her at the sink. "This is a matter of life and death."

"And we won't disturb the site," Tasha says. 'We'll just collect a couple vials of dust –"

"Bone dust," Lisa interrupts.

"Yes, bone dust. *Praful de strămoșii.* It's the missing ingredient."

"It's not the same as sweeping up broken glass," I tell Tasha.

Her body stiffens. "I'm not trying to trivialize it. I'm just trying to assure her – and you – that the bone dust will be collected with complete reverence."

Then I turn to Lisa. "It has to be done. You saw all the references at the library. It's the only way to save your father."

"It just seems so … sacrilegious. These 'artifacts' used to be people."

"Thousands of years ago," Carson says.

"Thousands of years from now, would you want your remains collected by strangers and put into some witch's brew?"

Carson returns her gaze, a sibling stare-down taken to a whole new level. "It won't matter to me what happens to my bones one minute after I'm dead, much less millennia from now. In fact, I plan to donate my body to science, hoping I'll help save someone's life, even if it's a hundred thousand years from now."

"Spoken like a true scientist," Lisa says.

"I'll take that as a compliment."

"Lisa, if it upsets you this much, you don't have to go. I'll stay here with you, and Carson and Tasha can go to Anina."

"I think that would be better," Tasha says. "This will be dirty work, walking in steep terrain and thick forest conditions."

Lisa strides back to the living room. "Maybe you didn't hear that we used to go camping all the time. We've hiked up Mount Mitchell, Mount Katadin, lots of rough trails to get to the best camping spots. I can handle whatever terrain you got."

"Good," Tasha says. "Then we'll all go."

Tasha breaks the bread, handing each of us a steaming half loaf.

Lisa glares at her and rips a big hunk of bread with her teeth. She chews it, swallows, and wipes her mouth with the back of her hand, staring at Tasha the whole time.

I hold my breath, wondering if Lisa is going to throw the rest of the loaf at Tasha.

"I have to tell you something," Lisa says finally. "Your grandma's bread is the bomb."

***

For the second night in a row, I can't sleep. I'm cold because Lisa has stolen the sheet, and when I manage to doze off, an inane YouTube video about what different animals say runs through my dreams. When it gets to the chorus, suddenly the actors are all dressed in wolf costumes. Blood dripping from their mouths, they shout at me, *What does the werewolf say?*

I sit up and shake the image from my mind.

Lisa is sound asleep, again curled into a tight ball with her knees tucked under her chin, the sheet wadded up at her feet.

I walk out to the kitchen, but instead of getting a glass of water, I just cup my hand under the faucet and let the water overflow and dribble through my fingers. It's cold and makes me shiver. I lean in to take a sip.

"You're sure the night owl." The voice comes from the living room.

Spurting water through my lips, I try to focus on the rocking chair that is filled by a shadowy figure.

"Carson, you scared the halo out of me."

"Sorry. I couldn't sleep either. Is Lisa asleep?"

I nod, then realize he might not be able to see my response in the dark. "Yes, she's even snoring a little bit. What about Tasha?"

He takes a long sip from a wine glass, then fills the glass with a bottle that he holds in his other hand.

When he doesn't answer, I ask, "Is Tasha okay?"

"She's ... out."

"You mean, out like a light, as in sleeping? Or out as in, not here?"

"The latter."

I sit on the couch and fold my legs under me. "Did you have a fight?"

"Only every time she leaves at night."

"How often does she go out at night?"

"Every night for about a week, every month."

So that's why she came in late last night, as well. "Where does she go?"

"It's some local folklore thing. Some sort of ritual her family takes part in."

"A religious ceremony?"

Carson shakes his head. "Tasha's Romanian Orthodox. It's a really traditional religion. No moonlight sacraments that I know of."

A shiver runs through me and I rub my bare arms. "Then what does she *do*?"

"I don't know the details, but I don't think it's safe for her to go out at night by herself."

"Why don't you go with her?"

Carson takes a swig straight from the bottle. "I tried, but she won't let me. She says when we get married, I'll be part of the family. But until then, I'm 'not allowed.'"

"I don't think I'd let Jace exclude me like that."

"Their families are completely different."

"Not completely. Jace is Roma, too. But maybe Tasha's family is more traditional than Jace's. At any rate, if she's with her family, I'm sure she's safe."

At that moment, the door opens and Tasha rushes into the room, shutting the door behind her as if she's being chased. She leans her quiver case against the wall by the door. "So, Mom and Dad, you both waited up for me."

"Are you okay?" I ask.

"Why wouldn't I be okay?" She stands behind Carson's

chair and drapes her arms across his chest.

"I told Lani how worried I get when you go out at night by yourself," Carson says.

She kisses him on the top of the head. "You know I wouldn't do anything dangerous. I would not put myself in danger."

"Carson says you're taking part in a family ritual."

"Yes, that's right."

"Is it --?" I think of a way to ask the question that won't sound ridiculous or overly nosy. "Is it something that would help Stan?"

Tasha laughs softly. "Am I a crusader for a cure for lycanthropy? Is that what you ask?"

I nod. "Well, is that what your family ritual is about?"

"No, it is not." Tasha strides to her bedroom door. "And unless *you* marry someone in my family, that is all I am going to say about it."

"I understand. I'm sorry if I overstepped my place."

Tasha taps a forefinger to her sculpted jawline. "Hmm, I have an idea. Would you like me to have Mihail court you? Then you would be family and I could tell you lots of secrets." Her tone is teasing and I know she isn't upset with me.

"No, that's okay."

"Really. I could call him now."

"Thanks, but I think I can contain my curiosity."

"Suit yourself. Carson, *Stea*, are you coming to bed?"

As Carson shuffles to his bedroom and Tasha closes the door behind them, I lie on the sofa, wondering what I'm doing here, what Tasha's doing at night, and whether, despite her denial, one has anything to do with the other.

In the dimly lit room, my eyes wander to the shadowy object by the front door – Tasha's quiver case. I've never seen her carry it during the day, so it must be associated with the nighttime ritual she takes part in, around the time of the full moon.

I can contain my curiosity, I had told Tasha. But my curiosity about what exactly is in that sack eats at my mind. Finally, I give in. I tiptoe to the door and pick up the sack by its leather strap. The sack's heavier than I expected. A zipper encircles the top, and I gently guide it open. Inside is a short bow and a quiver full of arrows. I slide one of the arrows out and look at it in the faint light from the window. The metal tip shimmers as it catches the light. Why would Tasha need an arrow with a silver point? And why would she only need it on and around full moons?

The full moon – How is Stan handling it? Will Mama be safe tomorrow night, when the moon comes up in Georgia?

When my Aunt Romelia was teaching me to shoot a gun, she had cautioned me only to use silver bullets for their intended purpose, because they are hard to come by.

I remember Tasha's necklace, missing a coin. Did it come loose accidentally, or had Tasha melted it down to replace a silver arrow tip?

A hard lump lodges in my throat, and tears sting my eyes. I slip the arrow back into quiver, re-zip the sack, and return it to its place by the door.

Tasha said she wasn't searching for a cure for lycanthropy. Now I see the truth in her words.

Tasha is a werewolf hunter.

PART II: THE HARVEST MOON - SEPTEMBER

CHAPTER 12

In the morning we gobble down a breakfast of fruit and granola, then hit the road for Anina.

Lisa sits quietly next to me, folding a straw wrapper into a star. She smiles at me and places it in my hand. "Have you ever wished on a star?"

I try to remember the last time. "When I was little. What about you?"

"Same here. Why do you think we don't wish on stars anymore?"

"I guess we stop believing in the magic when we grow up."

"That's sad, you know?" Lisa draws a deep breath and exhales.

I hold the paper star between my thumb and index finger. With one eye closed, I place the star so that, from my perspective, it covers Lisa's right eye. "Yeah, but I guess you'd be pretty disappointed if you made a wish every time you saw a shooting star, or the first star of the night, and your wishes never came true. You're better off doing what you and I are doing."

"What's that?"

"Making our own magic."

The car hits a pothole, momentarily bumping us out of our seats like a roller-coaster ride. I look out the window to discover we have left the city behind. The hilly pastures, woods, and an occasional, lonesome farmhouse in the middle of a vast field neatly planted in leafy green rows are like the piedmont region between the mountains of Cloud Pass, Tennessee, and my new home in the flatlands of Lafayette, Georgia.

I reach out and tap Carson on the shoulder. "Are we there yet?"

"It'll take all day, driving straight through," he answers, looking at me in the rearview mirror. "If you're getting hungry, you can tear off a hunk of that bread from Dama."

"Damn, Carson," Lisa says. "Now I'm hungry. Don't you know I'm trying to watch my weight?"

Carson shifts his gaze in the rearview to look at Lisa. "You *are* looking a bit hefty these days."

"Nonsense," Tasha says, swatting Carson's shoulder. "She is skin and bones. Your father must starve her."

"Actually, I'm the cook, ever since Mom died."

I want to ask Lisa more about her mom, but Tasha's train of thought takes the conversation in a whole 'nother direction.

"How is your father eating, while you are not there to cook for him?" she asks. "And, if you don't mind my asking, *what* is he eating?"

"My mom's taking care of him," I tell Tasha. "Don't worry; he won't be killing anybody, if that's what you're wondering."

Tasha adjusts the rearview mirror so that she can see me. "The full moon is tonight. Are you sure he can handle it?"

The image of Tasha's silver-tipped arrows pops in my

mind. I haven't told Lisa about my discovery. We need Tasha's medicinal expertise, so I don't want to alienate her by confronting her about her arsenal of specialty arrows. Besides, she's no danger to Stan as long as they're on separate continents.

"They'll both be fine," I say with more confidence than I feel.

My cell phone chimes that I have a text from Jace.

> Butt bone bruised, not broken. How's things there?

> On our way to see some ancient bones. Maybe even ancient butt bones.

> On way to charity event with Alex and her parents.

I tamp down the jealousy that tries to creep into my chest.

> Isn't it late there? Where are you going?

> Nightcrawler at Atlanta Zoo. Benefits Fulton County Library. Tell you about it tomorrow. Bye, Beautiful.

And a second later,

> Alex says hi.

> No moonlight kisses.

After a few minutes without a response, I put the phone on the seat between me and Lisa. As soon as I let go of it, it chimes again.

"Whew! I thought he got mad at me for that last text."

But it's not Jace; it's Mama.

I read the message out loud.

> Hello, daughter. Thought you all would like a Stan report. Each night gets better. Special diet working. Will take extra precautions tonight.

"Tell her to be careful, but if it's safe, to give Poppy a hug," Carson says.

I text the message. Mom texts back,

> Will give him a hug. He says tell you he's working on a new canvas. Says tell you this one is called "Bait-iful Friends."

"Tell him he's twisted," Carson says, apparently over his brief attack of sentimentality.

"Tell him I bet it's going to be even better than 'Bait-iful Sea,'" Lisa says.

"You're overruled, Carson." I text Lisa's message, not her brother's.

Mom texts,

> Had coffee at shop across from gallery. They have a bee problem.

> Is there a waitress...

I pause while I try to remember her name. Finally I just type,

> ...with big hair?

> LOL! Bees are NOT in her hair. They're in attic. Bee man says hive must have been there for decades, but they just found it when bees started dropping out of vents in kitchen.

> Maybe they'll add honey to menu.

> Not likely. Waitress wants bees gone. Shame. Local honey's good for your immune system. Sure would taste good on cathead biscuits, too.

THE HUNTER'S MOON

> How long will you stay with Stan?

> 2 more nights & I'll head home. Jace's G-Pa coming for a few weeks. Hope you will be home by then with remedy.

> Me too. What if???

> If you're not back by October's full moon, I'll come back up here. Stan sends Lisa and Carson his love. And mine to you. LHLH.

The phone beeps, indicating a low battery. I turn it off so it won't die on me while we're in the middle of Nowhere, Romania.

We climb through the Carpathians, navigating sharp curves and narrow roads cut into granite slopes. Tall trees hem us in. But we go around a turn and, like opening a children's pop-up book, a sweeping vista unfolds. A lush valley dotted with pointy, red-roofed houses, a pencil-thin stream glinting in the morning sun, a sky splashed with pink over the mountaintops at the other end of the valley.

"Wouldn't you love to live in that little village?" I ask Lisa. When she doesn't answer, I look at her and notice her face is pasty white. Her eyes and lips are clamped tight shut. For all her world travels, she is not handling the twists and turns.

As Carson takes a sharp curve too quickly, Lisa winces.

"How can you stand this drive?" she asks through clenched teeth.

"You forget, I grew up in the Smoky Mountains. My friend Ben had a hot rod, a '57 Chevy Bel Aire. He'd tear around the mountains in that car at ninety to nothin'. A lot like Carson drives, come to think of it."

I think of Ben and me, growing up in the small mountain town. We sat together in school and climbed the slippery rocks in the Garnet River. We raced each other up and down the narrow gravel road that ran from town all the way up to the top of the mountain with its spectacular views.

I am unable to reconcile the memories of my childhood friend with the snarling, murderous beast he became. By putting the "two Bens" into separate compartments of my mind, I can remember the good times, the way he really was, without tainting those memories with what came later.

With a twinge of guilt, I realize Lisa hasn't achieved this separation. How could she? She never met the Ben who was a kind, somewhat goofy guy.. She only knows him as the werewolf who attacked her father.

***

Finally we pull into the town of Anina. The sun has set, and we haven't eaten anything since we finished off the delicious bread and fruit Dama packed for us. "Keep your eyes peeled for a restaurant or an inn," Carson says.

Tasha points out a narrow, two-story building with a rocking-chair porch lit up by a pair of gas lamps. Carson pulls into a one-lane gravel drive beside the inn and parks.

We get two rooms – the one Lisa and I will share has two beds. "I bet you'll sleep better without me tossing and turning," I tell her as I toss my bag on one of the beds and sit down on the edge of the soft mattress, facing the other bed.

"What do you mean? I've been sleeping fine." Lisa sits on the other bed, leans back, and props her feet on my knees. "Have you been having trouble sleeping?"

"Well, yeah, I guess."

"Have I been taking up too much of the bed?"

I laugh. "You? You curl into a ball like a cat and take up about two square feet."

"Meow. Then why can't you sleep?"

I shrug and shake my head.

"Is something bothering you? Something other than, you know, Poppy's *condition?*"

When I'm silent, she says, "You know you can talk to me, right?"

"It's just, I have a strange feeling about Tasha."

"Tasha?" Lisa puts her feet on the floor and leans forward. "What about her?"

I shrug again, unsure how much I want to tell her. "Did you know she goes out at night? Some sort of family ceremony?"

"Yeah, Carson told me. It shouldn't bother you or him, though."

"How do you know it's not dangerous?"

"It's just a cultural thing. And she's with her family, so she's protected."

Should I tell Lisa about the quiver full of silver-tipped arrows? Again, I decide not to. I hate keeping a secret like this from Lisa, but if she confronted Tasha, Tasha might not help us any more.

"I guess you're right."

"Of course I'm right. I'm also hungry. Let's go find something to eat."

As we go downstairs, a rich aroma greets us. "I smell bread."

Lisa sniffs the air. "And veggies."

We follow the scent to the dining room, a small space crowded with a long mahogany table surrounded by a dozen chairs. Four places are set with plates of fresh bread and huge soup bowls.

"I was just about to come get you," Carson says, emerging from the kitchen carrying a ceramic kettle that he sets in the middle of the table.

Tasha opens the lid and a rich fragrance fills the air. "I heated up the stew I brought."

I sip the stew broth, which is hot and delicious. Bites of carrots, potatoes and onion dissolve like butter in my mouth. With each bite of stew, my worries about Tasha dissolve, too, at least for the moment.

***

In the morning we eat breakfast in the dining room. This time, the table is set for eight, and the other four places are taken by fellow travelers. One couple are retirees from Kansas, checking locations off their bucket list. "I've always wanted to see Dracula's castle," the woman says with gleaming eyes. "Ever since I saw Bela Lugosi on the Classics Movie Channel when I was a teenager."

The other two are mountain bikers from Italy. Both men are in their twenties, buff, wearing skin-tight biking shirts with short sleeves that expose firm biceps. Although I can't tell while they're sitting at the table, I presume they are wearing similarly tight-fitting biking shorts. Their helmets are slung across their chair backs. "We've followed the course the Tour de France takes through the Pyrenees," one man says.

"We've even biked the Blue Ridge Parkway, in America," the other man says.

"That runs close to where I used to live," I say.

"Have you ever been to Little Switzerland, in North Carolina?" the first man asks.

"It's so romantic," the second man says. The first nods in agreement.

"It's pretty," I agree, "but the next time you're in the Smokies, you should check out the waterfalls. I think they're even more romantic than a man-made town."

"We should add 'see Niagara Falls' to our bucket list," the man from Kansas says. He takes out a stubby pencil and a journal and scribbles a note.

"That's not in the Smokies, dear," his wife says.

"I know, Mabel. But I don't think either of us is in condition to hike up a mountain to see a waterfall. Heart failure is *not* romantic."

We all laugh and chat some more over our breakfast. "What brings your group to Romania?" Mabel asks.

"I live here," Tasha says. "I grew up on the Danube River."

"Now *that's* romantic," the two bikers say in unison.

Tasha squeezes Carson's arm. "I met Carson when he came to work in Bucharest. We are collaborating on a project to chronicle as many local medicinal remedies as we can."

"I'm a chemist," Carson adds. "We're combining old world knowledge and state-of-the-art medicine in hopes of improving treatments for cancer and Parkinson's disease."

"Among other things," Tasha adds.

"Which reminds me, I better check in to the office." He holds his cell phone in his lap and taps the screen. "Tash, I'm going to use Decebal for a reference. Can you spell his last name for me?"

She takes the cell phone and types in the name.

"What about you two?" Mabel's husband asks Lisa and me.

Lisa points at Carson. "I'm his sister. My friend and I are interested in folklore of different countries, especially how different cultures treat diseases."

"Lots of talk of disease," one of the bikers says. "I hope you are all healthy."

"We're fine," Lisa says. "We're just, um, passionate about knowledge."

"That's so refreshing in young people," Mabel says. "Seems most kids these days are just interested in music and video games." She notices Lisa's iPod and ear buds on the table next to her plate. "Not that there's anything wrong with music," she adds.

After breakfast, we bid our fellow travelers good bye and good luck. We'll be spending tonight in tents near *Peștera cu Oase*, the Cave with Bones, and the other guests will be gone before we return the following night.

"Why don't you girls hang out on the patio while Tasha and I find a guide?" Carson suggests.

"If the Cave with Bones is so secret, how are you going to find someone who knows where it is?"

"I'll ask around," Tasha says. "Since I'm local – or more local than any of you – I think I will find someone. Or someone who knows someone."

Lisa and I sit on the front porch in flexible metal-framed chairs that squeak when we rock in them. We scooch the chairs side-by-side so we can both listen to Lisa's iPod.

Within fifteen minutes, Carson and Lisa return. "Let's get this show on the road," Carson says. He swaggers toward the front porch like John Wayne. "We're burnin' daylight, pilgrims."

I hand Lisa my ear bud as we stand up.

"Did you forget something?" Lisa asks. "The guide?"

"They're coming," Tasha says.

"They?" I ask.

"Two brothers," Tasha explains. "They work together, in case we run into water hazards or wild animals. Sometimes rocks have tumbled onto the path, or a tree has fallen. With two guides, they can more easily remove any obstacles."

"Hey, I can help, too," Carson says.

"Yes, *Stea*, you are very strong. I know I can count on you."

Lisa backs away, waving her hands. "You didn't say the cave would be dangerous. You mentioned the wild animals, which is bad enough, but I don't want to be drowned and buried by rocks in some godforsaken cave."

"Come on, Sissa-Leezy. It's not going to be like that. Besides, it could be worse."

"Oh, yeah? How?"

"You could be drowned and buried by rocks, *and* eaten by wild animals."

Tasha scolds, "Carson! Do you think that is helpful? No.

It is not helpful."

"Sor-ry."

"Be nice or you might get in real trouble." Tasha softens her words by kissing his cheek.

I hear the whine of a small motorcycle – nothing like the rumble of Jace's Harley. From down the road, a light blue mini-bike approaches with two riders. The bike barely accommodates the riders' long legs, giving me the impression of circus clowns on a child-size bicycle. They pull to a stop in front of the inn.

The guides pull off their helmets. Both men have curly brown hair, gaunt faces, and high cheekbones.

"I'm Nicolai, Nicolai Damiano," the driver says. "You can call me Nick."

Carson introduces us. "This is my sister, Lisa, and her friend, Lani."

"Hello, pretty ladies," Nick says. "This is my brother, Željko."

His brother lifts his hand in a quick wave. "Zed. It is easier." He grins broadly, exposing a gold crown on his upper right canine tooth.

"No offense, but that bike doesn't look very reliable," I say. "You sure it can get where we need to go?"

"My brother can ride that bike anywhere," Zed says.

"But perhaps Zed can ride with you in the car?" Nick asks. "It has more room."

"Not by much," Carson answers. "But he's welcome to ride with us."

Zed curls himself into the back seat between Lisa and me

and we follow Nick out of town.

We turn off the main road onto a smaller road, winding our way up the mountain behind the mini-bike. The road turns from pavement to gravel. The mini-bike kicks up a pebble and it pings off the windshield right in front of Carson. He ducks as if to avoid being hit. The car swerves and he jerks it back onto the road.

Lisa holds her head in her hands, massaging her eyes with the fleshy part of her palms. "This is barely more than a cowpath. Are you sure we're going the right way?"

"My brother knows the way," Zed replies. "The road will get a little better."

"Good," Lisa says. "This road is making me nauseous."

"Unfortunately, it will get worse after it gets better."

"Lovely."

When the gravel road gives way to a weedy path, the ride is smoother. But then the path turns to a two-rut dirt road.

"You weren't lying about the road," Lisa says. "How much farther?"

Nick pulls the bike off the road into a grassy clearing that slopes gently up toward a thick forest.

"I think we're here," Carson says. He pulls the car into the grass and parks beside the bike.

Lisa climbs out of the car and leans over with her hands on her knees. "Oh, merciful Pete."

Zed unfolds himself out of the car and points to the meadow. "This is a good place to set up your tents."

The sun beams directly overhead, casting shadows

across the meadow from wispy clouds skittering by.

"Don't you have a tent?" Carson asks. "We only have the two."

"We don't need a tent. We will ride back tonight."

"Why don't we go back tonight, too?" Lisa looks around at the dark edge of the woods and at the heat-hazed sky.

"The mountain roads are no place for tourists at night," Zed says.

"But with you guiding us, it shouldn't be a problem," I say.

"No, I won't allow it," Nick says. "I would feel terrible if you ran off the road. Even a tiny mistake could be disaster-ful."

"Disastrous," Tasha corrects him. "*Dezastruos*."

"Yes, *dezastruos*. So pay me now and we will lead you to *Peștera cu Oase*," Nick says. He holds his hand out to Carson, palm-up.

Carson opens his wallet and hands Nick several bills.

Nick counts the money. "This is only fifty."

"Half now, half when we get what we need."

"You know you are not allowed to remove any bones," Zed says. "That is the deal."

"We won't take any bones. You have my word," Carson says.

Tasha says something in Romanian that apparently convinces the brothers that we can be trusted. They nod their heads. "Okay, everybody ready?"

"I will stay behind and set up the tents," Tasha says.

"Are you sure that's safe?" Carson looks to Nick and

Zed for the answer.

"*Stea,* you know I can look out for myself," Tasha says.

"I will be pleased to stay with you," Nick says. "Or my brother, if you prefer."

"*Mulțumesc mult.* Thank you, but that will not be necessary." Tasha pops the trunk and retrieves her quiver sack. "I can take care of myself."

"Suit yourself," Nick says.

"We should go," Carson says. "We're burning --"

"I know, I know." Lisa slings her backpack across one shoulder. "We're burning daylight."

Carson and the guides put on backpacks stocked with water bottles. Carson also carries two vials for the bone dust, tucked in a leather pouch in his backpack. I'm the only one without a backpack, but Lisa has extra bottled water for me.

Nick leads us uphill across the meadow and into the woods.

"Are there wild animals around here?" Lisa asks. "I mean, like predators?"

I hold a low-lying branch out of her way as we climb a steep slope.

"Do not worry, pretty lady," Nick says. The animals of these woods will not bother you."

The dense forest occasionally opens like a curtain to reveal outcroppings of jagged, grey rock. As we climb higher, the woods thin out and the ground becomes rockier, with boulders jutting out of the earth. If not for our guides, I would not have realized this was a trail.

A faint whisper of water gradually gets louder. At the next outcropping of rock, Nick and Zed stop and shed their backpacks. Both guides pull water bottles from their backpacks, tip their heads back and take giant swigs. Carson hands us each a water bottle from his backpack.

"Thanks." I take several deep swallows of the cool bottled water. "It's beautiful here."

At the base of a greyish-white rock, a rivulet spills in a pool at the base of an arrow-shaped split in the rock and tumbles down the mountain close to the path we took to get here.

"How much further?" Lisa asks.

"We are here, pretty lady." Nick points at the split in the rock. The opening is wide at the base, guarded by the shallow stream. The crevice narrows to a point about twenty feet high. "*Peştera cu Oase.*"

"The Cave with Bones." I can only see a few feet into the cave before it curves into shadow, hiding the bones and the dust of the ancestors and untold secrets that lie within. "I can't believe it. We actually found the Cave with Bones."

"Of course. Your guides are the best in Romania," Nick says. "Now let's have the rest of the money."

Carson takes out his wallet. "So, I'll follow you in and you'll show me where the bone dust is, right?"

"Yes, that is right. But you must take only dust. No bones."

Carson nods. "Let's do it, then. We're burning daylight. Do either of you want to come?"

Lisa shakes her head. "You know how I feel about going in there."

"I'll stay out here with Lisa."

"How long will it take?" Lisa asks.

"It could be a couple hours, depending on how much water we must go through," Nick answers. "We have had much rain."

"What if it's longer?" Lisa looks at her watch, then scans the sky. The sun is already way past its zenith. "What if it gets dark before you get back?"

"Željko will stay here. He can lead the girls back to your car if it gets dark."

"All-righty, then," Carson says, rubbing his hands together. "Let's get a move on."

Nick puts his backpack back on and pockets the cash that Carson gives him. "Follow me," he says as he slips into the cave.

"Guess we should sit back and relax until they come back." Lisa says. She offers me an ear bud and we sit with our backs against the rock, listening to tunes.

Zed produces a pocket knife out of his jeans pocket. He pushes a button on the side of the knife, springing the blade open. Finding a stick on the forest floor, he settles back against the rock to whittle.

Birds sing in the trees and a hawk cries its shrill call. The stream murmurs its way down the mountain.

Another animal sound, a cat-like cross between a howl and a growl, echoes through the forest.

Lisa pulls the ear bud from her ear and pops mine out, too. "Was that a tiger? That sounded like a tiger." She jumps to her feet and scans the woods around the little clearing.

I stand at Lisa's side. "I'm sure it wasn't a tiger, Leez. Tigers are in India."

"Lynx." Zed grins, flashing his gold-capped tooth. "There are lots of lynx in these woods. Bears and wolves, too. Half the wolves in all of Eastern Europe."

A shiver rattles my frame from head to toe.

"Are you cold, pretty lady? Or scared of the animals?"

"I'm not scared." I swivel my mother's ring around my finger.

"That's a nice ring," Zed says. "I bet my girlfriend would like a ring like that."

"You should get her one. Is there a jeweler in Anina?"

"Why would I need a jeweler?"

"To get your girlfriend a ring?" I say slowly.

"He understood you," Lisa says.

Realization dawns on me. I hide my hand behind my back. "No way."

Zed slices a curl of wood off the stick. It spirals to the ground. He tosses the stick aside and brandishes the knife at us. "Throw me the ring."

"I said no."

Lisa takes out her wallet and waves it at Zed. "Don't take her ring. I have money." She opens the wallet, but her hands are trembling so badly that she drops it on the ground.

When Zed bends down to pick it up, I ball up my fists

and hammer him as hard as I can, right between his shoulders. He falls to his hands and knees, and the knife drops from his hand.

I swipe at it, but Zed is too quick. He grabs my wrist and pulls me to the ground with one hand, grasping the knife with his other hand. He sits on top of me, pinning me to the ground.

Lisa steps toward us.

I feel the cold tip of the blade against my throat.

"No closer," Zed growls.

While he's holding the knife at my throat, my left hand is free. I twist to the right and Zed presses his weight on top of me. I'm on my side with my right arm pinned beneath my body. Zed grips my wrist with one hand and presses the cold tip of the blade against my neck.

"Try that again and I will not be such a gentleman." Zed jerks his head toward Lisa. "You. In the cave."

"Do what he says," I warn her. "He's so stupid he might actually cut my throat by accident."

"It would not be an accident," Zed snarls. "If she get any closer, I will cut your pretty face."

As Lisa backs toward the cave, I think of my mother, her face so much like mine, but with a jagged scar across one cheek. Instead of being scared, I feel the rush of adrenaline course through my chest.

"I mean it," Zed says. He pokes the knife deeper into my neck.

I feel something sticky drizzle down the side of my neck. The adrenaline turns to spewing lava. "That's enough!" I roll my body, twisting away from him. As soon as I'm free, I scramble to my feet.

Zed quickly stands as well. Pointing the knife, he herds me to the cave next to Lisa. With one eye on us, he kneels and retrieves Lisa's wallet.

"Have a nice night in the woods," he says, backing away. "The wild animals should be satisfied eating just one of you. You have until dark to decide which one."

We stand there blinking, stunned at how quickly a hike and a cave exploration have turned into a robbery.

I put my hand to the side of my neck and check for blood. My fingers are smeared with blood. "How's it look?" I ask Lisa.

"Not bad. Put pressure on it to stop the blood."

She guides my fingers to the side of the neck where I need to apply pressure.

Lisa slumps against the boulder. "He almost cut your jugular."

"That would have been real stupid of him."

"Lani, I'm not kidding. He's dangerous, and his brother's probably no saint, either."

From far away, the whine of the mini-bike's engine echoes up the mountain like a swarm of hornets.

"He took the bike?" I scoff. "At least we don't have to worry about him any more."

"We've got another problem, though." Lisa tips her head toward the cave.

Nick saunters out of the shadows, thumbing through the

contents of a wallet -- Carson's wallet.

"Where's my brother?" Lisa demands.

"Huh?" Nick looks around. "Where's *my* brother?"

"He took off," Lisa says. "After Lani whooped his butt for trying to steal her ring."

"I find it hard to believe a little girl like her could, as you say, "whoop" anybody's butt. Much less Željko's."

"Looks can be deceiving." I make a swipe for the wallet.

Nick holds it up over his head, out of my reach. "Yes, that they can, pretty lady. Ooh, that is a nasty scratch on your neck."

"What did you do with my brother?" Lisa asks.

"See for yourself," Nick says.

Lisa charges him, pushing him in the chest with both hands.

Nick stumbles backward but quickly regains his balance, laughing. "You are a fiery one. Would you like to be my girlfriend?"

Lisa and I reply in unison. *"Las-o baltă, tu pămpălău."*

Nick's laughter cuts off like a light. His face darkens and his upper lip twitches. "You are two silly, stupid girls."

He sidesteps around Lisa and jogs down the slope with the grace of a mountain goat. "Goodbye, pretty ladies," he calls over his shoulder. His laughter echoes through the forest.

"Have a nice walk home," Lisa yells after him.

Moments later, an engine growls to life like an angry dog.

"He's taking the car?" Lisa clenches her short purple hair

in her fists. "Unbelievable!"

I shake my head. "How did he get past Tasha?"

Lisa's eyes widen. "He's done something to Carson in the cave. He must have hurt Tasha, too."

I look at the dark, yawning mouth of the cave. "We have to find Carson. Then we have to find out what happened to Tasha."

"I know." Lisa chews her fingernail, spits out the nail tip, and squints at the dark slash that is the mouth of the cave. "I hope they're not hurt."

"Look, you don't have to go in there. I can do it. You can wait out here, or go on down to see about Tasha."

"I know," she says again. She takes a deep breath and steps to the threshold of the cave. "He's my brother. I have to go in after him. I think we should both go in."

I grab her hand and we enter the cave. We forge ahead, side-by-side until the passage narrows and we have to walk single file. "Keep hold of my hand."

"You don't have to tell me twice," Lisa says.

As we move deeper into the cave, the light dims until I have to run my free hand along the cold stone wall to feel my way.

"Carson!" I call. *Carson, Carson, Carson* echoes back at me.

My next step splashes and I pull to a stop. Lisa, right behind me, bumps into my back and I stumble forward, both feet now in water.

"What is it?" Lisa asks. Her voice echoes through the

cave. After it fades, she adds, "Why did you stop?"

"I'm standing in water," I whisper.

"How deep is it?"

"Mid-calf."

"What if it gets deeper?"

"Guess we'll cross that bridge when we come to it."

We creep forward, creating wavelets that slosh and echo.

"Carson? Can you hear me?"

"This way," Carson yells from somewhere deeper in the cave. His voice ricochets from wall to wall.

"Where are you?"

"Can you see the light?" *Light, light, light.*

I look up and notice a dim light dancing on the cave's ceiling, fifty or sixty feet above us.

"Yes! We see it," I answer.

"Follow the light!" *Light, light, light.*

We move slowly toward the beam of light until we turn a corner and find ourselves in a large cavernous room. Scattered around the edges of the cave, bones are stacked in pyramid-shaped mounds, with skulls on top, like exhibits in a gallery. Carson lies on the stony ground, his back propped against the cave wall.

"Gee, Carz. What happened to you?"

"Hurt my ankle. Didn't Nick tell you?" He waves the flashlight, aiming the beam at Lisa and me, then swiping it from side to side. "Where are they? Nick and Zed."

"Long gone," I answer.

"With both our wallets," Lisa adds.

"What about Tasha?"

Lisa and I look at each other, then back at Carson.

"We don't know," I admit.

"We had to find you first. C'mon, Bro. Let's get you out of here."

"Not until we get the dust of the ancestors."

"Where is it?" I ask.

"On that ledge." Carson swings his flashlight to illuminate a rocky shelf about six feet off the ground. "I twisted my ankle trying to get up there."

I look up toward the shelf, then around the room. "How did the bone dust get up there? Did somebody put it there?"

"It was washed there by rain water that seeped through a hole, somewhere in the roof of the cave."

"Then how'd these skeletons get down here, all arranged like this?"

"Probably a tour guide did it for the tourons," Carson answers through gritted teeth. "I don't think these are ancient bones. I think someone robbed a cemetery."

"No wonder Nick and Zed didn't want you taking any bones," Lisa says. "It's their source of revenue."

"Then why'd they need our wallets?"

I shrug my shoulders. "Easy money."

"Ha!" Lisa laughs. "Not as easy as they thought it would be.

I put my hand on her shoulder. "Give me a lift."

Lisa threads her fingers together, creating a stirrup. I put my foot in her hand and she boosts me up high enough that I can shimmy up on the ledge. It's very narrow, and so close to the ceiling of the cave that I have to shuffle on my hands and knees.

Lisa hands me the flashlight.

"Do you see anything?" she asks.

The surface is dusted with a fine powder. "I think so."

"Here. You'll need the vials," Carson says.

I look over the side of the ledge. Carson opens his backpack and takes out a small, leather pouch. He slides out two, four-inch long glass cylinders and hands them to Lisa.

Standing on tiptoe, she reaches them up to me.

"How do I know what's bone dust and what's rock dust or something else?"

"Fill up both vials, and we'll hope enough of it is bone dust for the recipe."

I feel like I should pray as I scoop the dust of the ancestors into the little glass tubes. "Please help us, Dust of the Ancestors," I whisper as I scoop the fine white powder into the vials. "Help us, *Peștera cu Oase.*"

CHAPTER 13

We emerge from *Peștera cu Oase*, drenched in sweat. Leaning against the cool granite outcropping, we uncap water bottles and guzzle the cool liquid. Carson bends forward and pours water over his head. It dribbles from his chin and he shakes his head, spraying Lisa and me with droplets.

We laugh and splash each other until Carson says, "Wait! Quiet!"

In the hush that follows, I clearly hear it: Someone -- or something -- crashing through the woods, heading right toward us.

Wolves. Bears. Lynx. We are completely unprotected against whatever it is.

Then Tasha breaks through the woods into the clearing.

Carson clutches his chest. "Tasha! You nearly give me a heart attack."

"What happened? Zed came rushing down the mountain and took off on the mini-bike. Then while I was running up here to find out what happened, Nick ran right into me. Knocked me over. He reached his hand out, I thought to help me get up, but he snatched my quiver and bow."

"Oh, babe! Are you okay?" Carson limps toward her.

"I am okay. But you are hurt, *Stea!*"

Carson stumbles against her and she plants her feet to support him.

"I'll give you a hand," Lisa says.

We take turns bracing Carson as we hobble our way down the mountain.

Back at the meadow, one tent is set up, the other is in a heap on the ground. A raccoon-sized animal is pawing through a bag of food.

"Hey, get away from there!" I charge toward the critter and it scurries away toward the cover of the woods.

Carson sits on the ground, his injured ankle propped on his backpack. Sweat streams along his cheeks and plasters his grey t-shirt to his chest. "They took my car?" He shakes his head. "How are we going to get back?"

Lisa and I slump on the ground on either side of Carson, but Tasha paces in a fury. "My bow, my arrows -- it is all gone!"

I take a long sip of water, tipping my head back to empty the bottle. "You can probably get another bow, but silver-tipped arrows must be hard to come by."

"Why would you need silver-tipped arrows?" Lisa asks.

"We're in the wilderness, miles away from the nearest town. I would prefer to be armed if I encounter a wild animal."

"But why silver --." Lisa looks at Tasha with horror as the implication dawns on her. "What kind of animal are you expecting to run into?"

Tasha bristles. "My arrows aren't silver."

I shake my head. "I saw them. They have silver tips."

"It was dark. You were imagining things."

"Oooohh," Carson moans. "Is there any ice?"

"No ice, *Stea*, but you can have some more water." Tasha

digs in the cloth bag that Nick and Zed have tossed on the ground. She unscrews the cap from a bottle of water and gives it to Carson, kissing him on the top of his head.

"We better finish setting up camp," I suggest.

Carson tries to stand and winces. He slumps back to the ground.

"Not you," Lisa says, helping him back to a sitting position. "You can supervise."

Carson gives her a weak smile.

By the time we have the second tent set up, the sun has disappeared behind the trees and the sky is shot with orange and purple.

"We should probably build a fire," I suggest.

"I will go with you to gather some firewood," Tasha says.

I press my lips together and mentally tamp down the apprehension that prickles my skin and makes my heart jump around in my chest. "Sure."

As we traipse through the woods, Tasha asks, "Why did you say that about my arrows? Do you want Lisa to hate me like you do?"

"I don't hate you. But I *know* the arrows in your sack had silver points. I saw them the other night."

Tasha laughs. "So you think I use silver arrows all the time? You Americans! You think because you are rich enough for such extravagance, that the rest of the world is. But even if I could afford such lavishness, I would not be so foolish. This is a difference between Americans and the rest of the world. We don't take our good fortune for granted."

"Some Americans might be like that; I guess some people in every country are." I add a small branch to my growing armful of firewood. "But that's not what I was thinking. I know you have a set of arrows with silver points. What do you use them for?"

Tasha stands up straight and still. "Shh!"

I stop my foraging for firewood and stand still as well. "What is it?" I whisper.

"We are being followed," Tasha whispers back. She kneels and drops her firewood to the ground, except for one long, spear-like branch. As she straightens up, she holds the branch over her shoulder like a javelin. She spins a quarter turn and focuses on a shadowy area of the woods.

I peer in the direction where her make-shift spear is aimed. A twig snaps and an animal emerges from the shadows.

A large brown doe, sleek as glass, steps into the clearing. She sniffs the air and twitches her tail.

"It's a deer," I whisper.

Tasha exhales and drops the branch to her side.

The doe spooks sideways and crashes away through the woods.

Tasha stabs the spear into the ground and breaks it in two with a swift kick. "It's getting dark. We had better go back to camp."

***

Lisa has arranged cannonball-size rocks in a circle for a fire pit several feet from the tents. She selects a few pieces of wood from the branches and twigs that Tasha and I gathered and arranges them in a pyramid in the middle of the circle. She shoves a handful of dry leaves into the center, flicks Carson's lighter and soon has a fire crackling.

Tasha rummages through the bag of food. "Here are some sandwiches."

She tosses us each a foil-wrapped sandwich and pokes around the bag some more. "Look what else I found!" She holds up a bottle of plum wine and passes it to Carson. "We have no ice for your ankle, but maybe this will dull the pain."

Carson pulls the cork out with his teeth. "Wish I had my cowboy hat."

"Your cowboy hat?" Tasha says. "Why on earth do you need that?"

Carson takes a long swig from the bottle and grins around at the group. "This is almost like a scene from an old Western movie."

"Please don't sing," Lisa says.

"Ah! I know what you mean," Tasha says. "But I think it's too late."

"I'm an old cow poooooooke, on the Rio Grande," Carson wails. "I give my coooooows, the-uh Rio brand."

Lisa covers her ears. "Ughh. Make it stop! Make it stop!"

"You don't appreciate my hidden singing talents." Carson takes another swig of wine.

"I might, if you actually used them," Lisa says. "But they're still hidden."

"Come on, Cowboy." Tasha helps Carson to his feet.

"Let's get you to bed. We're burning moonlight."

"I love you, Pilgrim," Carson tells her as he hobbles into the tent.

She follows him in and turns around to zip up the tent flap. "Goodnight, cowgirls. Be sure to stoke the fire and zip your tents before bed."

I sit as close as possible to the fire, hugging my bent legs and resting my chin on my knees.

Lisa pokes at the fire with a long, skinny stick. "Even stoking the fire right before we turn in, it won't last all night. What happens when it goes out?"

I shrug. "We'll probably get cold."

She jabs at the fire. "Cold, I can handle. I've camped out before. Do you think animals will bother us?"

"When I get cold, I'll wake up and stoke the fire again. Wild critters generally try to stay away from humans."

The night sky is perfectly clear, inky black like in the mountains where I used to live, and spangled with stars in constellations that I recognize -- Orion's Belt, the Big Dipper. We watch the stars for awhile, and when we get sleepy, we add several branches to the fire before crawling into our tent.

Near dawn, I awake, shivering. Once again, Lisa has claimed all the covers.

I step outside the tent into the foggy, grey light.

The fire is down to smoky embers.

I choose a hefty branch and a few smaller sticks from the stack of firewood and shove them on top of the remnants of the fire. I add a few leaves and blow on the embers to reignite the flames. At first, only a slender stream of smoke rises from the pile of wood and embers. Then a few flames shoot up and catch the twigs. From there, it's only moments before a substantial fire takes hold. I feel the pride of a cavewoman, a kinship with the prehistoric residents of this very mountain.

A shadow moves in the mist. I try to see what made the motion – an animal, or just a breeze pushing the fog.

I see the movement again, and then another. As the fire pushes the fog further away, widening the circle of light, figures come into focus at the rim of the mist.

Not one animal, but many.

"Lisa? Lisa!"

"What is it?" she mumbles from her blanket-wrapped burrow in the tent.

"We have visitors."

In a groggy voice, Lisa asks, "Is it someone with a ride home?"

"No, it's wolves."

I don't think wolves will attack people. They are probably just attracted by the scent of leftover food.

But what if they're not ordinary wolves?

Lisa pokes her head out of our tent's zippered door. "Wolves? Where?"

"All around us." I point at several shifting shapes in the mist.

Tasha emerges from the other tent. She peers through the fog. "Did you say we have wolves?"

"They're circling us."

"Dammit, I can't get up," Carson yells. He swats the tent flap out of his way and crawls half-way out of the tent on his belly. "Stoke the fire!"

"I did." I add more sticks to the fire.

The tent flap falls back across Carson's head. He yanks it so hard it rips along the seam. "Help me up, dammit!"

"Don't try to get up," Lisa says. She scrambles out of our tent and stands beside me. "You'll only hurt yourself worse."

She grips my upper arm and whispers, "I can't see them. Are you sure they're there? Are you sure it's wolves?"

"I saw them. They were closer when I first got up. Shh – listen!"

The soft padding of paws in the dewy grass, rapid panting as they circle the camp, leaves no doubt in my mind. They are wolves. But because they haven't attacked, I'm also certain they're not werewolves.

Then, the noises are gone, dissipated in the mist along with the animals that made them.

"Aloo? Aloo-ooh?" The voice comes from down the mountain, very close.

"Alo!" Tasha answers. "Who's there? *Cine este acolo?*"

Then there is more padding and panting, and a bark that makes both Lisa and me jump. A brown dog with a white cross emblazoned on his chest bursts through the mist and wildly sniffs around our feet, the campfire, the tents. He lifts his leg on Carson and Tasha's tent, missing Carson by inches.

"That's no wolf," Carson says. " That's an ordinary, pissing hound dog. Go away, dog!"

A vibrantly clothed man with a tall wooden walking stick emerges from the fog. He says something to the dog and snaps his fingers. *"Bruno, vino aici."*

The dog scratches the ground with his back feet, flicking bits of grass and dirt at Carson's head.

The dog trots to the man's side, circles and sits, leaning against the man's leg.

"Did ... did you see the wolves?" I ask the man.

The man's eyebrows shoot up. "Wolves? Many wolves, or just one wolf?"

"There was a pack, circling us."

Something about my answer seems to relieve him. He scratches the grey stubble on his chin.

"No, I see no wolves."

"They were here! I saw them."

The man pats the air with a bony hand. "I believe you, *copilul meu*. My dog, Bruno, must have scared them away." He smiles warmly at the dog, who returns his gaze of affection. *"Bun câine,* Bruno. Good dog."

"How did you find us?" I ask.

"But, *copilul meu*, I did not know I was looking for you." He looks around. "I am Eugen. Did you hike all the way up here on foot?"

"No," Tasha says. She explains the situation to him in Romanian and introduces us all.

"I have seen a car like you describe. Down the road a short distance."

"Maybe the jerk abandoned it," Carson says.

"I would have abandoned it, too," Eugen says. "It is against a tree."

He props his staff in the crook of one elbow and slaps his hands together. "Smooshed? It is the right word, *nu?*"

"Oh, no! Not my *car*," Carson wails. He crawls out of the tent, moaning, and grabs a tent tie-down to pull himself upright. Tasha rushes to his side. As slender as she is, Tasha is almost as tall as Carson and supports him as if he weighed no more than a feather.

"*Dor* Petrescu," Eugen says to Tasha. "How will you get home? You have no car; your boyfriend is lame."

"I'm not lame. Just my ankle is." Carson winces as he tries to put weight on his injured leg. Tasha adjusts his arm around her shoulder for a better angle of support.

The old man cocks his head and scrunches his eyebrows together. "Is this not the same? You still will not be walking off the mountain on that ankle."

Lisa steps up to the man. "Can you help us?"

The dog stands and sniffs her hand. Lisa instinctively jerks away, then stands frozen, as if to move would invite attack.

The dog sniffs her hands, her feet, her knees. His tail lashes the air. Lisa's breaths are rapid and hitched as the dog sniffs and circles her. Lisa's fingers twitch when the dog licks them, but other than that, she doesn't move.

"Does he bother you?" the man asks.

Lisa nods.

Eugen snaps his fingers. "Bruno, *vino aici.*"

The dog circles behind Eugen and returns to his place at his owner's side. Lisa's shoulders relax and she takes a deep breath. "*Mulțumesc.* Please, can you help us? Even our cell phones were in our car when our guide stole it."

"Except mine," Carson says. "It's around here somewhere."

"You will not get a telephone signal here. You need not even to try."

"Can you go back to town and get help?" Lisa suggests. "I mean, would you do that for us?"

The dog jumps to his feet and leaps at Lisa, putting his paws on her chest and reaching with his muzzle toward her face.

"No! Get off!" Lisa twirls to the side, dislodging the dog. "Lie down," she tells him.

The dog stares at her with chocolate eyes rimmed with mascara-like markings. He wags his tail and pants with his tongue lolling out the side of his mouth.

"*Vino aici și culcă-te,*" Eugen says in Romanian.

The dog pads back to the man's side and lies down with his head between his paws. He looks at Lisa and whines.

"Why did he do that?" Lisa's voice trembles.

"He likes you. He is a friendly dog, but to you, he seems to be especially attracted."

"She's a little dog-shy," I explain. "She and her dad were attacked by a ... dog recently."

"That is a shame. But this dog is not like the one that attacked you."

"I know you just walked all the way up here, but would you mind leading me back to town so I can get help?" I ask.

Eugen scratches his chin and shakes his head slowly. "No, I cannot do that. If I left the rest of you here, my wife would thrash me."

"Why would she be mad at you for going for help?"

"Because she is following me in the van."

"You've got a van?" Lisa smiles for the first time since we were listening to her iPod outside the Cave with Bones. "And your wife is driving it here, for realz?"

"*Da*. We are checking our bees. She comes behind me with the van and the Vanners."

"Vanners?" I ask.

"Our horses."

"Why do you need to drag your van up the mountain with horses?" Carson asks.

The man straightens his posture and taps his walking stick on the ground. "They are not just any horses. They are a pair of proper cobs."

"It's a wagon," Tasha explains. "A covered wagon pulled by a team of horses. They're called Gypsy Vanners."

"I thought you were supposed to say 'Roma.'"

"For a man who knows so much...." Tasha rolls her eyes.

"Mr. Eugen, is that a good thing? 'Proper cobs'?"

He winks at me. "The best."

"You've got a wagon? And horses?" Carson asks. "Why didn't you say so?"

"I did say so," the man replies. He leans in to Lisa and

cocks his thumb at Carson. "Is something wrong with this one's head, as well as his foot?"

"No," Lisa says with a laugh. "That's just the way my brother is. But they say he's a brilliant chemist. So he must have brains in that head somewhere."

The dog jumps to his feet, trembling all over and wagging his otter-like tail furiously.

The man kneels down on one knee and drapes an arm over his dog's back. *"Ce este, Bruno?* Do you hear Mama?"

The morning mist is clearing. I look down the road in the direction of the dog's interest.

The distinctive clop-clop of horse hooves echoes through the valley as a team of stocky pinto horses rounds the bend, pulling a covered wagon driven by a sturdy-looking woman. Insects hum lazily around the woman's head. I realize with astonishment that they are bees.

The woman clucks to the horses and slaps their backs with the reins. The horses jerk their heads forward and strain to pull the wagon more quickly on the steep grade.

"Eugen," the woman says. *"Nu ești!"* A bee lands on her nose and she blows it away.

"Yes, here I am," our new friend answers. "I found some American travelers who need our help."

"Alo, alo," the woman says, oblivious to the bees that form a floating halo around her head. She pulls the horses to a stop and ties the reins around a long wooden handle.

The man helps her down and she smoothes her floral apron. "I am Albine. You have met my husband, Eugen." As they stand side-by-side, they remind me of the pilgrim salt-and-pepper shakers from a holiday commercial: The slender husband with his hair swirled over a bald spot, wearing a puffy-sleeved shirt, light brown slacks, and a brightly colored, paisley patterned vest. The wife a little larger and an inch taller than him, wearing her grey-flecked dark hair in a long pony tail, and an apron to keep her flower-print dress from getting smudged.

We introduce ourselves, and Albine greets us all with kisses on the cheeks, like long-lost relatives.

"Tu nu sunt din America, nu?" Albine asks Tasha.

"No, I'm not from America. *"Sunt din Bucuresti,"* Tasha replies. "My boyfriend is from America, and his sister and her friend are, also."

Albine goes to the back of the wagon and returns holding a half-dozen canteens by their straps. "Here is water. You must be thirsty."

I help Albine pass the canteens around.

Carson tilts his head back and splashes water into his mouth. It spills across his stubbly face.

Albine tugs on her husband's puffy sleeve. "Help me, Eugen."

He follows her around to the back of the wagon and reappears carrying a huge cast iron skillet and a three-legged stool. Albine is laden down with a gallon jug, spice bottles, a spatula, and a couple rectangular packages wrapped in cloth. "Who is hungry?"

We all are, even Carson. With Tasha's help, he limps over to Eugen. "Breakfast, too? You are my guardian angels."

Albine ignores the compliment. "Why do you limp? You are hurt."

"I twisted my ankle a little bit. It's fine."

"It is not fine. Sit down and let me look at your ankle." She plops herself down on the stool and pulls Carson's pants leg up to his knee.

As Albine pokes at his ankle, Carson's lips are a tight line, but he doesn't make a sound until Albine removes his shoe. "Aah!" he screams, jerking his leg out of her grasp.

"*Lanina*," Albine says, "please look in the back of the wagon."

"What am I looking for?"

"A basket."

The covered wagon is packed with all kinds of supplies. Pots and pans and other items in lumpy cloth sacks. And in the middle of it all, , a stack of wooden drawers circled by bees. *Bees! What are they doing with bees in their wagon? And how am I supposed to get in there without getting stung?*

A red wicker basket is barely visible behind the wooden drawers.

I climb into the wagon, careful not to disturb the bees.

"Also bring another milking stool," Albine calls.

A three-legged stool hangs from a hook on one of the wagon's ribs.

I hold both items in one hand as I scooch backward out of the wagon. My foot knocks into the bee boxes, bringing a swarm out to investigate. *Do I stay still? Do I hustle on out of here?* I decide to get out of the wagon as quickly as possible.

I hand the items to Albine. "You have bees back there."

"*Da.*" She raises and drops her shoulders. "Carson, sit here on this stool."

Albine takes two small glass jars out of the basket. "This will help the pain in your ankle."

The jars are filled with an amber substance. "Honey?"

"*Da.*" Albine pops open the hinged lid of one of the jars.

"Can I eat some of that?" Carson asks. Without waiting for permission, he pokes his finger in the honey.

"Stop that," Tasha says, slapping his hand playfully.

"Mmm, it's tasty," Carson says, unapologetically.

"*Stea,* would you please let the woman apply her remedy? I don't want to hear you moaning and groaning all the way down the mountain."

"You mean, spread that honey on my ankle? Thanks, but no thanks. I don't want all the ants and flies in Romania swarming around me."

Lisa shakes her brother's shoulders gently. "You mean any more than usual?"

"You are the one studying local medicinal lore," Tasha says. "Don't you think you should give it a try?"

Carson shakes his finger at her. "Studying, not practicing."

Albine shrugs. "It is up to you."

"Do it, Carson," Lisa says.

Carson rubs his chin. "I don't know...."

Tasha blows gently in her boyfriend's ear, fluttering his hair. "Don't worry, *Stea*. I'll shoo the flies away for you."

Carson nods. "In that case, go for it."

Albine scoops the honey with a wooden spoon and smears it on the red, swollen area of Carson's ankle. She wraps it with gauze bandaging. "Now. If you are still hungry, I will fix some breakfast. Eugen, why have you not unharnessed the horses?"

Eugen removes the leather harnessing from the two draft horses and leads them to the middle of the meadow to graze.

"Can I help with breakfast?" I ask Albine.

"*Da*. The stove is in the back of the wagon. Can you slide it to the edge for me?"

I hop in the wagon and search for a stove. I see a cast-iron grill and try to pull it out. I land on my butt on the floor of the wagon. Bees burst from the boxes and fly around, buzzing loudly. I hold my breath and stay as still as a statue until the bees relax and return to the hive.

It takes me several tugs to get the stove to the edge of the wagon. The jerking and scraping upset the bees again. They swarm from the wooden drawers. Where there were a dozen, in seconds, there are hundreds.

Albine stands by the wagon. "Hush, children." The bees calm down and return to their hive-drawers.

"Wow! That was amazing. Let me get down and I'll help you carry that."

"No need," Albine says. She grabs the stove by wooden handles on either end and hoists it like a load of laundry. She squats to deposit the stove on the ground by the fire pit. Bees circle lazily around her head.

Albine wipes her hands together and goes back to the wagon. She retrieves a tall, slender jar of oil and an armful of cucumbers and tomatoes.

"Is there anything you *don't* have in there?" I ask.

Albine winks. "Well, horses would not fit back there, so we make them pull the whole thing."

Eugen lights a fire under the stove and places the skillet on top.

When the skillet is hot, Albine pours in a little oil. It beads and dances on the bottom of the iron pan. She shakes the jug and pours the contents in the skillet.

I tilt my nose toward the delicious aroma. "Mmm, cornbread."

In a few minutes, the bread is done. Eugen slices it up and serves us each a wedge. He saves back a morsel for the dog.

We eat the cornbread with slices of tomato and cucumber, all piled on top of pale yellow linen napkins with flowers and bees embroidered in the corners.

"How long have you kept bees?" I ask Albine.

"I am third generation of my family to keep bees," she replies. "My name means *bee.*"

"She married me so she would have an apprentice," Eugen says with a wink. "Not so much to learn the trade as to help with the heavy chores that require a man's strength."

"That is not true, Eugen." Albine stands behind her husband and wraps her arms around him. "You know I married you for your horses."

"And who could blame you. Even back then, I drove the

best team in Walachia. But I married you for the bees and honey. *Tu ești de miere pe buze."*

"What does that mean?" Lisa asks.

"I tell her she is the honey on my lips."

"What do you do with the bees? Do you sell the honey?" Lisa asks.

Albine pauses before answering. She glances at her husband. "*Da*, we sell it. Tourists love to buy things from the Roma. Trinkets, souvenirs, mostly. Honey is something they are familiar with."

"*Da*," Eugen agrees. "Honey is at the same time exotic and familiar."

"But you heal with it, too."

"That is not unique to the Roma," Eugen explains. "Many cultures know of the medicinal value of honey. And not just for people. We use it to keep the horses strong and healthy."

After breakfast, Lisa, Tasha and I take down the tents and roll them into tight bundles. Eugen removes the wooden drawers and sets them on the ground. He loads the tents into the wagon in place of the drawers.

"Where will you put the hives?" I ask.

"It is one hive. Many drawers, but one hive, one queen." Eugen waves expansively at the meadow. "I will set them up here. It is a good place."

"We were looking for a territory for the new queen. She is the ruler of this hive," Albine says.

Eugen pecks her on the cheek. "Like you are the ruler of my world."

Albine brings her hand to her face, but she can't hide the pink that has risen in her cheeks. The quaint exchange between this old married couple makes me think of Jace. Will we be together when we're old? My chest aches from missing him.

After the hive is situated and the wagon is packed up, Eugen whistles to the horses, which have been grazing in the meadow. Grabbing one last mouthful of grass, they lumber slowly to their owner. He hitches them back to the wagon and helps Carson step up to the bench. Tasha scoots in beside him, cooing to him and fussing over him.

"*Mulțumesc.* I don't know how to thank you enough for your help," I tell Albine as she helps Lisa and me find a place to sit in the back of the wagon. We sit with our backs against the tents and dangle our legs out the back.

"One day, you will show kindness to someone who needs help." Albine pats us on the knees. "You will understand, then, if not now, why *I* thank *you* for allowing Eugen and me to help you. It makes us feel good to be able to help someone."

"I understand," I tell her. I think of the community garden back in Cloud Pass, where my dad and I had helped underprivileged kids raise vegetables and flowers.

Lisa hands me an ear bud as we settle in for the ride.

The dog leaps into the back of the wagon and lies down between us, resting his head on Lisa's lap.

"Did someone forget to tell him I don't like dogs?"

"Guess he doesn't hold that against you."

Lisa tentatively pats the dog's head. "He's really not at all like the werewolf that attacked Poppy and me."

Ben. Again, I'm reminded of how many lives I've destroyed.

"I know what you're thinking," Lisa says. "But you're wrong. It's not your fault."

I nod my head. *She's* wrong, but I don't want to talk about it.

We bump down the mountain, and after my ear bud pops out of my ear for the third time, I give up the tunes and listen to the wagon creaking, the horses snorting, and the bees buzzing around the wagon.

Staring at the road disappearing behind us, I notice there are lots of bees. Some of them seem to be floating from the front of the wagon, possibly breaking away from Albine's halo. Others seem to appear from the trees and the sky, converging in the airspace behind the wagon.

Wherever they are coming from, they are definitely following us. They form a moving curtain, fashioned from thousands of bees, their bodies glimmering in the morning sun.

"There's my car," Carson yells. "Stop the horses!"

I peer around the edge of the wagon's canvas cover. The Volvo is accordioned against a tree. Smooshed, just as Eugen had described. Lisa and I hop out of the wagon to inspect the wreck. Bruno darts between Lisa and the car, pausing to pee on the tree.

"Serves him right," Lisa says. "I hope he's in pain, walking home."

Eugen and Albine join us in the road. "We saw no-one on the way up here," Eugen says. "Did we, Albine?"

"Nu."

Lisa opens the rear passenger door. She crawls in, searching the seats and the floor. "He left our cells. Catch." She tosses me my cell.

Tasha rushes to the driver's side of the car and retrieves the keys from the ignition. She presses a button on the key fob and the trunk pops open. "He took my bow and arrows."

Eugen asks her something in Romanian.

She answers in Romanian and slams the trunk shut.

A twig snaps and I look up in the direction of the sound.

Bruno, who has been busy sniffing around the car and the road, stands still and growls.

A wolf emerges from the tree line and stands in the road, sniffing the air. Brown with a darker face and tiny black eyes, it turns toward us and lifts its tail straight out behind it. The fur on its neck bristles.

I've seen this posture in wolves before.

It's a threat.

CHAPTER 14

"I think we need to get back in the wagon," I warn the others.

They follow my eyes to the wolf in the road.

"Both of you, get in the van and stay there," Albine says.

"What's going on back there?" Carson hollers from the front of the wagon.

"You, too, *Dor* Petrescu. And keep *domnule* Carson quiet."

Lisa and I climb in the back of the wagon.

Tasha goes to the front of the wagon. She tells Carson one word, *"Pricolici."*

Lisa grabs my arm. "Did Tasha say *pricolici?*"

I nod slowly, my eyes wide as I can't stop looking at the wolf.

"I have to help," Carson says. The wagon sways and he yells out in pain.

"Stay where you are," Tasha tells him. "You are no help. Neither of us are."

Eugen calls Bruno to his side. They advance toward the werewolf, narrowing the distance from a hundred feet to twenty. Eugen points his staff like a spear. *"Pricolici, fie plecat!"*

"They both think it's a werewolf!"

"Then why is he going *toward* it?" Lisa asks.

I stand on my hands and knees on the edge of the

floorboards. I gape in wonder and terror at the old man, armed only with a glorified stick, facing off against a werewolf.

Like a storm cloud, a swarm of bees gathers around Eugen and Bruno, forming a bubble around them.

The werewolf charges.

Bruno answers by running toward the beast. As if ruled by a single brain, the bees move with him.

When they are no more than a foot away from each other, both Bruno and the werewolf stop. Bruno stands with his head low, growling, encircled by the bee bubble.

The werewolf snarls, its teeth bared and its ears pinned to its head.

I scramble out of the wagon, not knowing what I can do, but unable to stay in the wagon and do nothing.

"Wait for me." Lisa jumps from the wagon and stands beside me. "Now what?"

"I don't know. Maybe we can distract it."

A hand grabs me from behind and I yelp in surprise.

The werewolf's head jerks up as his ears hone in on the source of the sound.

"Shh," Albine warns. She pushes us back toward the wagon. "Get back to the van, quickly. You do not know what we are dealing with. You will only be in the way."

"But we do know," I tell her. "That's a werewolf. *Pricolici.*"

"Then you know you must get back in the van. Eugen and I will deal with *pricolici.*"

"He can't stop a werewolf with a stick!"

"You do not have even a stick. And *Dor* Petrescu has no silver arrows. Eugen knows what he is doing. Now get back in the van. Stay out of sight." Albine grabs two tin pails from pegs in the wooden wagon frame and turns toward the fray.

Lisa and I get back in the wagon. This time, we crawl as far away from the edge as possible.

One of the horses whinnies as the wagon rolls with the sudden added weight.

Up front, Carson groans.

"Hush, *Stea*," Tasha tells him.

I peek around the tents and stacks of other stuff. "Look at Eugen."

Leaning on his staff with every other stride, the old man walks to within a few feet of Bruno and the werewolf.

Albine stands halfway between Eugen and the wagon, a tin pail in each hand and bees circling her. She puts the pails on the ground and swirls her hands around her head, corralling some of the bees. She opens her hands as she pushes them outward, directing the bees to join the others hovering around Bruno.

The reinforced group of bees expands their bubble to enwrap both Eugen and Bruno.

"It's a shield against the werewolf," I whisper in awe.

Eugen waves his staff.

The bees shift as if they are a single organism and surround the werewolf. The bubble shrinks until the bees are a blanket covering every inch of the animal. He howls in pain, falls to the ground and writhes around. He swats his eyes with his paws and rubs his side against the gravel in the road, trying to dislodge the bees. But the swarm is too large. The werewolf is stung hundreds, thousands of times.

The animal's moans grow fainter and the thrashing stops.

"*Albinele mele,*" Albine sobs. "*Albinele mele credinciosi!* My faithful little bees."

I jump out of the wagon and rush to her side. From here I can see the bees. Thousands of bee corpses cover the wolf's body and blanket the ground around it, like trout lily blossoms knocked to the ground by a storm.

"Give me the pails," Eugen says gently. He lays his staff on the ground.

Without taking her eyes from the mass of dead and dying bees, Albine hands her husband the two tin pails.

He places them on the ground near the werewolf. "We need firewood. *Lanina, Lisina,* can you find some branches in the woods? Dry wood, with dry leaves. Do not go far."

I look around at the woods, peering deep into their darkness. "What if there's another werewolf?"

"Bruno will protect you."

Lisa and I dash to the edge of the woods by the road. The dog scouts ahead, sniffing the road, roaming into the woods, and returning to us. In a few minutes, we return with our arms loaded with firewood.

Eugen arranges the wood in a rectangle around the werewolf's corpse. "More wood!"

Again Lisa and I scavenge the woods for dead branches.

We bring everything we can find, even small twigs and pine needles.

Eugen adds the material to the rectangular frame, forming a pyramid over the werewolf's body. He splashes liquid from the two tin pails over the animal's corpse and the tower of wood. He strikes a match and tosses it onto the werewolf's body. Flames erupt immediately, shooting twenty feet in the air with a *whoosh*.

"What are you doing?" Lisa asks. "Why can't we just go?"

"You have to burn the werewolf's body," Eugen explains. "Otherwise, the human part of the werewolf, the part with a soul, will never be at peace."

"Is – is that what will happen to Poppy if we can't cure him?"

I squeeze her hand. "No, no. We have the cure."

"Who is Poppy?" Albine asks.

"My -- my father. He was attacked by a werewolf."

"I am sorry, *copilul meu*. There is no cure for *pricolici*."

Lisa covers her mouth with both hands. A sob escapes as she turns and runs back to the wagon. She goes to the front and climbs up on the bench beside Carson. I hear her sobs and Carson asking, "What is it? Why are you crying, Sissy?"

Tasha joins us, covering her nose and mouth with her hand. "I will never get used to the smell. Why is Lisa so upset?"

"She's thinking about her dad, obviously."

Tasha nods. "Yes, it must be painful for her to watch this."

"Why can't we just leave it here?" I ask. "Let it burn."

"We must be sure the *pricolici* burns completely," Eugen says. "And even if it was not a werewolf, I would not leave an unattended fire in the woods."

"But Carson needs a doctor, and we need to get back to Oltenita." I look Eugen in the eyes. "We found the cure for werewolves. We did. We just have to prepare it and get it back to Lisa and Carson's dad."

Carson hobbles to the fire, leaning on Lisa's shoulder. "How long will it take?"

"Many hours," Eugen says. "I must add more wood to keep the pyre burning."

Albine moves closer to the fire. She kicks gravel at the animal's flaming carcass. "You dirty beast. I hope you rot in hell."

"You must have really loved those bees," Lisa says.

I put my arm around Albine's shoulders. I can feel her trembling. "It's more than the bees, isn't it, Albine?"

Struggling to hold back tears, she can only nod her head in response.

"Our son, Radi," Eugen answers. "He was killed by *pricolici*. Even the bees were unable to save him."

"Why not?"

"The hive was not big enough. A bee can only do so much. One sting, and she dies. Now, we establish new hives all around the city, the countryside, up here in the mountains. Sure, we get more honey for our business. But main reason is protection from *pricolici*.

We back away from the heat of the fire and the stench of burning fur and flesh. "How long ago was your son killed?"

"Three years," Eugen says. "Radi had just turned sixteen."

Albine pats my hand and moves from my embrace to her husband's. "Was happy time. Radi had proposed to his childhood sweetheart, Cosmina."

"At sixteen?" Lisa asks. "Isn't that kind of young? I mean, I know you can drink wine at sixteen in Romania. But get married?"

"It is the age of maturity in Roma culture. When most of our people get married."

It's also the reason Ben wanted to marry me before I turned sixteen. The reason my father and my Roma step-family feared I would become a werewolf if I didn't kill my mother before my sixteenth birthday.

The wind blows toward the top of the mountain, carrying the foul odor of the burning carcass away with it. We walk back to the wagon to watch over the werewolf's remains until it is burned up.

Eugen helps Carson into the back of the wagon. "We never identified the werewolf that killed Radi."

"We suspect it was a boy who liked Cosmina," Albine adds. "She never returned his affection, and he burned with jealousy."

"Željko was jealous to the point of distraction," Eugen says. "He could never accept that Cosmina's heart belonged to Radi."

"Željko!" Lisa and I say.

Lisa's whole body begins to tremble. I grab her hand to steady myself as much as to support her.

I don't want to ask, but I do anyway. "This Željko – did he ever go by 'Zed'?"

Eugen shakes his head. "I never hear him called that."

He looks to Albine, who shakes her head, too. *"Nu.* Maybe with his friends. But Radi never called him that."

I exhale, a sigh of relief.

"It would be too much of a coincidence," Lisa says.

"I know, right?"

Eugen spits on the ground. "But I will never forget his face. His *rânjet rău.*"

"Something about a smile?" Lisa offers.

"Yes, a smile, a grin."

Albine provides the English. "Mm. An *evil* grin."

"*Da*. An *evil* grin. With a gold ..." Eugen taps a tooth -- his upper right canine -- with a fingernail.

"A gold tooth?" My relief from a moment ago vanishes.

"Oh, god," Lisa says. She cups her hand over her mouth.

"Are you sick?" Albine fans Lisa's face with her apron. "Is the smell of the burning *pricolici.* Is awful. We need to move further away."

"It's not that," I tell her, even though the wind has changed again and the rank scent of death creeps toward us once more. "We think it's the same guy."

"You think who is same guy?"

"The guide. One of the guides that brought us to *Peştera*

cu Oase is named Željko. He has a gold crown, right there." I point to my top right canine tooth.

Eugen brushes the coincidence aside. "A lot of young men these days have gold crowns. It is the style."

"Ohhhhh," Carson moans. "I don't think the honey's helping my ankle."

Eugen speaks to Albine in Romanian. He grasps Carson's shoulder. "I will stay here to make sure the fire does not go out until the *pricolici* is returned to ashes. Albine will take you to hospital."

"We can't leave you out here alone," Lisa says. "What if there's another werewolf?"

"Bruno will stay with me."

Albine swipes her hands around her head and face, cups her hands together, and holds them out to Eugen. "Take these," she says.

I hear the bees inside her hands buzz as she transfers them to her husband's hand.

Eugen holds his hands to his face and uncups them. The bees float out, lazily buzzing around his head.

"I'll stay too," I say before I have a chance to think about it.

"Are you sure?" Albine asks.

I nod.

Lisa bites her fingernail. "I, uh, well, do you want me to stay too, Lani?"

"You go with Carson. Tasha will break her back if she has to keep supporting him by herself."

Lisa nods once. Her shoulders relax. She would have stayed if I'd asked. "Thanks, Lani. Be careful."

She bends down on one knee. Bruno sidles over to her and licks her face.

"Be careful, Bruno," Lisa whispers into the ruff of fur around his neck. "You're a good dog."

Albine reaches into the wagon and hands me a shovel. "Give this to Eugen." She climbs into the driver's seat and clucks to the horses.

The wagon lurches forward as they head down the mountain.

I watch the wagon roll down the mountain. Lisa, alone in the back, waves then turns her head to the side. Eugen whistles gently to the dog. Our odd trio returns to the werewolf's funeral pyre.

"I hope this person...." My voice trails off as I choke back tears, thinking not only of this particular werewolf, but of all the werewolves I have encountered. Ben, Mrs. Shoat, my mother, my father, Lisa's father, and this one, who I didn't know as a human.

"*Da, copilul meu.* The soul of this person is free from his prison."

Eugen goes to the side of the road and retrieves a large fallen tree limb. Every step he takes, he is followed by bees.

He snaps off the smaller branches and then stomps on the middle of the main branch, snapping it in two. He piles all the wood on top of the fire.

"Why do the bees do that?" I ask as I hunt for more

branches.

Eugen doesn't answer. When I look at him I see his eyebrows are wrinkled together.

"I mean, why do they attack the werewolf?"

He nods. "Ah. Albine could answer better. She has been around bees since the day she was born. And she has better English."

I toss my branches on the fire. He knows more English than I know Romanian, so I wait for him to find the right words.

He shrugs. "*Pricolici* are not of nature."

"They're not natural."

"*Da*. They are not natural. But it is more. They are not *of nature.* Nature did not make them. Nature wants no part of them."

"And bees?"

"Bees are of nature. In all the world, bees are most closely connected to nature, with the possible exception of a woman."

"What woman? Albine?"

He chuckles. "*Da*. Albine, and all other women who experience the natural wonder of pregnancy. Maybe one day, you yourself will experience this mystery of nature."

I think of Jace, and my ears and cheeks burn. I look away, pretending to search the edge of the road for more sticks.

"You do not need to be embarrassed," Eugen says. "You have never thought of getting married, having children, have you?"

"Noooo. Well, sort of. An old friend asked me to marry

him, but I wasn't even sixteen. And kids?" I laugh at the idea of me, being a mom. Too scary. "No."

"But you have someone. Not this friend you speak about, but someone else." Eugen squints at me and holds his hand up, gnarly fingers wavering slightly back and forth. "Yes, he will definitely be in the picture for a long time."

My ears burn again. "Are you reading my future in the air now? I just wanted to know about the bees."

"All right, all right." Eugen smiles broadly. "The old Roma will quit his fortune-telling tricks. What else do you want to know about bees?"

"How long has Albine's family been beekeepers?"

"How old are the bones in *Peştera cu Oase*?"

"Seriously? That long?"

"Ehh, perhaps an old man exaggerates *un pic*. But Albine will tell you: Her family has kept bee yards for generations."

"How long have bees been used to fight *pricolici?*"

"As long as there have been *pricolici*, bees have probably fought to destroy them. But I believe you mean, how long have people harnessed the bees' powers to kill *pricolici, nu?*"

"*Da.*"

He smiles. "Since the day Albine and I met. It was fate that we met, and chance that we discovered our combined talents."

"Because she's a beekeeper?"

Eugen wavers his hand. "Keeper, *da*, but more than that. She is *albine vrăjitor*. Like the man who brings snake out of basket with music of the flute."

"Charmer?"

"*Da*. She is bee charmer."

"Well, sure. I could have told you that. I think you have a little bee charmer in you, too."

He laughs. "*Nu*, the bees only do what is in their nature when they encounter *pricolici*."

"Then what do you do?"

"You see what I do." He points his staff at the carcass on the pyre. "I am *pricolici vânător*."

A shiver runs through me from head to toe, despite the heat coming off the fire. "Werewolf, um, vanquisher? Killer?"

"Only if lucky. *Vânător* means hunter."

"Oh," I say quietly.

"Does this bother you? That I hunt *pricolici*?"

"I guess. A little. I mean, I want to *stop* werewolves, but not by killing them."

"It does not bother you that *Dor* Petrescu is *pricolici vânător*."

"How did you know?"

"She told me earlier. This is why she was so upset at the loss of her bow and arrows."

I sigh heavily.

"What troubles you, *copilul meu*?"

"The reason we're here? In Romania?"

Eugen nods. "*Da*. Go on."

"Lisa's father was bitten by a werewolf. We're trying to find a cure."

He nods some more, strokes the stubble on his chin. "*Am*

înțeles. Now I understand."

"I know we had to kill this werewolf." I point to the remains of the werewolf in the fire. "He was going to attack us. But I'm hoping we will find a way to help Stan – Lisa's father – before he --."

"Before he kills."

I lower my head and nod. "Yes."

"Copilul meu, surely you know what you seek is impossible."

"I have to try. Stan is a werewolf because of me. Because of a Roma curse put on my family."

"A Roma curse is strong magic. But *copilul meu,* Roma are everywhere. Not just Romania. "Why do you think a cure is to be found anywhere in Romania?"

"The curse was started by my mother's step-family. Her step-sister and step-mother. They are Roma from Romania."

"So you are in search of local medicine."

"We found some ancient recipes that seem to be for a cure. Tasha's grandmother had everything except one ingredient: dust of the ancestors."

"Then that is reason why you are on mountain. *Peștera cu Oase* is more than a simple tourist destination for you and your friends, *nu?"*

I nod. "We collected some bone dust. I just hope it'll work."

"How will you test it?"

I shrug my shoulders. "Test it? I don't think there's a way to test it. We'll brew the potion and make Stan drink it."

A breeze rushes up the mountain, stirring the flames and sending embers twirling in the air.

Bruno leans into the side of his master's leg. Eugen lowers to one knee and strokes the dog's head.

I sit down on the other side of Bruno and pet his back. The dog wags his tail in appreciation of our attention.

"When was your friend attacked?" Eugen asks.

"In August. He changed on the full moon, but he knew something was happening. He locked himself in a room so he couldn't hurt anybody."

"What happened on the full moon of September?"

"My mother was there to help him get through it."

Eugen's eyebrows shoot up. "What sort of magic did she use?"

I shake my head. "No magic. She helped him satisfy his cravings. Don't ask how."

"The next full moon is coming soon. Do you think you will be able to get the remedy to him by then?"

"I hope so."

"But you must be protected, in case it does not work. Bees. Silver. Bring your best weapons."

"It has to work."

"Noroc bun, copilul meu. Good luck."

***

Several hours pass. Each time the fire begins to wane, we stack more wood on it. As the sun melts into the treetops in the west, splashing the sky with pinks and purples, all that is left of the werewolf is a few bone fragments. Eugen takes the shovel and spreads gravel and dirt from the road on top of the fire. Large billows of grey smoke gust toward the sky. After the clouds disperse, he strafes the shovel through the ashes.

"What are you looking for?"

"A gold tooth."

I move closer, peering into the dusty remnants of the fire and werewolf cremains. "You think this werewolf was Željko?"

"I did not want to say anything in front of your friend. She is troubled enough already."

"So you think our guide Željko and the boy who had a crush on your son's girlfriend are the same guy?"

"Is possible."

I catch my breath as I realize what that means. If it's true that the two Željkos are the same person, and that he was a werewolf, Lisa, Tasha, and I are lucky to be alive. His criminal tendencies were the least of our worries.

"Did you find anything?"

"*Nu.* No gold tooth. This *pricolici* was not Željko."

One shovelful at a time, Eugen moves the ashes into the meadow and spread s them around the bee boxes. It's a long, laborious process.

A small entourage of bees accompanies him back and forth.

"I wish we had two shovels," I say. "Can I take a turn?"

"*Nu, nu,*" he says.

When Eugen has scattered the last shovelful of ashes, he plants the shovel blade in the grass and crosses himself -- forehead, chest, right shoulder, left shoulder. *"Fie ca spiritul vostru merge cu Dumnezeu.*"

"What did you say?"

"I pray his spirit goes with God."

He's breathing heavily, and I feel guilty for not insisting he let me help.

"Bring me my staff, *copilul meu.*"

I jog to the spot in the road where Eugen left his staff.

I notice a small retinue of bees haloing my head. I hear them buzzing in flight. One lands on my nose and I look at it cross-eyed. "Honeybee, honeybee, fly away home," I whisper. The bee takes wing but quickly lands on the back of my hand. It vibrates its wings and dances a figure eight. "Please don't sting me," I ask it as I bend down to pick up Eugen's staff.

I become aware of a different kind of buzz. Whatever it is, is getting closer. I look down the mountain road, toward the source of the noise.

A second later, a mini-bike zips around the corner. The driver screeches to a stop inches in front of me and takes off his helmet.

My lips twist into a sneer as I spit out his name. "Zed."

He flashes his gold crown at me. "Hello, pretty lady."

"Did you suddenly develop a conscience and come back to help us?"

"Actually, I am looking for my brother."

I point at the wreckage of Carson's Volvo. "He probably shouldn't have 'borrowed' our car. It's a much more complex vehicle than your little mini-bike."

Zed glances at the car. It apparently doesn't interest him.

Dismounting the mini-bike, he sniffs the air. "What have you been burning?"

Removing his gloves, he strides to the place in the road where we improvised the funeral pyre. He squats beside the blackened area and picks up a handful of ashes. He holds them to his nose, then quickly stands up, casting the ashes to the ground. "What have you done with my brother?"

Eugen appears beside me. He hands me the shovel in exchange for his staff. "Alo, Željko."

"You," Željko says, his voice dripping with hatred. "I should have known you were involved. You have murdered him, then."

"*Nu*, not murder. He was an animal."

It was Nicolai! The werewolf wasn't Zed, but his brother!

"You admit you killed him," Zed says, his voice louder, muscles in his arms taut like a lion about to spring on its prey.

"I did no such thing." Eugen stares Zed in the eyes, as calm as milk.

Zed laughs, gestures at me dismissively. "Are you saying this, this *fetita* killed him?"

I don't know what he called me, but I don't like the way he said it. "Your brother was *pricolici*. You think I can't kill a werewolf?"

He spits on the ground. *"Fetita,"* he says again.

"You're wrong." My blood is pounding in my ears. I clench my fists at my sides.

"If you think you are done with *pricolici* because you killed Nico," Zed says, "it is *you* who is wrong. Dead wrong."

A shudder seizes Zed's body. His lips curl back.

Bruno growls. The fur across his shoulders forms a hump like a Brahma bull.

Zed drops to his hands and knees. His body is covered with blackish-brown fur. His face elongates into a muzzle and he bares his teeth.

"He's a werewolf, too!"

"Get behind me," Eugen commands.

"No. I'll fight him with you." I raise the shovel like a bat, knowing it is a stupid gesture. A shovel will be less than useless against a werewolf. But I won't cower like a fearful, defenseless child.

Then I notice the bees.

Where there were a dozen or so buzzing lazily around my head, there are now hundreds. Not the thousands that had died protecting us against the other werewolf -- Zed's brother, Nick. But a large swarm, nonetheless. I hope there are enough to protect me, Eugen, and Bruno.

I drop the shovel and spread my arms wide. The bees cover my clothes, my hands, my face and hair. I feel like an astronaut, and the bees are my spacesuit.

Yet I know the danger I'm in. Just as a single puncture in a spacesuit would spell death for an astronaut on a spacewalk, if just one area of my body is bare of bees, I will be vulnerable to the werewolf's attack.

"I don't want to kill you," I tell the werewolf. "I want to help you. That's why I'm here."

The werewolf snarls at me. He is only twelve or thirteen

feet away from me.

"It doesn't understand you," Eugen says.

I glance at him for a second, and what I see doubles my fear. "You have no bees!"

"*Nu*. The hive is decimated from attacking the other werewolf."

"Bruno has no bees, either!"

"*Nu*. It is up to you. You must kill it. You and your bees."

"*My* bees?" With my arms spread out like wings, I turn my palms face up. "Why am I the only one with bees?"

"There are only enough bees to protect one person."

"But why me?"

"Only the bees know why."

"What do I tell them? How do I get them to go? I mean, to transfer to the werewolf?"

"Walk toward it. The bees will know what to do."

I shake my head. "I'm not getting near him."

"You must," Eugen insists. "Do not fear. The bees will obey their nature."

The werewolf lowers its head, draws its lips back to reveal sharp fangs. One fang glints gold in the fading sunlight. The animal is intent on me, stepping closer on padded feet. I see the muscles ripple beneath the fur on its shoulders.

Behind me, Bruno growls. An instant later, he dashes past me toward the werewolf, but this time, he is not protected by a contingent of bee bodyguards.

"Bruno, come back," I yell at the dog.

"*Nu,* Bruno," Eugen commands. "*Reveni!* Come back!"

Bruno ignores us both, crashing head-on into the werewolf. He grabs the scruff of the werewolf's neck, but the beast spins in the air, forcing Bruno to let go.

The werewolf, much larger and more muscular than Bruno, charges the dog, ripping into the white cross on his chest. A bloody gash turns the cross red.

Bruno screams in agony but does not stop fighting. The two canines stand on their hind legs, pawing and snapping at each other.

"*Pricolici, fie plecat,*" Eugen commands, to no avail.

Although almost frozen with fear, I force myself to move toward the dog fight. "Help me, bees," I plead.

Step by step I approach the werewolf. As if waiting for my bidding, the bees hover a quarter inch over my body and move with me. When I dare not get any closer, I hold my arms out to my sides. "Zed, I beg you. Stop fighting now."

The werewolf responds by sinking his teeth into Bruno's jaw. He glares at me.

The dog whimpers in pain.

"Bees, I ask you to help us. Obey your nature."

This is the second time in two days I have asked a favor of the world around me. I wonder how many times I can be successful. I hope now, and I hope at least once more, when we use the Dust of the Ancestors to make a cure for lycanthropy. A cure for Lisa's dad.

The bees slowly peel away from my body and surround the werewolf. With the beast's fangs burrowed into Bruno's face, they envelop not only the werewolf but the dog's head as well.

"No! Don't sting Bruno!"

But the bees have no choice. They attack the werewolf and the dog. Both animals howl in pain. The werewolf lets go of Bruno. Bruno staggers away, pawing at his ears, muzzle, and eyes.

Eugen limps to the dog, picks him up and struggles to move him further away from the werewolf. He lays Bruno in the grass beside the road and returns to my side.

The bees continue their attack on the werewolf, dropping to the ground to die after releasing their stingers into the beast.

Soon all the bees are dead or dying.

But the werewolf is still alive.

He turns his eyes on me. His lips curl back and red-tinged saliva drips from his jaws.

I step backward, completely unprotected. Frantic, I look for the shovel on the ground.

In my nervous habit, I rub the ring my mother gave me. *Moonstone.*

I clench my fist around the ring and thrust my right arm toward the werewolf as if I hold a shield. "Get away, *Pricolici!*"

The animal pauses -- then resumes pacing toward me.

Eugen hands me the shovel, although it feels like deadweight in my left hand, ineffective compared to the moonstone ring I wield in my right.

The werewolf sneezes. I swear he is laughing at us, taunting us to stop him with a cane, a shovel, and a ring.

Then a howl echoes around the valley between the mountains. *A wolf!* "Is it another werewolf?"

During the fight, darkness has descended. Eugen's eyes scan the woods around us. "If it is, God help us all."

A second howl answers the first. Then a cacophony of howls erupts. It's hard to tell how many wolves there are, and how many of the howls are just echoes.

Eyes glow in the woods. Shapes emerge, surrounding us. Wolves. At least a dozen if not more.

As a werewolf, Zed has survived the attack of the last of the bees. Even my ring is a joke to him.

But these wolves have made an impression on him. His tail drops and he pants heavily, watching the wolves as they circle us.

"It's the pack from this morning," I tell Eugen. "I'm sure of it. I think they were there to protect us from the werewolves."

"I have never seen anything like it." Eugen stares first at one wolf, then another. "But I believe you are right, *copilul meu*. I pray to God you are right."

The werewolf takes another step toward me.

Immediately, the circle of wolves tightens. The largest one positions herself between me and the werewolf.

"De necrezut," Eugen whispers. "I do not believe what I am seeing."

The werewolf decides he is outnumbered. He sprints for a break in the ring of wolves and disappears into the woods.

I look at the big female, who I feel must be the pack's alpha, hoping she will return my look, give me some sort of signal. But she is just a wolf, a part of nature, fighting as the bees did, against that which is not of nature. She and the rest of the pack melt into the shadows.

The woods are silent. The only light comes from the moon and the stars.

Bruno whimpers, and I rush to where he lies in the grass.

Eugen limps up beside me and drops to his knees. He lays his hand against the side of the dog's swollen head. "He is badly hurt. He has much venom from the bee stings. But the worst is the injuries from *pricolici*."

"I know," I whisper. "We have to get him home."

"*Da*. I will not end his misery here."

I stare at Eugen. "You -- you can't kill him."

"There is no way to save him."

"A dog won't turn into a werewolf ... will he?"

"The poison is inside him now. He will either change, or die a horrible death. Rabies."

"No! He can't get rabies. Zed wasn't rabid. He was a werewolf."

"According to the ancient lore of the Roma, rabies originated with *pricolici*. And even if it is not technically rabies, I do not want to see Bruno suffer with an infection contracted from *pricolici*."

"You don't know he's infected! You have to give him a chance. Maybe the remedy from Tasha's grandmother will save him."

Eugen looks at the sky. The gibbous moon is very bright. "When will your remedy be ready?"

"As soon as we can get back to Oltenita. Dama will add the dust of the ancestors to the recipe."

"I know Oltenita. It is all the way across Romania." He struggles to pick up the dog and drape him across his shoulders. He gestures to me to pick up his staff.

I hand it to him and start to ask a question.

He silences me with a look. "How will you get there, with no car?"

My heart feels like a popped balloon. "I hadn't thought about that."

"Come. We will take care of first things first. It will be a long walk down this mountain."

As we walk down the moonlit road, I hear gentle whoofing noises from the woods to either side. The wolf pack is following us, our own protective escort against the werewolf that might still be stalking us.

"*Mulțumesc*, Eugen. I hope I can repay your kindness by helping Bruno."

In the moonlight, I see his lips press together. His chin quivers slightly. "*Mulțumesc*," he answers. "*Mulțumesc mult.*"

***

We must have walked for hours. If not for the brightness of the nearly full moon, we would not be able to see to make our way down the mountain.

Eugen's breathing is heavy, raspy.

"Do you want to stop and rest?"

"*Nu.*"

"Do you want me to carry Bruno?"

"*Nu.* I can hold him until we see Albine."

"How much longer will it take for her to get back?"

"Not long."

Sure enough, within the hour, I hear the clop-clop of the hooves of Eugen and Albine's Vanner horses. A ghostly light illuminates the road and the edges of the trees with a pulsing halo. As Albine and the horses come into view, I see the light is from a lantern swinging from a hook on the side of the wagon.

Albine pulls the horses to an abrupt stop and hastily ties the reins to the brake handle. She leaps from the seat and grabs a lantern from its peg on one side of the wagon. "I expected to find you much sooner. Why do you carry the dog?"

"Bruno is hurt."

She holds the lantern up so the light shines on the dog.

"He is so bloody! And so are you, my husband! What happened?"

In the lantern light, I see how much blood Bruno has lost. It is his blood that is all over Eugen.

Eugen answers his wife in Romanian; I hear the word *pricolici.*

They speak in Romanian as Eugen carries Bruno to the back of the wagon.

The wagon is almost completely empty now. Of all the meager trappings of Roma life, only the red basket remains. There is plenty of room for Eugen to gently place the dog on a scrap of carpet covering the floorboards.

"I will ride back here with Bruno," he says, climbing in the wagon. He reaches into the red basket for a jar of honey.

"You ride up front with Albine."

Eugen slathers honey with his fingers on the dog's wounds. Bruno lies still, barely breathing. I squeeze his paw lightly. "Good dog, Bruno. You are so brave. *Mulțumesc* for protecting us."

The dog whimpers softly.

Albine hugs my shoulders and steers me to the front of the wagon. She tucks a lap blanket around both of us and slaps the reins gently across the horses' backs.

"So, two *pricolici*."

I nod my lowered head. I can no longer hold back the tears. "I was so stupid," I sob. "If I'd done what Eugen told me, Bruno wouldn't be hurt."

"*Nu*, you must not think that. Eugen told me what happened. There were not enough bees to kill the *pricolici*. He said you were very brave."

I shake my head. "I was afraid. I've killed Bruno because I didn't believe the bees would save us."

"You did not believe they would respond to your commands."

I shake my head again.

"But they did, did they not?"

I nod, still crying too much to speak.

"Nature will behave the way it will behave. You must trust nature. And *copilul meu*?" She tucks her hand under my chin and turns my face gently toward hers.

I look in her soft brown eyes, so full of compassion.

She whispers, "You must trust yourself."

CHAPTER 15

Albine pulls the horses to a stop in front of the B&B. The gas lanterns have been extinguished for the night, and I never would have recognized it or been able to find it by myself. But I had given Albine the business card from the B&B and she knew how to find it.

Although late at night, almost morning, several people are strolling in the street. Either they are late-night partiers or on their way to work. One man, probably in his thirties, gives us the "okay" sign, which is confusing because he does not sound as though he thinks we are okay. *"Necurat Roma! Du-te înapoi la tabara vagabond!*

I leap off the wagon. I don't know what he said, except it sounds like he called us vagabonds, but I understand his tone. The "okay" sign must mean something different here.

After all I've been through, after all the help these Roma "vagabonds" have given me, my blood boils at the unfairness of his blatant discrimination. "Go to hell," I yell at him.

"Stupid American!" the man says in English. "She probably already stole you blind, promising a love potion, eh?"

"Pay them no attention," Albine says softly.

"They shouldn't treat you that way. It's wrong. And it's not fair."

"It is life," Albine says.

"On second thought," the man continues, "maybe it was

worth your money. You met me, right?" He cocks his head toward the B&B. "This is where you're staying? Why don't I come up to your room later?"

"*Las-o baltă, tu pămpălău.*"

The man's friends whoop out loud, punch him in the arm, and repeat the phrase in falsetto voices. They go on past without bothering us any more.

"Hey, wife," Eugen yells. "We need to get moving."

Albine gathers the reins.

"Wait, please," I ask before she slaps them against the horses' backs.

I rush to the back of the wagon. It's so dark that I can't even tell if Bruno is still breathing. I place my hand on his side. His fur is sticky with blood and honey, but I feel his chest rise and fall. The movement is shallow, but regular.

"Do you have a phone?" I ask Eugen.

"Of course. What do you think we are, hillbillies?"

I'm horrified by the thought that I've offended him. "No, of course not."

"It is a joke, *copilul meu.*"

We exchange phone numbers and I give Bruno a kiss, right above his eye. The long whiskers he has in place of eyebrows twitch. "*Mulțumesc,* Bruno. We'll get you well. I promise."

Their silhouette disappears into the pre-dawn greyness, but I stand on the porch until the staccato taps of the horses' hooves on the pavement have faded away.

The others have long since gone to bed.

I tiptoe into my room and take off my shoes. Lisa is curled in her little ball in one corner of her bed.

I use the bathroom and wash my hands and face in the tiny sink. My reflection in the mirror stares at me with puffy eyes.

The stench of the fire and its gruesome offering clings to my clothes. I take them all off and put on a clean t-shirt and underwear, then crawl into bed and pull the covers up to my chin. The room isn't chilly, but I want the feel of covers tight around me.

"Hey," Lisa whispers. "Did you just get in?"

"Mm-hmm."

"Everything go okay?"

"I guess." I don't want to tell her about Bruno. And Zed. Not yet. I'd just have to say it all again to the others. "I gotta get some sleep. I'll tell you about it in the morning. But hey, thanks for teaching me that Romanian phrase."

"I want a full report in the morning." She illuminates her cell phone. "Which is about two hours."

"Okay."

As tired as I am, I can't get to sleep. Despite Albine's reassurances, I feel horrible about Bruno's injuries. In the morning, when I tell the others how I failed, will they forgive me for putting Eugen in danger? For almost getting Bruno killed after his role in saving us? For the possibility that the dog might have to be put to sleep because of my slow response?

I promise myself I will be stronger next time.

Next time? When will the next time be? When we get

back home and give Stan the remedy? Will "next time" be when it doesn't work? What will I do? How will I be stronger?

Bring bees and silver, Eugen said. If the remedy doesn't work, will I be strong enough to use either of those weapons against Stan?

Never mind my failure with Bruno. If I have to kill Lisa's father, will she ever forgive me for that?

A knock on the door.

Lisa and I both bolt upright in bed.

"Who is it?" I ask.

"It's me. Carson. Breakfast is served."

"Is there coffee?" Lisa mumbles.

"And hot tea?" I add.

"Come downstairs and see for yourselves."

Fortunately, we're the only guests at breakfast, so we can talk openly about what happened.

The first thing Lisa asks is, "How is Bruno?"

"It's a good thing he was there," I say. "We were attacked by another werewolf."

I explain about Zed and the bees, how there weren't enough of them to kill the werewolf. How Bruno fought until he was too badly injured to go on. How the pack of wolves drove the werewolf away.

"So that asshole Zed is a werewolf too," Carson says. His appetite is in full-force, so his ankle must feel better. He slathers a pastry with butter and crams it whole into his mouth. It reminds me of Ben, before he became a werewolf.

"Poor, poor, Bruno," Lisa says. "Is he going to be okay?"

"I don't know, Leez. Eugen's taking him to the vet, and will use his own herbal remedies. But that won't stop Bruno from becoming a werewolf. I told Eugen we would share the remedy with him."

I look at Carson. "Do you think Zed will come looking for us? He knows where we're staying."

"We'll be gone in a couple hours. He has no way to track us back to Oltenita."

"Are you sure?"

"Well, I don't think werewolves are a super race of bloodhounds."

"I guess you're right." I sip a glass of juice. "How are we getting back, with no car?"

Carson looks at Tasha, who touches a hand to her throat.

"You sold your necklace?"

"Traded it, actually. For a car."

"How did you find a car so quickly?"

"The owner of the inn," Tasha says. "His wife was very impressed with it, and it turns out he was in the dog pen."

"In the dog house," Carson says.

"Yes, in the dog house for giving her a new stove for Christmas. This is a lesson to you, *Stea*. Jewelry will never get you in the dog house."

"So he traded their car for a necklace?" I ask in disbelief. "Don't they need a car?"

"Not really," Tasha says. "They have bicycles for getting around town, a taxi or the bus or train for longer trips. Not many people have personal cars here."

"I wish you didn't have to give up your beautiful necklace."

"Especially with Zed still on the prowl," I add.

Lisa looks at me quizzically. "What do you mean?"

Why did I say that? Now I have to explain that Tasha is a pricolici vânător. *A werewolf hunter.*

Before I can figure out how to respond, Tasha explains. "The coins are silver. Protection against *pricolici.* Like wearing garlic to ward off vampires."

Lisa narrows her eyes. "Are you sure it's just for protection? Not for killing werewolves?"

Tasha returns her stare silently.

"You kill werewolves? Is that what your bow and arrows are for?"

"I don't have them any more, either, do I?"

"But you kill werewolves," Lisa insists. "You hunt them and you kill them."

"*Da.* My family has protected our people from *pricolici* for generations."

Lisa stands up from the table. Every inch of her quivers as if she has taken a sudden chill. "You're supposed to be helping Carson and me cure our father. Are you trying to kill him instead?"

Carson and Tasha stand up too.

"Of course we can trust the remedy," Carson says. "Right, Tash? Right?"

Lisa moves slowly around the table toward Tasha. Carson moves in front of Tasha, and I slip out of my chair in front of Lisa.

"I only kill *pricolici* because there is no cure," Tasha says. "I want to discover a cure as much as you do."

"Prove it," Lisa challenges.

"C'mon, Leez." Standing in front of her, I grab her arms above the elbows. "Hasn't she been helping us find a cure this whole time? Including asking for her grandmother's help, and taking us to the Cave with Bones."

"Maybe. Or maybe she's just been leading us on a wild goose chase."

I have never seen the intensity of Lisa's glare, at least not directed at me. Stunned, I release her and step away from her.

"I can prove it," Tasha says.

"What?" I ask.

"How?" Carson asks.

"I'm listening, Lisa says, crossing her arms. "What's your proof?"

Tasha slumps into her chair. Propping her elbows on the table, she strafes her fingers through her white-blonde hair. "Your father is *pricolici, nu?*"

"Yes," Lisa says. "You know that."

"My father was once a renowned *pricolici vânător*. He hunted and killed more *pricolici* than any other hunter in Europe. Then one night, the *pricolici* he was hunting became the hunter. It ambushed my father. It is a wonder my father did not die from the attack itself, it was so brutal."

I move to Tasha's side and put my hand on her shoulder. "But he survived."

Tasha nods her head, takes a deep breath and exhales slowly. "*Da*. He survived. But as the next full moon approached, he became anxious. He paced and ranted like a lunatic. At first, he told us to keep away from him. But the night of the full moon, he begged me to kill him."

Carson wraps his arm around her and pulls her close. "Oh, my god, Tasha. You never told me."

Tasha turns in his arms so her back is to his chest. She grips his arms tightly around her waist. "I did not know your family believed in *pricolici,* much less was beset by them."

"Anyone else would have thought you were crazy," I say. "Before Lisa and I came to Romania, Carson would have thought you were crazy."

"No, I wouldn't have!"

"*Da*. You would have. And I would not have blamed you."

My chest feels like it's in a vice. "Your father asked you to kill him. Did you?"

Tears spring from Tasha's eyes. She nods again. "There was nothing else I could do. I shot him in the heart with a silver-tipped arrow. It was the hardest thing I have ever had to do."

"I'm so sorry, Tasha," Lisa says. "I didn't know."

"You had no way to know."

"So the recipes we found, they really are for cures?" Lisa asks. "Not for some sort of werewolf poison?"

"*Da*. The ancient texts speak of remedies. But they do not cite any successful cures."

"I guess that means Bruno will be the guinea pig," Lisa

says.

"Sissa-Leezy, I think the dog would rather be a guinea pig than a werewolf."

"A guinea pig?" Tasha asks. "Yes, Carson has mentioned people turning into guinea pigs in lab experiments. But I don't understand how a remedy for *pricolici* will cause the dog to turn into a guinea pig."

Lisa chuckles. "I think my brother has been confusing you with literal versus figurative expressions."

***

We pile our belongings into the new car, a powder-blue Cavalin 1100 which resembles a cardboard box spray-painted with synthetic metallic paint to make it look like a real car. The front bumper is held in place with a piece of twine.

While Carson checks the fluids and whatever else is under the hood, I lean against the side door and text Eugen. A moment later, my phone rings.

"I prefer talking to typing," Eugen says. "My fingers are too fat."

"So, how's Bruno?"

A heavy sigh rattles through the phone. "Very weak. How long will it take for you to return with the remedy?"

"A couple days. We'll come back as soon as we can."

Lisa pulls the phone from my hand. "Give Bruno kisses from me," she says, then hands me back my cell.

"Eugen?"

"*Da?*"

"*Mulțumesc.*"

He pauses. For a moment I think I've lost the connection. But then he says, *"Noroc bun, copilul meu.* Good luck."

The Cavalin is actually a little roomier than Carson's Volvo. It has a pleasant motion as we rock through the mountains. I soon fall asleep and begin to dream. For the first time in months, I dream my childhood nightmare. My mother, in werewolf form, crashing through our car's windshield as my father drives us through the rain, trying to get away from her.

I now know the dream was real. Although my mother survived the crash, and thanks to Romelia's sacrifice is no longer a werewolf, the dream still holds me in its terror.

"Wake up, Lani," Lisa says, shaking my shoulder. "You okay?"

"Yeah." I wipe sweat from the edges of my face, then grip my hands together to alleviate their shaking.

"Must have been quite a dream you were having."

I nod. "Mm-hmm."

"You don't have to worry, Lani. Everything's going to be okay."

Her eyes give her away. She is just as worried as I am. "I know," I tell her. "We have the secret ingredient that will make your dad well."

"I know he is, but -- but what if he doesn't get better? What if all the bone dust and basil in Romania don't work?"

"Carson, Tasha and Dama can keep looking for a cure." We hug each other tight. "Oh, Lisa. It has to work. It just has to."

CHAPTER 16

We pull into Dama's yard after midnight. I see movement at the front window, the curtain shifting slightly, then being tucked back in place.

Dama slings the front door open wide and stands in the doorway, a shotgun leveled at the car. She shouts at us in high-pitched Romanian.

"What's going on?" I ask. "Why's she pointing the gun at us?"

"She doesn't recognize us," Lisa says.

"She thinks we're here to rob her," Carson adds.

Tasha rolls down her window. "Dama," she calls to her grandmother. She yells something in Romanian.

"Tatiana?" Dama lowers her gun.

"*Da!*"

"This is not your car," Dama says in English. She raises the gun again. "How do I know it is you?"

"It's me, I promise!"

I tell Carson to turn off the headlights so she can see us.

He dims the lights and Dama squints out at us.

"We're getting out of the car, Dama," Carson says. "Don't shoot!"

"Do you have your flashlight?" I ask as he opens the door.

"It's in the glove compartment."

Tasha retrieves the flashlight and turns it on, pointing it at her face as she gets out of the car. "See Dama? It's me!" She points the light at Carson. "And there's Carson. Lisa and Lani are here, too."

Finally convinced, Dama rests the gun against the side of the house. *"Nepoată meu,* what happened? Are you okay?"

"Yes, we're okay."

Dama lumbers down the stairs to greet us. Cradling Tasha's face in her hands, she kisses both of her cheeks. "Come inside. I will make you tea."

She holds Tasha around the waist as they go up the porch stairs. "Tell me," Dama says. "Did you find *Peştera cu Oase*?"

"*Da*, we found it, Dama," Tasha says. "We brought back the dust of the ancestors."

"Then we shall start brewing at first dawn. After you have slept a few hours."

"Can't we start now?" Lisa asks. "There's no way I'm getting any sleep tonight."

Dama looks to Carson for approval. "Is this your wish?"

Carson nods. "I could easily sleep for a century or two. But Poppy needs the remedy sooner rather than later."

Just as I step across the threshold, my cell phone chimes. The illuminated screen shows the caller's name.

"It's Jace!"

"Stay out here where you have reception," Lisa says. "Come inside when you're done."

I push the button to accept the call and sit down on the

steps.

"Jace?"

"Hey, Beautiful."

"You sound like you're next door."

"Would you be happy about that, or am I interrupting something?"

"You should be interrupting my sleep. It's 2 AM here."

"If I was there, I'd love to be interrupting your sleep. What have you been doing?"

It's been so long since I've talked to him, or even texted him, and so much has happened. "I don't know where to begin."

"Begin with what has you awake at 2 AM." He continues in a fake Romanian accent. "Hopefully not some muscular Romanian with a lavish estate and a thousand-year-old castle."

I laugh at his accent. "That's pretty good. You sound just like Nicu."

"You saying I sound like an old man? Oh, my back." He moans into the phone, then sings, "First it was my tail bone, but the tail bone's connected to the back bone, and the back bone's connected to the neck bone, and the neck bone's connected to the brain bone."

"I miss you." It feels good to laugh.

"I miss you, too. When will you be back?"

"Soon. We just got back to Tasha's grandma's house, right when you called. The others are in the kitchen now, working on the remedy."

"So you had a successful trip to the Cave with Bones?"

"We had some, um, snags, but we got the bone dust."

"Snags? What happened?"

"I'll tell you when I get back. How's Stan? And my mom?"

"Your mom went back to Rock Bluff. It's getting close to the full moon again, and she didn't think Stan should be left alone."

"Has he tried to get out of the gallery? Oh, god, he hasn't hurt anyone, has he?"

"No, he's just feeling antsy, according to your mom. But she says that's not a good thing for someone in his condition."

"I better go see what I can do to help with the remedy."

"Okay. Come home soon. Alex doesn't want to put up with me much longer."

My mouth fills with the taste of rankled milk. "Then maybe you should quit hanging out with her. Go help my mom take care of Stan."

After a pause he says, "She's fine."

"Alex or my mom?"

"Both, but I meant your mom. Nicu drove up there yesterday with more, um, supplies. He's going to stay and help her out."

"Oh, good. Then there's nothing to keep you and Alex from chilling out together."

"Lani, it's not like that."

"Or better yet, go back to Lafayette. Aren't you missing school?"

"I'm taking virtual school the first nine weeks. Plus an

externship through Hotel and Restaurant Management, here at the B&B."

"That's convenient. How'd you manage that?"

"Medical necessity because of the pain in my ass."

When I don't respond to what I guess he considers a joke, he says, "Listen, I gotta go. I'll text you tomorrow night, about 10 my time."

I'm too tired to worry about Jace and Alex right now. Whatever's going on with them, I can't do anything about it from half the world away. "Okay. Talk to you then."

"Call ended" flashes on the screen of my cell.

I bend forward and prop my elbows on my knees. Twining my fingers behind my neck, I try to banish the doubts that swirl around my head and chew at my gut. Is this what they mean by a gut feeling? When you feel in your gut that something's wrong?

I tell myself that nothing's going on between Jace and Alex. Lisa swears Jace is over the moon for me. Jace himself says nothing is going on between him and Alex, but wouldn't he say that, especially if there was something going on?

"Damn it," I say out loud, pounding my fists on my knees. "I have more important things to take care of." I shove my cell into my jeans' back pocket and go inside.

Downstairs, the temperature is several degrees warmer and an herbal fragrance perfumes the air. Dama hunkers over the huge pot on the stove, stirring the contents with a long-handled spoon. She looks up when I enter the room.

"*Copil meu*, do you have the *praful de strămoșii*?"

I stare at her blankly.

"The dust of the ancestors," Lisa translates.

"Oh, that's right. It's still in the car."

"Please to go get it," Dama says. She brings the wooden spoon to her lips and sips. She nods, apparently satisfied with the brew. "We are ready for it."

I rush outside and take the front porch stairs too fast. I fall face-first in the yard, getting a mouthful of gravel and grass.

"Crap." I sit up and spit the debris out of my mouth. Other than the taste of blood in my mouth and throbbing in my palms where they took the brunt of my fall like I was sliding into home base, I'm not badly hurt. Just mad at myself for not paying more attention.

"Hello, pretty lady."

The voice sends a chill across my arms and makes the hairs stand up on the back of my neck. A silhouette in the darkness steps toward me. He steps into the light from the street lamp and flashes his gold-capped grin. As Eugen called it, his *evil* grin.

I spit out more grit. "Zed! How did you find us?"

I get to my feet slowly, looking around for some kind of weapon.

"What's wrong, pretty lady? Not as brave without your kung-fu sidekick?"

I step sideways, putting the car between me and Zed.

In the dim light from the street lamp, I see his mouth twitching in a vicious smile. His hands are tucked in his pockets in a nonchalant pose as he slowly tracks me around the car.

"I'll, I'll give you my ring."

"I think you know it's gone far beyond that. It will take more than a little ring to satisfy your debt."

"What debt? I don't owe you anything." I glance over Zed's shoulder toward the front porch. I can't make a run for it until I'm at the front of the car and Zed's at the rear. "You and your brother stole our car. I think you owe us."

"Ah, yes. My brother. The one you killed. That is the debt of which I speak."

"He was going to attack us. He was *pricolici.* Just like you."

"You don't have to remind me." As if to accentuate his point, Zed growls, a low rumble deep in his throat. "Nor do I suppose I have to remind you who you're dealing with."

"Zed, listen to me. We can help you."

"Help me what? Help me forget my brother? Help me reunite with my girlfriend? Help me get my life back?"

"Yes! I can't help you forget your brother, and I can't help you with your girlfriend. But I think we can cure your lycanthropy."

He cocks his head. "My what?"

"I can help you not be a werewolf any more."

"By shooting me with one of your silver arrows? Or do you prefer the traditional bullet?"

"I don't want to kill you. Do you know why we went to the Cave with Bones?"

"You wanted a souvenir. A ghoulish souvenir, but other tourists have requested worse."

I'm in line with the driver's door. Zed is opposite me, by the front passenger door. "It's not for a souvenir. It's for a remedy."

I dart my eyes toward the house. I don't know if Zed notices, or if he just chose that moment to change direction, forcing me back to the back of the car.

"Pretty lady, there is no remedy."

"Not now, but there may have been one, a long time ago. We think we've found it. I point to the house. "Tasha and her grandmother are preparing it now."

Suddenly Zed leaps on top of the car. From there, in one smooth motion, he jumps on me, knocking me to the ground. As he straddles me, his face inches from mine, he growls once more and morphs into his werewolf form.

A scream of terror rises in my throat. I twist and struggle to escape, but his paws pin my shoulders to the ground. I try to knee him, but that just infuriates him. He curls his lips back, exposing his fangs, including the gold one. His breath reeks of carnage. I strike him with my fists, but he rips at my arms with his bloody fangs. Pain sears through my arm as he bites me over and over.

A door slams. Dama stands on the front porch, her shotgun aimed at the werewolf.

"*Pricolici, fie plecat!*"

The werewolf huffs at her. The sound brings an image to my mind of the three little pigs and the disdainful wolf huffing and puffing their houses down. Two of the pigs did not fare very well against the wolf. Would Dama and I meet an even worse fate?

The wolf steps toward the front porch and Dama, ignoring the gun.

I can't let him kill her. I might have hesitated before, and it could have cost Eugen his life. It might have cost Bruno his life.

I won't make that mistake again. "Hey, *pămpălău!* Kill me if you want, but don't go after the old lady!"

The beast returns his attention to me. He snaps his jaws together a hair's breath away from my cheek, before turning his back on me once again.

"That's it?" I stand up and grab his tail.

With the speed of an arrow, the werewolf spins around and lunges at my throat, gnashing his fangs.

I thrust my arm up to ward off the attack. I scream in pain as the animal's jaws clench on my arm.

Suddenly a shotgun blast thunders through the night.

The werewolf yelps, releasing my arm. It growls at Dama and slowly, steadily advances toward her.

"Dama, you have to have silver to kill him!"

"That was just the first barrel," she says. Her voice is calm, matter-of-fact, belying the fact that a werewolf is about to attack her. "It is loaded with bear shot, to get *pricolici* away from you. The other barrel is filled with silver shot. And now, *pricolici*, you can go to hell."

She fires the second barrel, straight into the werewolf. The force spins him in the air and knocks him back several yards. He lands at my feet, bloody and lifeless.

I stand there, dazed, gripping my injured arm.

Dama props the gun against the side of the house and comes to my side. "Come inside, *copil meu*, and we will dress your wounds."

Suddenly dizzy, I lean into her for support. "Oh, snap. I've been bitten by a werewolf."

CHAPTER 17

Lisa cleans my wounds in Dama's tiny washroom. It's only big enough for Lisa and me, so the others gather around the open door, peering in. "I'm not the bearded lady at the circus, you know."

"Not yet," Carson says.

"Thanks for that vote of confidence."

"Sorry, Lani." He hangs his head and raps his knuckles against the doorframe. "I guess I say stupid things when I'm worried."

Lisa dabs rubbing alcohol on a scratch that runs down my left cheek from just below my eye. Watching her in the mirror, I could be looking at my mother, with an almost identical scar on her right cheek.

"So he followed you all the way here," Dama says, pacing in the hallway right outside the washroom. "Only true love or true hate will possess someone to do that."

"Three guesses which one," Lisa says.

"And the first two don't count," Tasha replies.

Carson beams. "I taught her that."

Lisa throws the pile of used cotton balls in the trash can and screws the cap back on the bottle of rubbing alcohol. "Arms, hands, face. That's it. We're done."

Carson hitches his thumb over his shoulder in the general direction of the front door. "What should I do about the dead thing in the yard?"

"Put on gloves and drag it around to the back of the house, please," Dama says. "In the morning, I will call animal control."

"Will they cremate him?" Even though Zed attacked me, I don't want his soul to go to hell.

"Yes, *copil meu*, they have a pet crematory outside town. I will say he was my dog. They will cremate him and bury the ashes in a little plot I own."

"Do you have a pet?" Lisa asks.

"Nu. No pet." Dama shakes her head slowly. "But one day, I will die. It is cheaper than buying plot in human cemetery."

"Will they let you do that?" I ask.

"Nu. I will have to sneak in." Dama grins and winks. She pulls Lisa and me close like a mother hen cradling her chicks under her wings. "Now I must tend to the recipe."

"How can we help?" I ask.

"You, *copil meu*, must rest and stay away from the kitchen until the remedy is ready."

"Are you afraid of contaminating the work area?" Lisa asks.

"Da."

"But I cleaned all her wounds."

"Da."

She gently steers me to a rocking chair with soft, pillowy cushions and pushes me gently but firmly to sit down. There is no arguing with Dama. She props the door to the kitchen open so I can watch a bit of what's going on and listen to the conversation.

As soon as she opens the door, I am blasted with a stench. "Snake oil smells an awful lot like scalded collard greens, if you ask me."

Lisa pokes her head out of the kitchen. "I think Poppy's going to love it. And you better love it too, girlfriend."

I take an exaggerated sigh, which stretches something the wrong way in my side. "Mmm, ow!"

"What's wrong?" Lisa rushes to my side.

"I think I might have sprained something in here." I softly rub my ribs just under my left breast. The gentle touch brings another stab of pain.

"Pull up your shirt."

When I do, we both see the problem. A four-inch gash, cross-wise on my left rib cage. Protruding from one end is a thorn-like object.

"What is that?" Lisa asks.

I pull it out and hold it between my fingertips. "I believe that's a wolf claw."

"Better give it to Carson to cremate with the rest of the carcass."

Dama comes out of the kitchen with a sunflower-yellow pottery mug. She hands it to me. *"Noroc.* Cheers."

I hold the mug in front of my mouth, but I can't drink it.

"What is wrong, *copil meu?*"

"This is probably the worst-smelling stuff that's ever come out of your kitchen."

"You must drink it. Every drop."

Shaking my head, I try to hand the mug back to Dama. "The remedy is for Stan. And after yesterday, for Bruno, too. Will there be enough for all three of us?"

"You have to drink it, Lani," Lisa says. "If you don't, I couldn't bring myself to shoot you when you turn into a werewolf."

Her tone is light, but there it is: If I don't drink it, I'll turn into a werewolf. All Romelia's efforts to keep me from that fate – including sacrificing her own life – will have been in vain.

"I'm sure Alex would be happy to take care of that."

"Would somebody just shoot you now so you quit thinking that way?"

Dama puts her hand on my cheek. "Please, *copil meu*, drink the potion." She lifts the mug to my lips.

I take a small sip. Its warmth trickles down my throat.

"More," Dama says. "Drink the whole cup."

I gulp the remaining liquid. The warm sensation fills my chest. My fingers tingle.

"My thung ith nlumb," I say.

Tasha gasps. "Is she turning into a guinea pig?"

"It's the wolfsbane," Carson explains. "It can cause numbness. Also vomiting."

"So she isn't turning into a guinea pig?"

Lisa ignores her. "Isn't wolfsbane a poison?"

"Ye-e-e-es," Carson says slowly.

"It is sometimes used on arrows," Lisa says. "To kill wolves."

"I *am* a henny bwih," I try to say. "A dead henny bwih."

"You are *not* a dead guinea pig," Lisa says. She turns to Tasha. "Tell her she's not going to die."

"The potion will not kill her," Tasha says. "Or your father."

"How wih we know ib id wooks?"

Talk about bad English! I can hardly understand myself.

"How will we know if it works?" Lisa translates.

We all stare at Dama, four culinary students looking to the Julia Child of Romanian recipes for the answer.

"We won't know for sure until …."

Lisa nods. "Until the Hunter's Moon."

I wipe away a stream of drool from the corner of my mouth. "Wha'zath?"

"The full moon of October. It's less than a week away."

"So we take the remedy home, give it to Poppy…."

"And wait and see what happens?" Carson finishes for his sister.

"To both of us," I say.

"*Da*. That is all we can do. The sooner he drinks the potion, the better chance he has to survive the full moon."

"Or die of wolfsbane poisoning."

"If he dies," Dama says, "it will not be from the wolfsbane."

"Let me take your cup," Tasha says. She goes back to the kitchen with the mug.

"His only hope," Dama continues, "is to drink the remedy before the full moon."

"He's already been through two full moons as a werewolf." Lisa rubs the back of her neck. "Will it still work?"

"It will work, or it will not work," Dama says with a shrug.

"Curing a werewolf has never been attempted successfully before," Carson says. "I hope it works for Poppy."

"And for you," Lisa says, hugging me.

Dama nods. "*Da*. They will either be cured, or not cured. You will know on the full moon. But you must also be prepared for the next full moon. As Carson said, a cure for the *pricolici* has never been tried successfully. I do not know if this potion will be permanent, or will be required for the rest of your lives."

"Carson, please come to the kitchen for me."

I watch from my vantage point in the rocking chair as Dama retrieves a funnel and six, one-liter glass jars from a shelf. "You will hold the cauldron for me."

Carson grips the cauldron's ears with hot pads and tips it gently to fill the jars.

"Six jars. That's not a lot," he says.

"Five," Lisa says. "We have to take one to Bruno."

"Who is Bruno?" Dama asks.

"He's the dog that helped us fight the werewolves," Lisa says. "He was hurt real badly."

Dama shakes her head. "He will get rabies. This is not a cure for rabies."

"We don't even know if it's a cure for lycanthropy," Carson points out. "But we wouldn't be here to try it if the dog hadn't helped us. We have to try to help him."

"Where is this dog?"

"He's in Anina."

"You have no time to waste," Dama says. "It will take you two days to get back to Anina and return to Bucharest. Those are days you do not have."

"Den oo hab to tay id to imm."

Dama stares at me, trying to decipher what I've said. It must be hard, trying to translate gibberish spoken in a language that is not your first language.

"You have to take it to him," Lisa says. "You have to contact Eugen and Albine and give them some of the remedy for Bruno."

I get my cell phone out of my pocket and pull up Eugen's number.

Dama writes the number on a scrap of paper. "I will call him. I promise."

She exhales a long breath and slumps heavily into a rickety wooden chair.

Tasha rushes to her side. "Are you okay, Dama?"

"I am tired. There is much work here for one old lady."

"I'll stay and help you," Tasha says. "Carson can drive the girls back to Bucharest to catch a flight. I'll call Mihail in the morning to help us here."

***

Carson drives back to Bucharest like he's in the Daytona 500. "This baby can really move out," he says as he squeals the tires around the curves.

I cling tightly to a soft-sided cooler. Inside: Two one-liter bottles of the lycanthropy remedy.

We stop by the apartment to gather our belongings and make flight arrangements.

Carson removes a pile of papers from the little dinner table, uncovering a laptop computer and a printer. Carson checks flights on the Internet, types in reservation information, and prints out a departure schedule. "Your flight leaves in six hours."

Lisa looks at the itinerary. "This is only tickets for Lani and me. Aren't you coming?"

"Those were the last two seats," Carson says. "I'm on the next flight."

"When does it leave?"

"Tomorrow."

"A full day? You have to get the faster!"

"Sissy, I'll get there as fast as I can. Believe me, I would have been there yesterday if I could have."

Lisa's shoulders slump. "I know."

Carson turns back to the computer. "There's one more thing I need to print."

"Boarding passes?"

He shakes his head. "Labels."

"Labels?" Lisa cocks one eyebrow. "We have luggage tags."

He prints two labels and hands them to us with a flourish. "Ta-da!"

The labels are printed in English and Romanian. The English says, "Expressed human breast milk. Do not run through x-ray."

"Why are we taking breast milk?" I ask, no trace of numbness left in my voice, or in the way I feel.

Lisa adds, "*Whose* breast milk?"

Carson looks from me to Lisa and back. And he's not looking at our faces. His gaze comes to rest on my chest.

Self-consciously, I cross my arms. "You can't be serious."

"As a heart attack."

"We're teenagers, Bubba," Lisa says. "And you expect airport security to believe she's a mom?"

"This is Romania. You're both practically old maids by Romanian standards."

A memory flashes in my brain: Ben telling me he wanted to marry me even though I was an old maid by mountain standards.

Carson bumps his hip against Lisa's. "Do you even *have* a boyfriend?"

She notches her chin a few degrees in his direction and glares at him. "There's … someone."

"Oh, really? And you didn't tell me? How could you keep a secret like that from your big brother!"

"Did you tell me about Tasha?"

"Yes. Yes, I did."

"Not until I told you we were coming to Romania."

Carson grabs his sister in a bear hug and twirls her around. "Don't try to change the subject. What's his name?"

"Uh-uh. No details until I find out if it's serious. I might not even be on the radar."

He puts her down with a sigh. "If you're interested in someone, and he doesn't know it, he must be awful dense. Maybe I should give him a call. What's his cell number?"

"Nice try."

"Awww," Carson pouts. "Guess I'll have to get it out of you later. Just as well. We've got work to do. We have to get our story straight. Lani, what's your husband's name?"

"Huh?"

"Wrong answer! You have to be able to answer the questions."

"His name's Jace, but he's not my husband."

"But he is the father of your baby?"

I remember my conversation with Eugen.

"She's blushing!" Lisa says.

"How quaint to still be in love with the man who put you through the agony of childbirth."

I shake my head, hoping to shake the redness off my face. "Yes! He's the father of my baby!"

"Boy or girl?"

"Girl," I answer quickly. "No, boy!"

"Make up your mind. And you better have a name for the little ankle-biter." He shakes the bottles of lycanthropy remedy – aka breast milk – at me. "Or nipple-biter, as the case may be."

"His name is Frank, after my father. He was born on August First, and if I don't express my milk, my breasts get so engorged that I scream in pain! And if you don't let me take these hard-earned bottles of breast milk back to my baby, I'll start screaming right now!"

Carson and Lisa both laugh.

"Damn, girl," Lisa says. "You could win an Oscar!"

I can't help laughing, too. But then the reality of the situation hits me again. "What if I don't convince airport security? What if they pour the remedy down the sink? What then?"

Carson winks and saunters to the kitchen. He retrieves an old coffee can from on top of the refrigerator and opens it, breathing in the aroma.

"We're going to buy them off with coffee?" Lisa grabs the can and looks inside. "Oh, okay, then."

"What is it?" I ask.

Lisa gives Carson a grin. "The richest kind," she says, rolling the *r*.

"What *is* it?"

Lisa hands me the tin.

I look inside and pull out a one-hundred dollar bill, US currency. "Yep, that should do the trick. But are you sure you weren't saving this for something important?"

Carson takes back the empty tin and replaces it on top of the fridge. "If this isn't important, I don't know what is."

***

The airport is crowded with travelers, vendors, and an occasional huddle of Roma children. As we pass one cluster of kids, a boy who looks about twelve breaks away from the group and steps next to me. His muddy yellow shirt must have once been the color of the Tweety Bird on the front, and his pants are three inches too short, exposing toothpick legs. "Hello, would you like a flower?" He holds out a purple flower with a wilted stem.

"Go away," Carson yells, clapping his hands as if to shoo a stray dog.

The boy skitters away, but soon returns, accompanied by a girl wearing a denim jacket that swallows her and a flippy white skirt. She looks much cleaner than the boy but just as skinny.

"Please. It's only one American dollar," the boy says.

"Why don't you give it to your girlfriend?"

"She likes chocolate better. I can buy her lots of chocolate with the dollar you give me for this flower."

"What kind of flower is it?" I ask.

"Lani," Carson warns. "Don't talk to him!"

"A very pretty flower, just like you."

"Now you've done it," Carson says. "Go away, you little ruffian."

The boy points his dirty chin in the air. "Not unless the lady asks me to leave."

He thrusts the flower in my hand so I reflexively grasp it.

"One dollar, please."

"Okay, okay." I have to stop and put down the little cooler Carson gave me for the bottles of potion. Remembering our first day in Romania, I keep a tight hold on the strap as I zip open a pocket on my backpack.

I hand the boy a dollar and watch him and the girl scamper away.

"You know, that skirt looks awful familiar," I muse.

"Whatever. Let's get while the getting's good," Carson says.

As we stand at the ticket counter, Lisa glares silently at Carson.

"What?" he asks when he finally notices.

"You were really rude to those kids."

"They're beggars, Sissy. If you encourage them, they will just rip you off."

"They're obviously starving. I bet they haven't had a decent meal in months."

"Lisa, I hate to break it to you, but you can't save everyone."

"Each one counts," she replies.

"First save Poppy. Then if you want to come back and save all the orphans in Romania, be my guest."

"Maybe I will."

"Look," I tell them. "It's our turn."

Carson approaches the counter. I catch the words *Atlanta, Georgia,* and *Statele Unite ale Americii.*

"He said Atlanta. Isn't there another airport closer to you?"

"Chattanooga," Lisa says. "But we can probably get to Rock Bluff quicker going through Atlanta."

"Not according to what I've heard about Atlanta."

Carson looks at us over his shoulder. "Chattanooga's a no-go. Flight takes longer and the next one isn't until tomorrow. I checked back at the apartment when I made the reservations."

I shrug my shoulders. "Atlanta it is."

Carson walks us to the security station. A guard who looks straight out of a Russian spy movie -- drab green uniform, pants tucked into black boots, beret, rifle slung over one shoulder by a strap -- looks at our tickets.

He waves Lisa and me through to the next checkpoint, but this is as far as non-passengers can go.

Carson gives Lisa a hug and a peck on the cheek. "Good luck, Sissy. Tell Poppy I love him. I'll be home in a couple days."

He gives me a quick hug as well, then he is swallowed in the tide of relatives bidding their loved ones farewell.

As we wait in line to have our bags run through the x-ray, I glance up at a model airplane suspended from the ceiling. "I hope our plane's not made of cardboard," I tell Lisa.

"Don't be silly," she says. "It's balsa wood."

"With a rubber band for a propeller?"

"Don't worry. It's a *big* rubber band."

"What if it's not big enough to get us to Paris?"

"The pilot will climb out on the wing and wind it back up when we start losing altitude."

"Bags go here," a man in a camouflage uniform barks at us. He wears a feathery blonde mustache that he probably – and mistakenly – thinks makes him look more mature.

Lisa puts her duffel bag on the conveyor belt of rolling metal rods, and I put my backpack next to it.

"This too," the man says, tapping the cooler on my shoulder with a long pointer.

"It doesn't get x-rayed," I say, hoping my voice isn't

trembling so badly it gives me away. "It's breast milk."

"Everything goes through x-ray."

"Not this." I point to Tasha's pink TSA lock that Carson fastened to the cooler.

"*Da*. Everything." He reaches for the strap but I twist to the side.

"BUT IT'S BREAST MILK," Lisa shouts. "FOR HER BABY!"

The man jerks back as if she slapped him. He recovers his facade of power a second later. He pokes the cooler with the pointer, accentuating his words. "Every. Thing. Gets. X. Rayed."

I straighten my back and swat the pointer away. "I want to see your supervisor. *Now!*"

He narrows his eyes at me.

I narrow mine at him. "Now," I repeat.

The line is backing up behind us. People shuffle around, trying to see what the hold-up is. Angry voices rumble. "What are they saying?" I whisper to Lisa without breaking my stare-down with the security guard.

"Hurry up, we'll be late. They're not happy."

"You hear that?" I tell the security guard. "They are not happy. You better call your supervisor before a riot breaks out."

Finally he shifts his eyes away from mine. He tugs a walkie-talkie off his belt and speaks into it. A moment later, a response bursts through the speaker. The security boy holds the device at arm's length. "*Da*," he says, and re-clips the radio to his belt.

"You will wait there." He points to a row of chairs.

Lisa and I grab for our bags, only to have our knuckles rapped with the pointer.

"What the hell?" Lisa says.

"You will get your bags after you speak to my supervisor," the security guard says. "*As you requested.*"

"C'mon, Lisa. Let's just do what he says. He's in charge, after all."

A smug grin spreads across the guy's face. He obviously doesn't recognize sarcasm.

We wait in the chairs as instructed until a Pillsbury dough boy approaches us. His sharp features, buzz hair cut, and bushy uni-brow contrast with his doughy body.

"I am Captain Grigor. You have problem?"

"Yessir," I reply, standing up.

"Captain *Katarina* Grigor.

That's when I realize the captain is a woman.

"I'm sorry, ma'am," I sputter.

"Can you help us?" Lisa asks. "The security guard is telling my friend she has to have her cooler of breast milk X-rayed."

"Breast milk?" Captain Grigor asks. "Are you a mother?"

I nod. "Mm-hmm. My son is waiting for me back home in the U.S."

"How old is your child?"

"Just nine weeks."

"Why are you traveling without him?"

"I ... I." This wasn't one of the questions Carson asked in our practice session.

"Her grandfather is very sick," Lisa jumps in. "On his death bed, we thought."

"That's right. And I didn't want to risk the baby catching the disease."

"Your grandfather, he lives in Romania?"

"Yes."

"In Bucharest?" the captain asks.

"Yes," I say.

"No," Lisa says at the same time.

Captain Grigor raises half of her uni-brow. "Oh?"

"He lives in Oltenita," I quickly explain. "But he's in the hospital in Bucharest."

She doesn't seem completely convinced. "Please to open the case for me."

I fumble for the key to the tiny lock.

Captain Grigor stops me with a pointer, identical to the one the security guard used. "Wait. This is TSA lock?"

"Yes."

"I will unlock."

She unzips the cooler, revealing the two bottles of milky liquid.

"Take them out," she says.

I hold the two bottles of lycanthropy potion for her inspection.

"Would you be willing to drink it?"

"Drink my own breast milk?"

"Just a sip. Either that or we pour it down the sink right now."

"Do you have a cup? I don't want to get my germs on the bottle."

The captain barks an order into her walkie-talkie. A moment later, another guard with a rifle slung across his shoulder rushes over to us and hands the captain a tiny paper cup.

I screw the top off one of the bottles and pour the liquid into the cup. *"Noroc,"* I say, using the toast I just learned from Dama.

After I down the remedy, the captain looks at me for a minute. Then another minute.

My face hasn't turned purple and I haven't stopped breathing, so I guess she figures the potion really is breast milk. She nods approvingly. *"Bine, bine."*

"So we tan go?"

"Nu."

"I mean *can* we go?" I repeat, forcing my numb lips and tongue to form the word correctly.

"Nu."

A cold fear slides down my spine. I look at Lisa for help.

"Why not?" Lisa asks.

The captain points at the other bottle. "You must drink some from the other bottle."

I do as she says.

Again she waits.

When I don't keel over dead or go into a seizure, she nods again.

I run my tongue around my gums. The tingling

sensation has worn off. "Ith it okay for uth to go now?"

Apparently, it hasn't completely worn off.

But Captain Grigor doesn't seem to notice my slurred speech. She wipes the corner of her eye.

Is that a tear? Is she crying?

"Ma'am, are you okay?" I tighten the bottle caps and repack the bottles in the cooler.

"*Da*. Is just, I wish I could have fed my daughter breast milk. But I was dry."

"I'm sorry." I don't know what to say. "How old is she?"

"She is about your age. She is sixteen."

"I just turned sixteen."

"My daughter, her name is Elena. She is having her own baby in January."

"Congratulations! What happy news."

"Excuse me," Lisa interrupts. "We're going to miss our flight."

Captain Grigor whips out her walkie-talkie again. "I will call escort boos."

"Boos?" I ask.

"*Da*. Boos. Little electric car."

"Oh, *bus*."

"*Da*, boos. I am sorry my English is not too good. My accent needs work."

I shake my head. "You have a wonderful accent. And I only wish I could speak two languages. Sometimes, I can barely speak one."

Lisa clears her throat. "The plane?"

The captain calls for our escort, and in a few minutes, we have collected our packs and boarded the airport car.

As we speed away, Captain Grigor calls out after us, "Good luck to your grandfather! And your son!"

The driver zigzags around people and their luggage like he is racing through an obstacle course. He pulls in front of the gate and salutes. We jump off the bus and hustle through the tunnel to the plane.

***

"Thank our lucky stars for the bond between mothers," Lisa says as the plane lifts off.

"And that I already knew Stan's Snake Oil wouldn't kill me."

Once we reach cruising altitude, a flight attendant walks down the aisle carrying a tray of tiny paper cups. "Coke? Water?"

"Just a straw, please," Lisa says.

"Diet Coke, please," I say.

"Nu. Only regular." The attendant hands me a cup and walks away before I can say I really don't want a sugary soda.

"Was I slurring again?" I ask Lisa, looking for a place to put my cup. There are no fold-down trays in the backs of the seats.

"Sorry, Sailor. You can't blame that miscommunication on your drunken slurring."

Lisa turns silent for a few minutes, intent on the straw-wrapper she's folding in her lap. When she's done, she puts it in my hand. "Your lucky star," she says.

I hand it back to her and fold her fingers around it. "Keep this one for Stan."

PART III: THE HUNTER'S MOON - OCTOBER

CHAPTER 18

When the plane touches down in Atlanta, I am simultaneously exhausted and exhilarated. As soon as we make it through Customs, I'll see Jace.

But the first voice I hear, the first face I recognize, is Alex's. "Eeeeee! There she is! Lani, Lani! Over here!"

Her blonde hair is tucked under an Atlanta Braves baseball cap. She's wearing skinny jeans and a men's white button-up shirt.

"Can I carry that?" She tugs at the shoulder strap of the cooler without waiting for a reply.

"No, I got it."

She frowns and turns her attention to Lisa. "Can I help you with your bag?"

"Thanks, it's not heavy."

"C'mon, you guys gotta let me help somehow!"

"You're our chauffer, right?" I remind her.

Alex's smile returns, beaming at me like I'm her long-lost best friend. She taps a finger to the bill of her cap. "That's right! And, a certain gentleman's waiting in the limo who might be less of a gentleman when he sees you."

"Why didn't he come to the gate?"

"Re-injured his tailbone," Alex says.

"Oh, dip! What happened?"

"Well, we were dancing, and he got a little tipsy and

fell."

"Wait, you were dancing? Together? And he was drinking? I didn't even know he drank."

"Yeah, well, he doesn't normally." She giggles like it's a big joke, but I am not amused. "That's probably why he got so drunk."

"Why was he drinking, then? And dancing? I thought he's supposed to be recovering."

"We were celebrating your coming home."

"Oh, why didn't you say so! You were drinking and dancing with my boyfriend, but it's okay because I was coming home soon."

Lisa slips her arm around mine. "Lani, chill."

I tug away, the fire too hot to be doused that easily. "You really think it's okay to play house with my boyfriend, just because I'm not around?"

Alex's eyes are wide. "It's not like that!"

"The hell it's not." I stop dead in my tracks.

"Sorry, sorry," Lisa says to the people who have to swerve around us like a river around a rock formation.

"He's just a friend, Lani," Alex says. "A drop-dead gorgeous friend, but he's not interested in me."

I glare at her, silently daring her to go on.

"I won't lie," she says. "When I saw him again, all the old feelings came rushing back. We went out a couple years ago, when we were both freshmen. But then my family moved to Jasper. He visited, we texted and talked on the phone. But one day he came to see me out of the blue. He said he was in love with someone else." She shrugs. "That someone was you."

Suddenly I feel like a possessive, paranoid bully. "Oh."

"Not to say I told you so," Lisa stage-whispers. "But I told you so."

"Alex, I --. I'm sorry I jumped to conclusions. It's just you're so, so beautiful, and perky, and I'm so blah. How could I compete with someone like you? Especially when you're here and I'm halfway around the world."

"First off," Alex says, her smile returning. "You are hardly 'blah.' And second, *perky*? How could you be so cruel as to call me *perky?*"

"It was a compliment, honest."

"Paging Lani Morgan. Paging Lani Morgan," Lisa says. "If we're all buds again, can we *please* get out of this madhouse?"

Laughing, we follow Alex to the parking lot. We are all still laughing and chatting so intently that I don't see Jace until I almost bump right into him. I drop my backpack and jump into his arms, knocking him into the back of Alex's car.

"Ouch," he says, wincing.

"Jace! Your butt! I'm so sorry!"

He repositions himself against the car and pulls me up against him. "I'm not. It's worth it to see you again, Beautiful. You're a sight for sore eyes, and sore butts."

He takes my face in his hands, threading his fingers through my hair, and kisses me gently on the lips.

I press my mouth to his.

"Mmm, honey chestnut ice cream," he murmurs, his

breath hot on my mouth. "Emphasis on the honey."

When he moves his hands, he notices the scratch on my face. "What happened?"

"Fought with a pricker vine when we were hiking up the mountain."

"I'll get you some aloe when we get back to the B&B." He kisses me on my forehead, unscratched cheek, and again on my lips.

"Hate to break this up," Lisa says, "but have you heard anything from Poppy?"

Jace moves away from the car so Alex can open the trunk.

"Mrs. Morgan's been checking in daily while she's in Tennessee," Jace says. He turns to me. "She's had problems getting texts through to you, and so have I."

"What's going on? Is Poppy worse?"

Jace waits until Alex has gotten in the car. "Mrs. Morgan says we're not in danger until the full moon."

"Which is two nights from now," I point out. "We don't have any time to waste."

Jace packs my backpack and Lisa's duffel bag into the trunk. "So did you find an antidote for Stan?" he asks. "I'm hoping that's what's in your new cooler."

"I hope so, too."

Jace and I sit in the back seat on the drive back to Jasper, his arm wrapped around my shoulder. I snuggle as close to him as the seat belt will allow, until a jolt of pain shoots through my injured arm.

"You okay?" Jace asks. I'm glad I have on a jacket so he can't see my wounds.

"Yeah." I nestle against him with my arm repositioned. Other than the throbbing pain in my arm, I feel no different than before the attack.

I don't feel werewolf-ish -- or at least, I don't feel any unusual cravings or anxiety which I could attribute to a lycanthropy infection. If I do, I'll lock myself up in the room with Stan. The last thing I want is to take a chance that I'd be a danger to my family and friends.

But for now, I don't want to waste a minute of being near Jace, just in case the antidote doesn't work. I snuggle next to him the whole trip back to Jasper.

The parking area behind the B&B is full, but Alex has a reserved spot. As we pull in, a man with dark blonde hair and beard and a woman who looks like an older replica of Alex explode through the back door and dash to the car to meet us.

"You have got to be Lani," the woman says. "You look just like your mother."

"You must be Alex's mother," I respond. "You look like sisters."

"I was going to say that about you and Melani," Alex's mother says. She gives me a big hug; she's stronger than she looks. I grit my teeth to bear the pain in my arm.

"I'm Zander, Alex's dad," the bearded man says. "And you've met Milly. Hope she didn't break any ribs with that hug."

"I'm a southern girl. Hugs are great."

Milly hugs Alex while Zander shakes hands with Jace. "Guess I should give up on you and Alex ever getting back together. I hope that doesn't mean an end to our friendship, or your apprenticeship."

"Don't worry, Mr. B," Jace replies. "You and I will always have Paris. Paris, Tennessee, that is."

Zander laughs and slaps Jace on the back. "Let me help you with the bags."

Lisa gets her hug from Milly. "I don't know about Paris, Tennessee," Milly says. "But the boys in Jasper, Georgia, had better watch out with the three of you girls in town. I swear, I've never seen a trio of more beautiful girls since they cancelled *Charlie's Angels*."

As we walk up the back steps, Alex asks, "What's in the cooler?"

"Stan's Snake Oil," I blurt.

Lisa coughs, a reminder that we don't know how much Alex and her parents know, or how much information they can be trusted with. "It's the medicine for Poppy that my brother helped us develop in Romania."

"I hope it helps," Milly says. "Melani told us about the rabies."

"Right, the rabies," Lisa says. "He got the shot series, but he's in a lot of pain. Nothing local seemed to help."

"Well, you kids relax here tonight, and you can go see to your daddy in the morning."

"Thank you, Ms. Book," Lisa and I say together.

As we enter the B&B through the back door, a delicious

aroma surrounds us. "Who's up for some Brunswick stew?" Zander asks.

"Sounds great." I feel a rush of saliva fill my mouth like Pavlov's dogs when the dinner bell rang.

"Zander, will you put their luggage in Jace's room?" Milly asks.

"Yes, ma'am." Zander grabs our bags and heads upstairs.

"It's the only room in the house that isn't booked," Milly says. "I'm afraid the three of you are going to have to bunk up tonight."

Jace ducks his head, looking at me out of the tops of his eyes. "I've been staying in the room you and your mother were in."

I pull his chin up with my fingertips. "Are you blushing? Why are you blushing?"

"I want to stay in their room, too," Alex says. "Like a sleepover."

"You'll sleep in your own room, dear."

"Oh, Mom. You're such a killjoy."

"The girls have been traveling. They don't need a sleepover. They need sleep."

"Then Jace can sleep in my room."

"Hello, your mother is right here." Milly turns to Jace. "But if you'd prefer, you can sleep on the couch in the front parlor. It's very comfortable."

"Thanks, but I'll be fine sharing the room with Lani and Lisa."

Alex holds open the door to the dining room. It's full of people in 1860s costumes. Some of the men are dressed like Union soldiers, others in Confederate uniforms. Most of the women are dressed in long-sleeved black dresses with high necklines and low hemlines, but a couple younger women have Scarlett O'Hara gowns with wide hoop skirts. Everyone is chatting and laughing without regard to their role-playing sides of the war.

We weave our way through the crowd to the kitchen. Zander serves me a bowl of steaming hot stew. I polish mine off before he's through dishing out the others' stew.

"Goodness, little lady. You're welcome to another bowl."

"Yes, please."

"I don't know where you put it," Milly says. "Y'all help yourselves to cornbread in the oven. Jace and Alex both know where the drinks are. Holler if you need anything else."

After finishing all of the stew and most of the cornbread, Lisa, Jace and I go upstairs to our room. The bed is made, but one of the pillows and a blanket are on the sofa. "You've been here at the B&B the whole time we were gone?"

"Yeah," Jace says.

"You haven't had to go home for school?"

"Virtual school, remember?"

"Yeah, I remember now." I roll my eyes and rub my hand over my mouth.

"You're okay with that, right? That I've been staying here at the B&B?"

"Jace, I owe you a big apology. I had no reason to doubt

you, and I never will again, as long as I live."

"Hey, you don't have to get all emotional." He wipes away a tear from my cheek. "Listen, I've been working in the kitchen here to satisfy my Hotel and Restaurant externship.

"I only have three classes, and one of them is an externship for Hotel and Restaurant Management. I'll make you something new for breakfast. It's a savory pastry I invented."

I hug him and nuzzle his neck. "Nothing against the food in Romania, but I've missed your cooking."

"So, do you guys want to share the bed?" Lisa asks. I'd almost forgotten she is in the room, too. "I can take the sofa."

"Tempting, very tempting." Jace pushes me to arm's length. "But I'm used to the sofa."

"Why have you been sleeping on the sofa when you could have used the bed?"

"Okay, this is going to sound strange. But by *not* sleeping in the bed you slept in, I kind of felt closer to you. Like by sleeping on the couch, I could pretend you were sleeping in the bed."

"What a romantic," Lisa says. "But now that she is here, really, I don't mind the sofa."

"Uh-uh." Jace shakes his head. "I don't think I could control myself."

"I could lend Lani my stun gun."

"You have a stun gun?" I blink at her incredulously. "Why didn't you use it on those creeps, Nick and Zed?"

Lisa laughs. "I left it at home. But if I had had it with me, those jerks would have been feeling the business end of it."

Jace stiffens, as if the danger is right outside the door. "Why? What happened? Who are Nick and Zed?"

"Just a couple two-bit criminals," Lisa says.

"No, they were more than that," I tell her. "He's going to find out sooner or later."

"What do you mean, Lani?"

I take off my jacket, exposing the bandages on my upper arm and scratches between my elbow and wrist. My hair hides the bite marks on my neck.

"You were attacked? My god, Lani! Is that the 'snag' you mentioned? These guys attacked you?"

"They weren't just guys."

Jace stares at me with dark eyes beneath furrowed brows. "Then, who were they?"

I watch his face as the truth dawns on him. "You were attacked by a werewolf."

"Werewolves were old-world before they were new-world."

"Why didn't you tell me?"

"So that you could do what, exactly?" I hug him with my face buried in his chest. "I took the potion. Stan and I will either recover together, or not."

"You'll recover," Lisa says with only a slight tinge of fear quivering around the edges of her words. "You and Poppy both will."

After a sniffling pause, Lisa takes a deep breath. "Okay, so tell me for realz. How's Poppy doing?"

Jace takes my hand in both of his, twining our fingers. "He hasn't had any problems since the last full moon."

"But the next full moon is coming up in two days," Lisa says. "What if ... what if the potion doesn't work?"

That question has been running through my mind as well. What if it doesn't work?

The Red Moon, the full moon of August, when I had my birthday and Stan had his first werewolf episode – was a close call. Stan could have killed Lisa. And if he'd escaped, who knows how many victims would have died? How many would have been wounded and become werewolves themselves?

And then the Harvest Moon – the full moon of September. Stan wouldn't have survived if my mother hadn't been there to help.

Now the Hunter's Moon approaches. If the remedy doesn't work, it will be the death of both Stan and me.

Lisa gets a faraway look like she's in shock. "If the potion doesn't work, I'll have to kill my own father."

I look Jace square in the eye so he knows I mean what I'm about to say. "And you'll have to kill me."

"Don't think that way," Jace says.

"No, we have to think that way. If it doesn't work, Stan and I will both, well, we need to get ahold of two silver bullets, just in case it doesn't work."

"I can't," Jace cries, his voice cracking. "I can't. I love you too much."

I touch the side of his face, feel the rough stubble on his cheek. "I know you do. I love you, too, Jace. And that's why you'll do it. *Because* you love me."

He throws his arms around me and buries his head in my shoulder. I feel his body shake as he sobs. All I can do is hold him.

What could have been, if I hadn't been a werewolf waiting to happen?

Would he have taken me to prom? I imagine standing next to him in a frilly, pale gold gown that stops right above my knees in front, draping longer in back. I try to imagine him in a tux, but I can't. The image keeps morphing into his black leather biker pants and jacket. He's wearing a t-shirt with a lopsided bow tie.

Would we have gotten married? Had kids? What would they have looked like? A boy with my red hair and pale skin? A little girl with Jace's dark brown hair and olive complexion? I don't realize I'm crying until I taste salt on my lips where the tears have trickled down my cheeks.

Jace looks up at me. He kisses the tears off my cheeks. "You won't die," he states, like it's the absolute truth. "Not until you're an old, old lady."

"I'll hold out if you promise to take me to prom."

He grins at me and just like that, the crushing weight breaks free of my chest and flies away. "It's a date," he says. "I was going to ask you, you know."

Suddenly I'm super thirsty. "Can we go down to the bar? I'm still on Romanian time."

We go down to the bar. Jace takes on the role of bartender. "What'll it be, ladies?"

"I'll have a LaCroix," Lisa says. Jace opens the mini-fridge and offers her a lime and a raspberry. "Lime, thanks."

Jace winks at me. "You don't have to tell me what *you* want." He puts a measuring cup of water in the microwave and prepares a china cup with an Earl Grey teabag.

We fill him in on our Romanian adventures -- the cruise on the Danube River, the beautiful landscapes between Bucharest and Anina, the cathedral-like Cave with Bones.

Alex comes in with a FedEx package. "Thought I'd find y'all in here. Jace, fix me something that'll put hair on my chest."

"Sure thing. What did you use before?"

"You turd. Just pour me a cranberry and Sprite."

"What's in the box?" Jace asks as he mixes her drink.

"Delivery for Lani. Here ya go."

I take the slender cardboard envelope from her and rip the package open by the pull strip. "Who would FedEx something to me here?" A bubble-wrapped rectangle falls into my hands. When I untape it, I know instantly who sent the package, and why.

Inside are two silver *lew* coins.

"Ooh, those are pretty," Alex says. "Are they silver?"

She holds her hands open so I let her hold the coins.

"I thought she sold her necklace," Lisa says.

"She must have held back a couple coins for an emergency."

"Who is 'she'? And what's the emergency?"

Jace holds his hand out and Alex places the coins in his

palm, one at a time. "These are silver, aren't they?"

"Can you take care of this?" I ask him.

"Take care of what?" Alex asks.

"Not until morning," Jace says. "And I'll have to find someone who can handle the job, quickly and discreetly."

"Handle what?" Alex stomps her foot. "Why won't you tell me what's going on?"

"Just some family business we need to tend to," I tell her. I turn to Jace. "I think Aurelia used a silversmith in Atlanta. I'll call Mama."

I step out the back door, but some of the re-enactment crowd are standing around the parking lot, yakking.

I walk around front and dial Mama.

"Are you back?" Mama says when she answers. "I haven't heard from you since you texted me that you had made your connection in Paris."

"We're at the B&B. I need you to do something for me."

"Of course, sweet daughter. Anything."

My chest fills with warmth. When my mother says she'll do anything for me, she means it. Right up to and including dying for me. Which, thank God, she didn't have to do, and hopefully never will.

"Do you know what silversmith Aurelia uses?"

"Oh, Lani. Does this mean you didn't find a remedy?"

"We've got the remedy, but we don't know if it'll work. We have to be prepared for the worse."

"I understand. Do you have the silver?"

"Yes. Carson's girlfriend FedExed me two silver coins

from Romania."

"I'll call you right back."

"Mama, wait. How's Stan?"

I hear her exhale before she answers. "Antsy. The sooner you get here with the remedy, the better."

"Okay. We will."

The night is chilly, and I go back inside to wait for Mama to call me back.

Alex is telling corny jokes. I'm sure Jace put her up to it to stop her torrent of questions.

"A horse walks into a bar," Alex says. "The bartender says, 'Why the long face?'"

Jace laughs and Lisa groans.

"No mas! No mas!" Lisa pleads.

Jace catches my eye. "What'd she say?"

I glance at Alex as I pull out a barstool. "I'll tell you later."

"You can talk in front of me," Alex says. "We're all friends, here, right?"

"Absolutely." Jace grabs Alex by both hands and pulls her behind the bar with him. And that's why you're going to tell us your secret recipe for a virgin dark and stormy."

"Oh, really? You want my ten-thousand-dollar award-winning recipe?"

"Get out," Lisa says. "You won ten K on a recipe?"

Alex hip-bumps Jace. "Not yet. But I will one day!"

"It's good, but not that good." Jace squirts Alex with the club soda nozzle.

"You goofball. Now I have to go get another shirt."

Once Alex leaves, I tell Jace and Lisa what Mama said about Stan.

Lisa props her elbows on the bar and cups her hands over her eyes.

"Don't worry, Leez. We have the remedy. It's gonna work."

My phone rings. "I'll take this outside."

I zigzag through the crowd in the dining room and go out on the front porch. The October night is cooled by a gentle breeze. "Hi, Mama. What did you find out?"

"Aurelia says her silversmith will be ready whenever you get there. His name's Cosmas Cojocaru. I'll text you the address."

"Cojocaru?" The name sounds familiar, but I can't place it. "Is he Romanian?"

"Yes, that's right. Lani?"

"Mm-hmm?"

"If Carson's friend sent you silver, she knows why you need it, right?"

"Yes. She knows. She helped us a lot in finding the remedy."

"Why didn't she just send you silver bullets?"

"She probably didn't want to raise a lot of questions by the FedEx people, or by anyone who happened to see when I opened the package. Such as Alex. Who, believe me, was plenty curious about the coins as it is. Besides, how would Tasha know what caliber?"

"Good point."

"What caliber is it, anyway?"

"Nine millimeter."

I pause and look around to make sure no-one can overhear. "Mama, how bad is Stan, for real? What does 'antsy' mean?"

She exhales loudly enough for me to hear through the phone. "He's getting real worked up. He doesn't think he can resist the full moon. It's only two nights from now. Lani, he ... he asked me to kill him, before he can kill anyone."

"You won't have to do that. If the remedy doesn't work, Lisa will shoot him. And Jace will shoot me."

"What do you mean? Why would *you* need to be shot?"

"Mama, I don't know how to tell you this, so I'll just say it. I got hurt. By a werewolf."

"Oh, Lani, after all you've been through...." Her voice cracks. "It should be me, not you."

"Mama, listen. You wanted me to shoot you, and I didn't think I could do it. But if Romelia hadn't jumped in the way, I guess I would have, to save Aurelia. If I'm strong enough to do that, I'm strong enough to beat this."

Mama takes several deep breaths to control her tears. "I hope you're right, Sweetheart. I just got you back in my life. I don't want to lose you again, with no hope of getting you back."

"Me too, Mama. We'll get ahold of the silversmith, and see you tomorrow."

"I love you, Daughter."

"I love you too."

I lower my head, not feeling near as strong as I let Mama think.

I itch all over. My scalp itches. My back itches. My arms and the bottoms of my feet itch. I kick off my shoes and pace in a small circle in the front yard. The dew feels cool on my toes, but not unpleasant. A night breeze makes me shiver. I stop pacing and arch my back, staring at the cloud-strewn sky.

Where is the moon? I think to myself. *It should be out.*

"Where are you?" I ask the moon.

"Right behind you, Beautiful."

I smell the musky incense that is Jace's scent. Turning to face him, I let him enfold me in his arms. His body warmth quickly wards off the coolness of the night and quells my nervousness.

"You'll make it, Lani. You will. Look at that moon." He raises his face to the sky, and I follow his gaze. The moon appears from behind a silver-lined cloud. "It's almost full. Tomorrow night, you'll be able to look at the Hunter's Moon and know you are not, and never will be, a werewolf. We'll look at it together and I'll wonder how anything could be more beautiful than the full moon." He looks down at me and gently pulls my face to his. "Except you."

"I hope you're right. I want to sit in the moonlight with you for all the full moons in my life. But in case tomorrow's my last one, I guess we better take care of Plan B."

He opens his hand, revealing the silver *lew*. They glimmer in the moonlight. How innocuous they look. Not like something that could lodge in my heart and end my life -- and

Stan's -- tomorrow night.

I scoop the coins into my hand and clench my fist tight around them. "I hope for Lisa's sake, we don't have to use any silver bullets."

Jace envelops me in his arms again and kisses the top of my head. "For all our sakes."

CHAPTER 19

Lisa decides to drive to Rock Bluff tonight. She takes the cooler filled with Stan's Snake Oil. That leaves Jace's Harley for our ride to Atlanta.

"I don't have a spare helmet," Jace says. "So you'll have to wear mine."

"Wait," Alex says. She disappears down a corridor and returns with a helmet. It's neon pink with chocolate-colored skulls. "Jace gave me this last year when we were still kinda going out. You can have it."

She tugs the helmet over my head and helps me adjust the chin strap. "It looks great on you."

Jace plugs the silversmith's address into his cell phone's GPS app and we hit the road, headed back to Atlanta.

As soon as Mr. Cojocaru opens the door, I know why the name sounds familiar.

"Are you any relation to Decebal Cojocaru?" I ask as I shake his hand.

"My brother is Decebal Cojocaru. How do you know him?"

"He was a big help to my friends and me in Romania. He has a fabulous library."

Mr. Cojocaru laughs. "When we were children, he was always stealing my books. It did not matter if it was my book, or a school book, or a book I had borrowed from someone else. Did he tell you, he made his fortune buying and selling antique books?"

"No, but it doesn't surprise me."

Mr. Cojocaru escorts us through his house and out the back door. A covered breezeway leads to a workshop. A brick oven is set in one wall; twin fires crackle under iron grills surrounded by chalky white bricks. "Do you have the silver?"

"Yes." I drop the coins into his outstretched hands.

He rubs them between his fingers, then holds them up to the light, one in each hand. "These are silver *leu*. Very old, valuable coins. Are you sure you want them melted down?"

"Absolutely. You know my grandmother Aurelia sent us to you. So you must know, Mr. Cojocaru. They aren't worth anything to me unless they are bullets."

"I knew, but I was hoping I had misunderstood. God help you, *copil meu*."

"Thank you, Mr. Cojocaru."

"My dear, you must call me Coco, both of you. It is my American name, for only my closest friends to call me."

"Thank you, Coco." I search my memory for the phrase I used so much in Romania. *"Mulţumesc mult."*

Coco smiles. He drops the coins in a vessel on top of one of the grills. "Would you like to watch me work? Or wait inside where it's cooler."

"I'm not too hot. I'd like to watch."

Jace nods. "Me too."

"Bine. What caliber bullet?"

"Baretta, nine millimeter."

"Ah, same as before." Coco selects a large, egg-shaped rock off a shelf stacked with similar rocks. He buries it three-quarters of the way in a sand pit that is fitted into a table near the oven. There is a hole in the top of the rock. "This is the mold for your bullet. The molten silver will go in here. How many bullets do you want me to make?"

"Two."

"Two?" Coco asks, looking at Jace.

Jace nods his assent. "Yes. We want two bullets."

Coco weighs the *lew* in his hand. "Yes, it should be enough." He drops the two coins into a kettle on one of the grills in the oven.

As the silver melts, it turns as red as molten lava.

Coco pulls on a pair of heavy-duty gloves that stretch almost to his elbows. "The *pricolici* you are hunting. He is in Atlanta? Or is he in the town where Aurelia lives?"

"Neither. He's in Rock Bluff, up near the Tennessee border." I clear my throat before continuing. "And we're not hunting him; we're trying to save him."

Coco cocks an eyebrow. "Then why the silver bullets?"

"It's in case the cure doesn't work."

Coco swishes the kettle back and forth with a giant pair of fireplace tongs. "You must know that there is only one cure for a *pricolici.*"

"A silver bullet. Yes, I've heard that saying. I'm hoping to prove it wrong."

"But in case *you* are wrong, you have the silver bullets? One for the kill, and one in case the first shot misses the mark."

"Yes, that's right." Again, I look at Jace, but his eyes are on the floor. "In case we need more than one to finish the job."

Coco grabs the tongs in both hands and hoists the kettle to the mold which waits in the sand pit. Deftly, he pours the red-hot liquid into the mold, one gooey drop at a time. A tiny red dot at the top of the mold is all I can see of the newly formed silver bullet.

"How long will it take to cool?" I ask.

"Not long. I will submerge the mold in cold water once the silver has solidified."

When the mold cools enough, Coco holds it with a long pair of tongs and submerses it in a steel drum filled with water. Steam rises and the water hisses. Coco removes the mold from the water and drops it on a cloth on his workbench. He cracks open the mold, revealing the bullet, which glimmers like a silver charm. I suppose that's what it is.

Coco reheats the rest of the molten silver in the cauldron and repeats the process with a duplicate mold to make the second bullet. He opens a drawer and removes a small velvet pouch. He drops the two silver bullets inside, pulls the drawstring tight, and places the pouch in my hands. "Here you are, *copil meu*."

Jace pulls his wallet out of his hip pocket. "How much do we owe you?"

Coco waves his hands at arms length. "No, no, no. You owe me nothing. Aurelia and I have an arrangement in such matters. The bill is paid in full."

"That's very kind of you," I say. "But there must be some

way to repay you."

"Just give your grandmother my love." A glint of a tear wells in the old man's eye. I feel there must be some connection between them other than the professional silversmithing services Coco provides.

"Why don't you tell her yourself? I'm sure she'd enjoy a visit from you."

"I'll make you two a candle-light dinner," Jace offers. "Whatever your favorite dish is, I can prepare it."

Coco smiles, showing yellowed teeth, tiny like baby's teeth, just like his brother's. "That is a tempting offer."

He clasps his hands around mine. "I hope your magic elixir proves successful, and that you never need to use these."

"Me too, Coco. Me too."

***

By the time we get back to the B&B, I'm dog-tired and a bit antsy.

"You okay?" Jace strokes my hair and rubs the knots in my shoulder muscles.

"Yeah. I guess I'm just anxious about Lisa. She must be as exhausted as I am. I hope she was okay to drive."

As if Lisa is reading my thoughts, I get a text as we're climbing the steps to the back door.

> I'm here. Your mom sends a hug & says get a good night's sleep & drive safely tomorrow.

> How's Stan? Did he take the remedy?

> Not yet. Your mom gave him a sleeping pill so he could get some rest. He's sawing logs. Just like I'm going to be doing in a few minutes. I'll wait till we're both awake to give him the remedy.

> K. We'll be there in the AM.

> Love ya, Sis.

Tears sting the corner of my eyes. I draw in my breath and wipe my cheek.

"What's wrong?" Jace asks. "Did something happen?"

"No, everything's okay. She called me 'Sis.'" I tap the keypad.

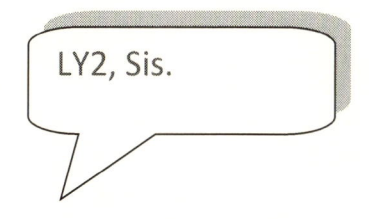

> LY2, Sis.

Jace opens the door for me. "Let's try to get some sleep. We've got a big day tomorrow."

We go back inside, and Jace opens the door to our room.

A chill runs through me as he locks the door behind us.

Could this be the night? The first night we give ourselves to each other?

Tomorrow, I could be a monster.

Jace takes off his shirt and throws it in the corner. His chest is smooth, with just a line of hair that starts just above his navel and disappears under the waistline of his jeans.

I am a trembling pillar of magma, tingling, waiting to erupt and devour him whole, like a lamb caught in the flow of lava.

Why would I think that? That's not what I want! I shake my head to clear my mind of the image.

Jace presses his body to mine and folds his hands around my face. He kisses me long and deep and I feel his heat melt with mine.

My shoes, which I carried inside, drop from my hand with a thud. The sound seems to break the spell.

Jace releases me with a sigh. "Good night, Beautiful."

"Like I'm supposed to sleep after a kiss like that!"

He smiles and nods his head. "Yeah, I know what I'll be dreaming of tonight."

He lies down on the sofa, resting his ankles on one of the sofa's arms so his head will fit, and kicks off his shoes.

I line my shoes up on the floor beside the bed and turn away from Jace to take off my jeans. I crawl under the covers and shut my eyes. In moments I am asleep, and not long after – in the altered timescape of sleep, anyway – the nightmare returns.

Papa and I are in the car, speeding away from Lafayette. He stops on the covered bridge. I hear the rain pummel the old tin roof.

Then he drives off the bridge, onto the muddy dirt road.

A figure appears – Mama, standing in the road, illuminated by the headlamps.

But this time, she's not alone. Jace and Lisa stand beside her.

Papa turns the wheel and slams on the brakes to avoid hitting them. Instead of Mama coming through the windshield,

I'm ejected from my seat. Glass shards sting my body as I land on the hood of the car.

I am no longer myself. I am a hot ball of consciousness wrapped in fur. My werewolf body tingles with hunger as I look at the three shapes in front of me. Their names float above them, the letters drifting apart and dissolving into new words: Malice. Jaws. My mother's name, Melani, fades into mine, Lani. Then all the words are swept away in the rain and all that is left is the one thought, not even a word, just an overwhelming need.

Hunger.

I wake up, curled in a ball with my knees tucked under me, on the floor next to the sofa.

The room is bathed in light from the near-full moon.

Jace's arm is draped across my back.

For a minute I'm afraid I've killed him.

Then he snores.

I laugh silently. His grandmother warned me about that.

I stand up and look at my arms and my hands.

No fur. No claws.

My legs and feet – normal.

I go to the bed and pull off the comforter, then return to the floor by the sofa.

I sleep there till morning. No more nightmares.

CHAPTER 20

In the morning, we dress quickly and grab a couple pastries from the breakfast buffet.

Alex greets us, handing me a large plastic thermos with cartoon kittens all over it. "Hot Earl Grey. I didn't know how you like it, so I left it black."

"Perfect. Thanks, Alex." I shove the thermos in my backpack.

"Are you sure you don't want some bacon and eggs before you go? Grits and toast?"

I give her a hug. "We'll take a rain check."

On the back of Jace's bike, the cold morning wind bites through my jacket. I hug Jace closer to stay warm. He must be frozen solid, taking the brunt of the wind as we race along the interstate toward Rock Bluff.

Finally we turn off the highway onto a two-lane blacktop. We cross a small bridge and a sign welcomes us to "Rock Bluff, GA Pop. 5,504." I hope we aren't too late to keep the town's sign painter from revising the count to 5,503.

My metallic green SUV and Lisa's old-fashioned VW Bug are parked in front of the gallery. Jace pulls the Harley in between the other two vehicles and I jump off, peeling the helmet from my head as I burst through the gallery's front door.

The room is empty and silent. Leaning against one wall is a giant canvass with charcoal outlines of the painting Stan is working on. I know it's "Bait-iful Friends." There are two mermaids, arm in arm. I recognize their faces -- me and Lisa.

"Mama? Lisa?"

The door to the back opens and my mother rushes to me. "Baby, I'm so glad you're here."

"I missed you, Mama. Where's Stan and Lisa?"

Jace comes in and Mama hugs him as well.

"They're in back. Stan's asleep." She leads us to the back part of the gallery, a converted 1920s bungalow. A former bedroom serves as an office with a small cot for late nights. A bathroom down the hall is available for gallery patrons and is where Stan keeps his live bait; I hear crickets chirping.

Mama opens the door to the office where Stan has been staying. The room is dark, lit only by a small lamp on the nightstand. A clear plastic tarp is tacked over the window; through it I see iron bars.

Stan lies on the cot, asleep with his mouth open, breathing softly.

His arm is raised above his head in an awkward position, but I see he has no choice. His one remaining wrist is handcuffed to an iron ring that's bolted into the wall behind the bed. The stump of his other arm, bandaged neatly, hangs off the side of the bed.

Lisa sits in a chair beside the bed, reading. She looks up when we walk in and immediately rushes to me. I squeeze her in a hug and she squeezes back. "Hey, Leez," I whisper. "How'd it go?"

"He woke up about 4 AM and we were able to get some of the remedy in him. He wasn't happy about it, said the name fits 'cause it tastes like snake oil."

"I can vouch for that."

"But he kept it down. A big mugful, about half the bottle. Do you think he should have some more?"

"Wouldn't hurt, and I should probably take some more, too."

A voice booms from the bed. "So, you came to see my new masterpiece?"

"You're awake," Lisa says.

"Hi, Stan. How are you feeling?"

"Been better. Afraid I haven't made much progress on 'Bait-iful Friends' these last couple days."

"It looks great so far. You'll be working on it again in no time."

"How about breakfast?" Stan says. "I'm starved."

"We don't have much in the gallery," Lisa says. "Just some granola bars."

"Why don't you all go across the street to the café and have breakfast," Mama suggests. "You can bring something back for Stan and me when you're done."

Lisa pecks Stan on the cheek. "Bye, Poppy. I'll bring you back Cary's extra tall flap-jack stack."

"That's why I had a daughter," Stan says. "Do you think her brother would do that for me? Noooooo."

"But just wait till you need a cure for lycanthropy, then he's your favorite offspring."

"Only if it works, LP. Only if it works."

At the Rock Bluff Café, only one of the four tables is

taken. A scrawny older man with a grizzled grey beard sits at the table nearest the door.

"I guess we're in between the breakfast crowd and the lunch crowd," I remark.

"Actually, it's the bees, hon," the waitress says. Her name tag says CARY, and I recognize her from my first visit to the Rock Bluff Café.

I look suspiciously at her tall hair-do.

"No, child, they ain't in there." She pokes a pencil into her hair. "They're in the attic. But they won't be for long. The fumigator's coming in the a.m."

"Oh, no," Lisa says.

"You can't just kill them."

"I can and I will."

"Why don't you get someone to move them?" Lisa asks.

"Move 'em where? Lisa gal, I don't reckon your pa would welcome them over to the gallery."

"Doesn't anyone around here have hives?" Jace suggests.

"Only after getting into the poison ivy," the old guy at the table by the door says. He laughs at his joke until he erupts in smoker's coughs. He wipes his mouth on his sleeve, takes a sip of coffee, and shakes his head. "Yeah, hives. Good one."

I grab Cary's elbow. "No, for real. I'll find someone to remove them."

"Hon, we got a lot of beekeepers in these parts. Problem is, they're all out of town right now. The Georgia folks are down in Milledgeville for their annual shindig, and the Tennessee folks are up in Cookeville getting ready for theirs. Everyone that's still home has to tend their own bees."

"If I have to do it myself, I will."

"Must be some sorta bee charmer herself," the guy in the corner says. "Buzz, buzz, buzz!"

"C'mon, Cary," Lisa pleads. "We've learned a lot about bees lately. It means a lot to us."

Cary scratches her scalp with her pencil nub. "Reckon I can hold off a bit. But if those bees are still here come morning, it will be the last sunrise they see."

"Thank you! I'll take care of it! I promise."

Lisa and I squeeze each other's hands, but my delight is short-lived. A chill runs through me and I shiver. Will *I* see tomorrow's sunrise? Will Stan?

"Now that *that's* solved," Jace says, "can we order some breakfast?"

"Anything you want, hon," Cary says with a big smile. "Including my phone number, if you like."

Jace winks at Cary and she blushes clear to her bleach-blonde roots. She puts three menus on the table for us. "I'll be back in a few."

I practically salivate as I inspect the menu. The photos are mouth-watering. Piles of bacon crowd a mound of scrambled eggs. Another photo is of sausage, accompanied by hash browns and grits. I jab my finger at a photo of a rare steak. "That's what I want, right there."

"That's a huge steak," Jace says. "Do you want to share it?"

"I think I could eat the whole thing and half of another

one."

"Okay, Beautiful. Whatever makes you happy."

Cary returns and we place our orders.

"How do you want that steak, hon?"

"Rare is you can get it," I answer. "Bloody."

"You know tonight's a Blood Moon," Cary says.

"The full moon?" I ask. "I thought it was the Hunter's Moon."

"That too. But there's a full lunar eclipse, and the moon's gonna turn red. It's called a Blood Moon."

"Wow, a lunar eclipse! That's awesome," Lisa says. "Hope I'm able to watch it, what with looking after my dad."

"I'm sure he'll let you step outside for a bit. The eclipse'll start around seven or so. Even with my early bedtime, I'll get to see it."

Soon breakfast arrives and I rip into my steak. I close my eyes to savor the feel and the flavor of the juice in my mouth. When I open my eyes, everyone is staring at me, including Cary.

"Girl, you really know how to enjoy a steak," Lisa says. "Almost makes me wish I wasn't a vegan."

"You have a little dribble," Jace says. He dabs my chin with his napkin.

I can feel my face blush hot red. "I'm sorry. I'm just so hungry."

"It's okay, Beautiful. You make carnivores sexy."

"Anything else I can bring y'all?" Cary asks.

"An extra tall flap-jack stack for Poppy."

"He still got the fever, hon?"

"Yes, ma'am," Lisa drawls. I doubt she realizes that she has adopted an accent that mirrors Cary's. "But we got him some special medicine that I'm hoping will do the trick."

"Well, at least his appetite's improving. He hasn't been eating much, far as I can tell. Least, he hasn't been over here in a coon's age."

"My mom's been cooking for him."

Cary slaps her thigh. "That's why you look familiar! You could be sisters. Well, do you think she'd like anything?"

"Cheese grits and toast, please. Whole wheat, light butter."

"You got it, hon."

After breakfast, I ask Cary if I can see the bees.

"Sure, hon. Look all you like." She leads me to the kitchen, which is twice as big as the dining area and filled with industrial-quality, stainless steel appliances. It reminds me of Dama's basement kitchen.

"The bees are over yonder," Cary says, pointing to a latticed metal vent cover in the ceiling. A dozen bees swirl lazily, occasionally landing on a nearby window screen before returning to the vent.

"Is there attic access to that vent, or just a crawl space?"

"I don't reckon you'd call it crawl space, exactly. It's vent work, so it's not very wide."

"Do you think they'd leave if you opened that window?"

"Tried it, hon. Took the vent cover off and opened the window, but we ain't got no way to shoo 'em out. We called the bee man over in Chattooga County. He came out and looked at the hive. Said it was the biggest he'd ever seen. Must have been there for years. We never knew about it until the hive got so big, the bees started getting pushed out through the vent."

"Why didn't you have him remove the bees when he was here?"

Cary scratches her scalp with her pencil. "Wish I'd'a done just that. But the café was just so darn busy that day. I would've had to send away my customers while Twitch – that's the bee man, Twitch Rogers – while he did his bee wrangling."

"Can't you get him back out here?"

"He's booked solid through the end of the month. The bees'll take over the place before then. I got no choice but to fumigate 'em out."

"Maybe I could call him, get him to make an emergency run."

"I'll find his card for you. But I'm not paying no overtime."

"I'll pay whatever he charges."

"All right, hon. But the fumigator's coming first thing in the morning, before we open for breakfast."

I wait with Jace and Lisa in the dining area until Cary returns with the beekeeper's business card and a Styrofoam to-go box. She hands me the card and gives the box to Lisa. "Tell your dad we miss him over here, hon. Tell him to get well soon."

"Thanks, Cary."

Back at the gallery, Lisa sings, "Poppy, who wants breakfast?"

She peeks in to the little bedroom and her song stops abruptly. "Poppy's gone."

The bed is empty. Stan and Mama are nowhere to be found.

Then I hear humming.

"The bathroom," Lisa says. We follow her down a short hall and around a corner.

Mama stands guard at the bathroom door.

"What's going on?" I ask.

"Stan's shaving his beard."

"Poppy, no!" Lisa bursts through the bathroom door.

Behind her, I see Stan standing over a porcelain pedestal sink with a straight razor like the one I used when Dad got sick and I had to shave him.

"Why are you doing that?"

"It was time."

"But you've had a beard ever since Mommy got sick. She asked you to always wear a beard, because she loved it so much."

Stan pauses. "And I loved that she loved it. But it has to go."

"But why?" Lisa is in tears.

Stan puts the razor down on the sink behind the faucets. "Because of what might happen tonight when the moon gets full. I want to see the very first signs of change."

"Nothing's going to happen," Lisa says. She spins her father around to face her and pokes him in the chest, accenting her words. "Nothing's going to happen."

"Okay, LP. Okay. But look at me." Stan turns his head first to the left, then to the right. One side of his face is shaven, the other side bearded. "I'm like one of those kabuki masks we saw in Japan."

"Well, I can't take you anywhere like that," Lisa says. "Go ahead and cut the rest off, then you can grow it again. But Poppy, nothing is going to happen tonight. Do you understand me."

Stan tweaks his daughter under her chin. "You sound just like your mother. I could never tell her 'no,' either."

"Then do as I say and wash off your face. I got you Cary's big stack of flap jacks, and they're getting cold."

"Yes, ma'am."

Stan shoos Lisa out of the bathroom and we all go to the tiny kitchen. It's cramped but comfortable, with a pub-height table surrounded by bar stools and a ceiling fan suspended from the high ceiling, its blades lazily plying the air.

For some reason, I feel antsy and pace the tiny room, bumping into Mama, Jace, and Lisa on my circuit around the table.

"Why don't we go outside?" Jace suggests.

We go out to the front porch where there is more room for me to walk back and forth.

"What's wrong, Lani?"

"You have to ask? Really?"

Jace shrugs his shoulders. "No, I guess I don't."

"I'm just so nervous. I know there's nothing else I can do. The remedy's either going to work, or it's not. We should know in an hour or two."

"But the moon won't be full until tonight."

"It's already night in Romania."

I stop pacing and wrap my arms around him. He folds his arms around me and waits for me to explain.

"There's a dog, Bruno. He belongs to the beekeepers, Eugen and Albine. He got attacked by a werewolf, too."

"Did you give him some of the remedy? Is he your test case?"

"That's right."

"Can a dog turn into a werewolf?"

"I don't know. He might just start foaming at the mouth like Ole Yeller."

"You mean, the werewolf might have given him rabies?"

"It's possible. Either way, Bruno is our canary in the coal mine. If he survives the full moon, so will Stan and I."

"Are they going to call you?"

"Yes, Eugen has my number, and I have his."

I call Rogers, the bee man. When I tell him Cary wants to have the bees fumigated, he says he'll take personal leave from his day job. It might take him a couple hours to get things squared away at work, and then he'll drive right over.

I put the phone in my jeans pocket and rub my eyes with the heels of my palms. "I'm so tired."

"Why don't you get some rest? I'm sure Lisa wouldn't mind if you crashed in her room for a while."

Mama's been using Lisa's room. A pale-sage sweater with crocheted sleeves is draped across the foot of the bed. I spread it across my shoulders and breathe in Mama's scent, like gardenias, but more subtle. I curl up in the bed and am asleep before I know it.

In my dream, I stand in front of the bathroom mirror with Stan's straight razor. As I slide the blade across my cheek, my smooth skin is replaced with fur. With each stroke, more fur appears. I wash my hands under steaming hot water and towel them dry. When I replace the towel on the rack, I stare at my hands. They are covered in fur. I sniff the air. My sense of smell is heightened and my nostrils fill with the sweet yet pungent aroma of dragon's blood incense. I drop to all fours because standing upright suddenly feels wrong. I pad down the hallway to Stan's room. Jace stands at the bedside, his back to me. Stan sits up in bed, looking past Jace at me. Stan's beard is fully grown. His thoughts race to me through the air. *It's time. He's our first prey.* Jace turns to look at me, an expression of horror on his face. Simultaneously, Stan and I leap on Jace. His screams are too much to bear, and I jerk myself awake.

I stumble out of bed and down the hall to the bathroom. I flick on the light, expecting a werewolf's reflection to stare at me from the mirror. But it's only my own face, no fur, just my familiar bird's nest of auburn hair, more disheveled than usual after my restless nap.

I splash water on my face to rinse away the vestiges of the dream. The remedy will work. It has to. No more deaths on my account. If killing myself would stop the curse from claiming Stan, I'd do it in a heartbeat. But that's not the way it works. If the remedy doesn't work, Stan will have to be shot with one of the silver bullets. And the other one will be for me.

The apartment is still. I peek in Stan's room, but it's empty. Walking through the gallery, I hear voices on the front porch. Stan leans against the corner post, rubbing the stump of his arm. He's still clean-shaven; the beard hasn't grown back like it did in my dream.

Lisa and Mama sit in a porch swing, rocking gently. Jace sits on the front steps, texting.

"This is such a peaceful scene."

Jace turns and his face lights up. "Hey, Beautiful. Feel better?"

"Yeah, a little." I sit beside him on the step and he wraps his arm across my shoulders.

"Have you heard from your friend in Romania?"

"No, but they should know something by now." I take out my cell and send a text to Eugen,

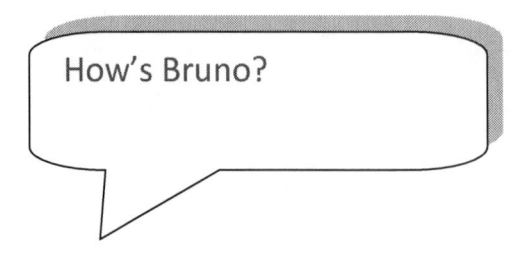

> How's Bruno?

A few minutes pass as I stare at my cell.

Finally a message pings through. I read it out loud.

> All is well. He is sitting in Albine's lap and she is feeding him more honey.

"Woohoo!" Lisa jumps off the swing and rushes to her father.

Stan picks her up and spins her in a one-armed bear hug.

Jace squeezes me close and kisses me. "That's great news."

Mama is the only one who isn't caught up in the celebration.

"Mama, isn't that good news?"

"It is good news, but it doesn't mean you and Stan are in the clear yet. The dog is, well, a dog. As little as there is in the literature about a cure for lycanthropy, there's even less about what happens to a dog who is bitten by a werewolf."

"I know, but –."

My thoughts are interrupted by the arrival of an extended-cab pick-up truck that pulls in to the parking lot of the Rock Bluff Café. A magnetic sign on the driver's door has the words "Willow Springs Apiary" arched over a cartoon of a smiling bee. Below the bee are the words, "Twitchell Rogers III, Summerville, Georgia," and a phone number.

"That must be the bee man." I leap off the step and jog across the street. "Hi, I'm Lani. I'm the one who called you. Thanks for coming out so quickly."

"Twitchell Rogers. Call me Twitch. All my friends do."

Twitch drops his tailgate and slides four boxes to the edge. He stacks three on top of each other and hoists them out of the truck. "You wanna grab that last box, there?"

I pick it up and follow him toward the café.

"After you," Twitch says.

I open the door to the café and Twitch strides in on daddy-long-legs legs.

"Why, Twitch Rogers. Thought you couldn't get out here till the end of the month," Cary says, smiling. "Maybe you just couldn't stay away from me."

"Guilty as charged. Plus, you should have told me you were gonna call in a fumigator."

"Didn't think it would make a difference."

Twitch and Cary gaze at each other, Cary swishing her hips from side to side and Twitch matching her movements with his load of boxes.

I clear my throat. "Ahem. The bees?"

"You got time for a cup of coffee, dontcha, Twitch?"

The man opens his mouth to reply, but I butt in before he can accept. "I don't have a lot of time."

Cary gives me a scathing look.

"I'm really sorry," I continue, making things up as I go, "but Stan was asking for some of the honeycomb, and he's been awful sick, and I thought if he was asking for it, maybe I could also order some biscuits and take them on over to him. Miss Cary, I hear you've got the best cathead biscuits in the tri-state area."

Cary's glare turns to a shy smile. "I do make a mean batch of biscuits. I'll put in an order for ya, hon."

"We'll need to set these boxes in the kitchen, Miss Cary."

She holds the swinging door open for us. "But if y'all are gonna be all up in my kitchen, it might take a while for those biscuits."

"That's okay."

We put the boxes on the stainless steel counter and I gaze around. "Where are they? Where are the bees?"

I don't know why I'm so antsy. Why do I need to see those bees? It might even be dangerous for me to be around them. When Albine's friendly, protective swarm embraced me, I had not been attacked by Zed. Will these bees, thousands of miles away from the scene of my attack, sense that I'm infected? I don't know, but something inside me pushes me toward them.

Twitch points at a ceiling vent in the corner. Several bees move in and out of the vent cover. The counter underneath is cluttered with dirty dishes waiting to be washed. I slide them to the side into a deep-sided sink, cringing at the sound of several plates cracking. Looking at the vent, at the mesmerizing movement of the bees, I crawl up on the counter and reach toward the screws that hold the vent cover in place.

"Hold on a minute," Twitch says, snapping me out of my trance. "If you wanna wrangle some bees with me, you're gonna have to suit up."

"I don't have a bee suit."

"You mean one of those costumes that looks like a giant bee? I've got one I'd let you borrow, but I'm gonna be wearing it myself on Halloween."

"No, I mean those outfits that look like what astronauts wear for space walks."

Twitch laughs. "I know. And fortunately, I've got two of 'em out in the truck. You're not allergic to bees, are you?"

"I don't think so."

"All-righty then. Let's get this show on the road. You know what they say about us beekeepers, dontcha?"

I shake my head.

"There's no bees-ness like show bees-ness."

"Very punny."

Twitch winks and points his trigger finger at me. "Good one."

Twitch opens the side lid of a toolbox in the truck bed. He retrieves two white jumpsuits, two veiled hats, and two pairs of gloves. He helps me pull my suit over my clothes, then puts his suit on.

"Last but not least," he says, removing a tin can with a spout from the truck bed. The can is attached by a wire cage to a bellows.

"What's that for?"

"That's my smoke can." Twitch pumps the bellows and smoke puffs out of the spout. "It riles up the bees."

"You mean, you *want* them to be mad?"

"Where there's smoke, they'll think there's fire. They'll want to eat as much honey as they can, as quick as they can. That'll make 'em slow and sleepy, and less likely to sting."

As I head back into the kitchen, Twitch puts his hand on

my shoulder. "Let me take the lead on this, okay?"

He looks around the kitchen walls at ceiling height. His gaze lights on a smoke detector. He pulls a small step ladder out from under one of the counters and climbs up to the smoke detector. "Gotta disconnect this sucker before I stoke the smoke can."

After he disconnects the smoke alarm, Twitch opens the lid of the smoke can. He reaches into his pocket and pulls out a pile of wood shavings which he tamps down in the can. A stream of dark grey smoke swirls toward the ceiling. Twitch replaces the lid, pumps the bellows of the smoker, and climbs up on the counter beneath the vent. He removes the screws and gently jimmies the vent cover off.

The vent space is crammed with honeycombs. They hang like dozens of thick golden pancakes, lined up with narrow spaces in between. Clumps of bees move about the cells.

"Damn if it hasn't gotten bigger since the first time I was here." Twitch aims the spout of the smoke can toward the hive, waving his arm back and forth as he pumps the bellows so the smoke puffs out over the entire gilded structure. The bees retreat deeper into the hive.

"Open that closest box," Twitch says. "I'm gonna hand you honeycombs to put inside."

Twitch saws at the comb with a pocket knife. "Careful of the bees," he says as he hands me the first slice.

I quickly take off my gloves and hat. As soon as the first comb is in my hands, my mouth fills with saliva. Part of the comb oozes with honey. I break it off and tip my head back, holding the comb over my mouth. It drips profusely, running down my chin and through my fingers. I shut my eyes and lap up the amber goo, reveling in the sensation. I'm simultaneously warmed and cooled, comforted and protected, like when I used to lean against the stone statue, Boulder Man, that Dad built in our back yard in Cloud Pass.

"Good, huh?"

I open my eyes to see Twitch smiling down at me from the counter.

Cary is in the doorway, holding a paper bag, her mouth agape. "God, girl. You gotta give me some of that."

My cheeks burn, wondering how I looked to these strangers as I lost myself in the pleasure of eating the honey.

"Um, are those the biscuits for Stan."

"Uh-huh," Cary says slowly. "Baked 'em in the second kitchen."

"Sorry, I didn't mean to be so messy. It's the first time I've eaten wild honey."

Cary shakes her head. "It's not that."

"Holy cow," Twitch says softly.

Then I notice what they are gawking at.

Bees.

Dozens of bees swirl around my head, like Albine's halo of bees.

A chill runs through me. Are they here as my protectors, like Albine's bees, or as *pricolici vânători*, werewolf hunters who will swarm all over me and sting me to death?

Twitch eases himself off the counter. "Lani, can you get

those bees to the box?"

My heart feels like it's going to spring right out of my throat. "I don't know."

I remember how Albine scooped bees into her hands and passed them to Eugen. My arms trembling, I cup my hands at the back of my head, then bring them forward over my head. Holding them cupped together before me, I feel the bees buzzing around inside.

Twitch slides two new cakes of honeycomb into the box. I hold my hands over the box and open them. The bees waft around over the box and settle onto the comb.

"Young lady, I know I said to let me take the lead on this, but would you mind getting up there on the counter and charming some more bees out?"

I do as he asks, standing up on the counter so my face is inches away from the rows of golden combs. My heart beat has calmed, and I am no longer afraid that the bees will try to kill me.

The remedy must have worked! Otherwise, the bees surely would have attacked me as swiftly as Albine's bees swarmed on Nick.

I gaze at the combs, mesmerized by the movement of the bees across the surface.

For the next several hours, Twitch and I alternate roles. I gather bees from the hive and transport them to the box, then Twitch cuts more comb and hands it to me to place in vertical rows in the boxes.

It's almost dark when I notice one bee that is larger than

the others. She has a bulbous abdomen that is a rich golden color. I reach my hand out to her and she crawls onto my palm. Other bees join her in my hands or hover around my head.

With Twitch's help, I climb back down from the counter.

"The queen! You found the queen," he whispers.

I hold my hands over the box and tilt my fingers down. The queen and her entourage crawl onto the combs in the box. The bees hovering around me follow their queen.

Cary comes back to the kitchen door, where earlier she stood with a bag of biscuits. "How's it going in here?"

"Oh, Cary, I forgot about the biscuits," I say. "I guess they're cold now."

"I took 'em on over to Stan, but he said he wasn't hungry. He stormed inside without so much as a thank you kindly."

"I'm really sorry. He must be feeling poorly again. Let me pay you for those biscuits."

"Your mom and Lisa both offered the same, and I'll tell you what I told them. If y'all can get that bear of a man to eat even one little ole biscuit, it'll warm my heart more than any price."

"Thank you, Cary. I'm sure he'll appreciate it when he feels better."

I cover a yawn with my elbow.

"I think we're just about done for tonight," Twitch says. "Thanks for the help, Lani. I'll cut the rest of the honeycomb. We'll have to leave those boxes here for twenty-four hours to make sure all the bees move over."

"Take a break and have dinner with me?" Cary asks.

"Love to," Twitch answers with a smile.

"I'll pass." I yawn again. "I'll just wash up and go see how Stan's doing."

"Just shuck out of that bee suit and drape it acrost the tailgate."

"Will do."

"Don't forget, tonight's the Harvest Moon. Should be up soon."

"Thanks, Cary. I'll try to catch it."

Back at the gallery, Jace sits on the steps. I sit next to him, and he takes my hand and twines his fingers in mine.

"Everyone else is inside," he says. "But I wanted to be out here. I couldn't go with you, but I wanted to be … I don't know. Available."

I pull our hands to my mouth and kiss the back of his hand. "Things went fine. The bees liked me. I think that means I'm cured. That Stan and I are both cured."

"I don't know about Stan." Jace looks down at his feet. "The remedy doesn't seem to be working."

"I better go see if there's anything I can do. Do you want to come too?"

Jace nods and follows me inside.

Stan's room is hotter than the rest of the house. I notice a space heater humming at the foot of the bed.

Stan lies in bed with his arm chained to the wall. Mama stands just inside the doorway, and Lisa leans back in a chair beside the bed, her legs crossed and her feet propped on the foot of the bed.

I hug Mama. "So our patient's not hungry."

"Not for biscuits."

A chill runs through me.

"He's having carnivorous leanings," Lisa says.

Stan glares at me.

I feel like a mouse in a cage with a python. I'm caught in his intense stare. "Does it have to be this hot in here?"

"Poppy's cold," Lisa says.

Stan continues to stare at me. "You better go ahead and get your gun, Lani."

I finally tear my gaze away from him. "No, we won't need it. The bees like me!"

Stan and Mama look at me like I'm crazy, but Lisa understands the implication. She leaps to her feet and tackles me with a bear hug worthy of her father.

"Woohoo! The remedy works!" She dives onto the bed beside her father and gives him an equally expressive hug.

"Lisa Marie Puckett! Get off this bed immediately! I could change any minute."

"But Poppy, the bees don't like werewolves. If Lani was a werewolf, they would have killed her."

"Maybe I should go over to the café and let the bees do their work on me," Stan growls. "I can tell you, I'm hungry, and a steak won't cut it."

"I'll get you something," Mama says. "But it's the last of the supplies from Mr. Lovari."

Mama leaves for a few minutes and returns with a long,

slender package wrapped in a white plastic garbage bag. It's the shape of a boomerang. "You might not want to watch this," Mama warns.

"I might not want to," Lisa says, "but I need to."

Mama looks at Jace and me.

Standing behind me, Jace puts his hand on my shoulder.

"We'll stay," I say for both of us.

Mama unwraps the package, exposing a charred human calf and foot still in its sneaker.

I cover my mouth to stifle a sob. "What happened?"

"House fire," Mama says, her voice hushed. She steps to the side of the bed and places the grisly package on Stan's chest. With his one arm chained to the wall, Stan waves the stump of his other arm and strains his head forward, teeth gnashing.

"I'll have to unlock the handcuff," Mama says. "Someone needs to be ready with the pistol in case he gets out of control."

"He's pretty out of control now," Jace says. He opens the top dresser drawer and retrieves the Baretta. He points it at Stan.

"Hand me the gun," Lisa says. She reaches a trembling hand toward Jace.

"Leez, I know you feel it's your responsibility since he's your father. But are you sure you can do it if you have to?"

"Yes." Lisa's eyes are cold, determined. "If I need to shoot him, he won't be my father any more. At that point, Poppy will be gone."

When Mama unlocks the handcuff that chains Stan to the

wall, he grabs the gruesome meal and tears into it like it was a turkey leg at Thanksgiving.

"I don't understand," I say. "I'm fine. Bruno's fine. Why didn't the remedy work on Stan?"

"Bruno's a dog," Lisa says. She has the gun trained on her father. "The werewolf attack must have a different effect on dogs than on humans."

"Then what about me? Why aren't I werewolf-ing?"

"Maybe there's something in your blood, from your family," Mama says.

"Maybe because the werewolf that attacked you was from Romania, and the remedy had Romanian ingredients."

"But *I'm* not Romanian."

Stan has finished his blood meal. He wipes his mouth with his sleeve and calmly presents his arm to Mama to re-handcuff him.

The heat is starting to make me light-headed. Watching Stan eat doesn't help. "I've gotta go outside."

I spin and bang my shoulder against the doorframe, then pinball my way through the gallery, bumping into the edge of the cashier's stand and a pedestal with a red-streaked vase. As the vase wobbles, I grab for it, but I'm too late. It crashes to the floor and shatters.

Once outside, I stand on the porch and take deep breaths. *The moon! Where's the moon?*

I stumble down the stairs and stand in the yard, looking skyward. There it is! Huge and buttery-yellow, low in the eastern sky. It looks like one tiny sliver has been dipped in ink.

As I gaze at it, my racing heart calms and my breathing returns to normal.

The breeze brings a whiff of dragon-blood incense and I know Jace is beside me. I reach out and find his hand.

"You okay?"

"Look at that moon, would you? It's the same moon as in Romania, the same ancestors, the same wolfsbane. Why am I okay and Stan isn't?"

"I don't know."

Across the road, the bee man's truck engine cranks to life. Twitch rolls down his window and waves at me. "Any time you want to take up beekeeping, give me a call!"

He backs out of the café parking lot, and stops in the road in front of me. He holds out a mason jar filled with honeycomb. "Here, thought you might like some more honeycomb. You certainly seemed to enjoy it."

I clutch the jar to my chest and watch as Twitch drives away. I turn my attention to the jar so I'm not watching him out of sight. Some of the honey has oozed out of the comb and pooled at the bottom of the jar.

What had Mama texted me about honey? It's good for your immune system.

And Albine. She used honey to heal both Carson and Bruno. She and Eugen had praised honey's medicinal value. They said it was both exotic and familiar.

I remember how nervous I was when I went into Cary's kitchen with Twitch. Drawn to the bees, and simultaneously fearful. Then as soon as I ate the honey, I felt normal.

"Trust nature," Albine had said. "And yourself."

"It's the honey," I murmur.

Jace taps the mason jar. "Yeah. Nice of him to give you some."

I rush inside, Jace on my heels.

"He needs honey," I yell. I dash to the bed, unscrewing the jar lid as I go.

Jace grabs me from behind.

"Lani, get back."

I look up in time to duck as Stan snaps at me.

Or what was Stan.

Chained to the wall by one paw, a snarling, three-legged wolf twists and lunges. In his writhing, he knocks against the bedside lamp. It crashes to the floor and the room is momentarily dark, until my eyes adjust to the moonlight pouring through the window.

Lisa stands with the pistol gripped in both hands, tears streaming down her face. "It didn't work, Lani. The remedy didn't work."

"Don't shoot! He just needs honey."

"A spoonful of honey and all that?" Lisa takes a jerky breath and lets out a keening sob. "It won't make a silver bullet go down any easier."

"Lisa, listen to me. Both Stan and I took the remedy, but I ate honey and Stan didn't."

Lisa flicks her eyes at me briefly before returning her attention to her father. "So?"

"It's the missing ingredient."

She looks at me again, eyes wide with hope. "For realz?"

Jace asks, "How are we supposed to get him to eat it?"

"Mama, what did you do with the, um, bones from before?"

"I'll get them."

Mama leaves and returns with the grisly remains.

Holding the bone by one end, I drench it in honey poured from the jar. The werewolf stops thrashing and watches my movements intently.

I toss the bone onto the bed.

The werewolf lunges for it, but it is out of his reach.

I don't want to get any nearer to the beast, but I know I must. For the sake of Stan, who still lives somewhere deep inside this werewolf's coat.

I inch toward the bed.

The werewolf twists and lunges, snapping his jaws.

"Poppy, sit," Lisa commands.

The werewolf doesn't obey, but does turn his attention to her, long enough for me to fling the bone a little closer to him.

The werewolf sinks his teeth into the bone, splintering it and chewing it up. When he is done, there is nothing left but a spot of honey on the sheet. The wolf licks it with long, slow strokes.

Looking from one of us to the other, the werewolf snarls but makes no move to attack.

Lisa drops her arms to her sides, but keeps a hold of the gun. "Oh, Poppy, I just want this to be over."

The werewolf turns his muzzle toward the window and

sniffs. He tips his nose skyward and lets out a howl that sounds as desolate as a train whistle in the night.

Outside that window is the full moon. The Hunter's Moon. Is it still calling to the werewolf, or will Stan break its grip?

A knock on the front door of the gallery startles us all.

The werewolf growls and barks, thrashing to get free of the chain.

"Anybody home?" a woman's voice calls. I hear her heels clicking across the gallery floor.

"Customer. I'll get rid of her," Lisa says. She leaves the gun on the dresser on her way out.

"A customer at this time of night?" Mama asks.

"That voice sounds familiar," I say. "But it couldn't be. She's in Romania."

I hear Lisa's voice. "No, you can't go back there!"

"It is her! It's Tasha!"

"A friend of yours?" Mama asks.

"Hardly. She's Carson's girlfriend."

"Carson's girlfriend?" The voice comes from the bed. Stan has morphed back into himself. "Why isn't she your friend if she's Carson's girlfriend?"

"She's a werewolf hunter, Stan. She's here to kill you."

"Lock the door," Lisa yells from the front of the gallery. "She's coming for Poppy!"

I hear sounds of a scuffle, then a thump. Tasha must have knocked Lisa to the floor.

I shove past Jace to shut the bedroom door, but I'm too

late. Tasha is there in the doorway, a quiver of arrows strapped across her back, a bow in one hand.

"We weren't expecting you, Tasha. Where's Carson?"

"He was held up at security. A problem with his passport."

"And yet you were able to make it through with your bow and arrows. New set? I don't even have to ask if the tips are silver."

"That is right. I decided I could not count on you and your Carson's sister to get the job done."

"Didn't you hear? The remedy worked."

"Nu. I heard the remedy did *not* work." She pushes the door with her elbow and it flies open, knocking me against Jace. He moves me behind him. "In fact, I saw it for myself a few minutes ago, through that window."

"You heard wrong. Bruno's fine, I'm fine, and now Stan's fine.

I notice the gun, lying on top of the dresser where Lisa left it.

Tasha follows my gaze. She shoulders her bow and picks up the gun. "I trust this is already loaded with your silver bullets. I don't want my *lew* to go to waste, do I? Now move." She waves the gun, indicating she wants us all to go stand between the bed and the wall.

Mama, Jace, and I walk single file and line up in the narrow space.

"So are you going to kill us all?" I ask.

"If I have to," Tasha replies.

"But what about your father?" I ask. "I thought you wanted to find a cure so no-one else would suffer his fate."

"I want to kill every last werewolf so no-one else will suffer his fate."

"I'm afraid I'm going to have to tell Carson to stop seeing you," Stan says. "You have a violent personality that just won't fit in our family."

"And *I'm* afraid that won't be possible, since you'll be dead."

She aims the Baretta at Stan.

"No," I yell, leaping onto the bed and jumping toward her with my arms outstretched.

The gun goes off and I feel a searing pain in my side. As I crumple to the floor, I grab for Tasha's leg and yank. As she falls to the floor on top of me, the gun goes off again.

"Aahh!" I can't tell whose voice it is, but someone has been hit.

A moment later, Jace leaps across the bed and tackles Tasha, knocking her off me. He rips the gun out of her hand and throws it to the corner. He yanks Tasha to her feet, wrapping one forearm around her throat and wrenching her right arm behind her back with his other arm.

I struggle to my feet and press my hand to my side. I know without looking that the warmth oozing between my fingers is my own blood. "I'm shot," I say.

"Me, too," Stan says. "Can somebody take this damn handcuff off of me?"

Mama fumbles in her pocket for the key and releases

Stan. He feels the stump of his arm, where blood drips from a dime-size hole. "This is gonna need a Band-aid."

"Someone check on Lisa," I say as darkness closes in and I slump to the floor.

CHAPTER 21

I wake up in a hospital bed. The moonlight coming through the sheer curtains has a ruddy glow.

Jace sits in a chair by the bed, slumped over with his head at my side. I stroke his tangly hair and he wakes up.

"Hey, Beautiful." He gives me a radiant, lopsided grin that reaches all the way to his deep blue eyes.

"How's Lisa?" I ask.

"Small bump on the head. Not even a concussion."

"And Stan? And Mama?"

"Slow down," Jace says with a laugh. "Don't you want to know how *you* are?"

"I'm alive, which means I'm not a werewolf. How are the others?"

"Your mom's fine. Worried to death about you, but fine."

"Where is she?"

"Down at police HQ. They already took statements from me and Lisa. They'll want statements from you and Stan too, I'm sure."

"For what?"

"They've got Tasha in custody for attempted homicide."

"So Stan's alive. How badly was he hurt?"

"He has a stump of steel." Jace chuckles and points to a spot on his own arm just above the elbow. "Bullet lodged in the bone, right about there."

"What about the bullet that hit me?" I twist to look at my side, but a pang shoots straight up to my brain stem and down to my toes.

"You're very lucky. It almost punctured a lung, but passed all the way through you without hitting any major organs."

"What about minor organs?"

"I don't even know what those would be." He kisses my forehead, then cups my face in his hands and kisses me on the mouth.

"I'll never get tired of the way you taste like chestnuts and honey," he murmurs.

I kiss him again and run my fingers through his hair. "*Tu ești de miere pe buze.* You are the honey on my lips."

Discussion Starters

1. The terms *Roma* and *Romani* are endonyms, meaning names by which people of a particular ethnic background refer to themselves or their geographic region. *Gypsy* is an exonym, a term for an ethnic group or region used by people outside that group or region. Why is it important to use endonyms rather than exonyms? Can you think of other examples where use of endonyms reflects cultural sensitivity?
2. When Lani and Lisa first see the Danube River, Lani says, "But it's brown." She and Lisa both expect the Danube to be blue. They have probably heard of *The Blue Danube,* a waltz written by Austrian composer Johann Strauss II in 1867. In the intervening centuries, what turned the Danube from blue to brown? Why does this matter if you live near the Danube? Why does it matter, even if you don't live near the river?
3. In American Indian lore the Hunter's Moon is the name given to the full moon of October. What other full moon names are included in this book? How did the full moons get their nicknames?
4. Roma experience discrimination in many cultures around the world. Recently, a sweep of a Roma camp in Greece fed the population's belief that Roma are "baby snatchers." (The girl who was taken into "protective custody" by authorities during the raid was actually a Roma child.) In Paris, a teenage Roma was brutally beaten by a group of 20-plus teens who accused him of stealing. Were these appropriate responses to suspicion of wrong-doing? Here is a link to more information about discrimination against Roma: http://globalpublicsquare.blogs.cnn.com/2013/11/04/time-to-drop-the-roma-myths/?hpt=hp_bn2
5. Has anyone ever discriminated against you? Was this discrimination in education, employment, or another aspect of your life? How did it make you feel? How did you respond?

ABOUT THE AUTHOR

M.R. Street is an award-winning middle-grade and young adult author. She is a member of the Society of Children's Book Writers and Illustrators, the Florida Writers Association, Florida Library Association, Leon County Reading Council, and Tallahassee Writers Association. She loves to gaze at the night sky, whether or not there's a full moon. Contact her at www.turtlecovepress.com.

ALSO BY M.R. STREET

The Werewolf's Daughter

2013 Gold Medal - Young Adult Fiction
Florida Authors and Publishers Association

"A taut, heart-pounding tale."
~~Adrian Fogelin, Author of *Crossing Jordan*

"The story of Lani Morgan will pull you in and not let you go."
~~Judi Rundel, Eastside Branch Manager,
Leon County Public Library

Blue Rock Rescue

2010 Royal Palm Literary Awards – First Place
Published Elementary/Middle-Grade Fiction:
"emotional whitewater"
"subtle thread of tension"

Writers Digest Self-Published Book Awards
Honorable Mention:
"reader is hooked by the first page"
"heart-rending"

TeensReadToo.com:
★ ★ ★ ★ ★
"A heartwarming story about family, friendship, love, redemption, and trust"

Made in the USA
Charleston, SC
16 July 2014